Enjoy!

Jamie Hall

Duty-Honor-Courage

By Janie Hall

authorHOUSE®

AuthorHouse™
1663 Liberty Drive
Bloomington, IN 47403
www.authorhouse.com
Phone: 1-800-839-8640

First published by AuthorHouse 4/7/2010

ISBN: 978-1-4520-0677-2 (sc)
ISBN: 978-1-4520-0678-9 (hc)
ISBN: 978-1-4520-0679-6 (e)

Library of Congress Control Number: 2010904543

Printed in the United States of America
Bloomington, Indiana

This book is printed on acid-free paper.

I dedicate this book to the firemen, volunteer firefighters, EMS and EMT in our family and to all firefighters past, present and future who serve their communities.
God Bless You All

Contents

1

Reminiscing

September 25, 1972

When John first went to work for the fire department in 1904, he learned fire fighting the hard way, by fighting the fires. Now they had a new Fort Worth Fire Department Training Center. A picnic was being held today for all firemen and retired fire fighters at the new training facility.

It would be interesting to see the training center and how they train the men these days. John wondered if he might run into some old retirees he knew, but he believed they were all dead by now or wouldn't remember him. John's daughter and son-in-law talked him into going and they would take him, as he no longer drove his car.

They arrived on time to find about a hundred people already there. One by one they came up to him.

"Hi, Chief, remember me? You trained me in '32 when I joined the department."

"Hello, Chief," said his ex-driver. "I'm retired now. You need me to drive you anywhere, just call."

"Hello, Chief, remember me? I was one of the neighborhood kids that played ball in the vacant lot next door to the fire hall."

"Chief, meet my son, Joe, Jr. He's a fireman now, too."

"Glad to finally meet you, Sir. My father has spoken of you often."

John couldn't believe so many people had remembered him, after all these years.

After they made their way to their designated table, the present City Fire Chief L.R. Hines walked up to the podium to make an announcement.

"Ladies and Gentlemen, we are here tonight to honor a man who worked diligently for better equipment and better training for the men during the early years of the fire department development. He taught most of us here today when there was no fire school. He taught us not just how to fight fires, but how to live a life of integrity, dedication and honesty. He earned the nickname of being the 'daddy of all North Side firemen.' After forty-three years on the fire department, he retired in 1947, as Battalion Chief of the four stations in the North Side District Three."

John thought, "*That sounds familiar.*"

Chief Hines continued. "We are here today to honor this man for his dedication and service, but also to celebrate his birthday. At ninety-two years old, he is the oldest living firefighter in Fort Worth. Ladies and Gentlemen, Retired Battalion Chief John Whittenburg."

"*What? That's my name. He was talking about me?*"

The sound of applause rose and John's mind began to reminisce. "*Me? This can't be for me. I was just doing my job. Look at all those faces, faces of the men I trained and worked with and their families. Has it really been seventy years since I joined the fire department? What happened to all those years? Jennie, my love, why aren't you here with me?*"

*****

September 24, 1880

Elmos helped Cornelia climb into the seat of the covered wagon. Grandpa helped Ida and Clemmie into the back of the wagon threatening each with a spanking it they got into the picnic basket of food. Grandma handed little Charlie to his big sister Fannie. Grandpa waved and Grandma wiped tears with her apron and the children yelled "Goodbye" till the wagon rolled out of sight. It had been a good visit, taking the children to see their grandparents and the rest of the family in Dublin, Texas. Now they were heading back to their farm close to Stephenville, an all day trip in the wagon.

The rutted, dirt road was bumpy, so Elmos reined in the horses to a slow walk, trying to make it easier for Cornelia, who was carrying their fifth child. Time passed slowly and the further they went the worse Cornelia felt. "*Surely, I can make it home*", she thought, "*I don't believe the baby is due for a few more weeks. It must be something I ate.*" A few more turns of the wagon wheels on the bumpy road and suddenly, Cornelia had to lean over the side of the wagon to throw up her breakfast.

"Whoa!" Elmos called as he pulled on the reins to bring the horses to a stop.

"No, keep going," Cornelia replied, "I'll be alright now. Let's get on home."

"You sure? You want to lie down in the back with the children?"

Cornelia felt a slight cramp, "I think I will."

Elmos wound the horse's reins over the hook and set the brake on the wagon.

Retrieving the step stool out of the back of the wagon he brought it around to the side and helped Cornelia get down. Moving the stool he helped her climb into the back.

"You children move over and sit on the quilts and let your Ma lay down on the bed. Fannie, tend to your Ma, a drink of water and a wet rag to wipe her face. Clemmie, you watch over Ida and Charlie."

"Yes, Pa." they answered as they did as they were told.

Elmos climbed back on the wagon and flicked the reins, signaling the horses to start pulling again.

A few minutes later, Cornelia felt another little cramp. *Oh, dear,* she thought, *we are too far to turn back now. Maybe I can make it home.* But within an hour, she was grimacing in pain. "Elmos!" she yelled. "We have to stop. The baby's coming. I can't make it home in time!"

Elmos looked over the countryside, "We're almost to Green's Creek. That will be a good place to stop. Can you make it a few more minutes?"

"Yes, I'm guessing.....Oh,h,h,h,....maybe......about an hour or two to go."

"Oh, no, that doesn't even give me time to go back for help and I don't know where the nearest farm is and there may not be a woman there to help," Elmos thought. He could see the creek now and started looking for a level piece of ground. He guided the horses into the shade of some big Scrub Oak trees and jumped down to tie the reins to one of the trees. Helping the children out of the wagon, he told them, "Stay close and stay together. Fannie, get one of those quilts and the picnic basket. You and Clemmie take care of the young'uns and ya'll get something to eat, while I help your Ma."

Getting the children settled down to eating, Elmos climbed into the wagon and began helping Cornelia get undressed and into a nightgown to make her more comfortable. Cornelia instructed him where to find her sewing scissors, the handmade diapers and everything else they might need. Remembering one more thing, he called, "Fannie, gather some wood to start a fire. We're going to need some warm water to wash the baby."

After gathering the wood, Fannie went to sit with her mother. Elmos grabbed a bite to eat and made sure the rest of the food was put away for their supper. He unhitched the horses and walked them to the creek for water, getting a bucket full for the family as well. They would have to spend the night out, so he secured the horses to the trees, so they wouldn't run away if they heard a predator. His gun was under the wagon seat and could be reached easily. While setting up camp, he checked on Cornelia every few minutes. It was getting close to time now, so Elmos told Fannie, "You go take care of the other children and set the bucket of water on the fire to start heating. When it's warm bring it here. Watch it doesn't get hot." He took over letting Cornelia squeeze his hand with every pain. Elmos was nervous. When the other children were born there was always a lady family member or a midwife to help. He wondered if he was capable of the situation. All he could do was pray nothing went wrong and Cornelia could tell him what to do.

September 24, 1880, mid-afternoon, a baby's cry echoes across the rolling hills of central Texas. A boy with thin locks of blond hair and fat little arms and legs, sturdy build like his German heritage has been born in a covered wagon. *"Like a lowly manger,"* Cornelia thought. Elmos and Cornelia sighed with relief as Elmos held the baby over the warm water, rinsed him off and wrapped him in one of the hand sewn diapers and thin summer quilt. Elmos went to the back of the wagon and called, "Fannie, I need your help now." Fannie quickly ran to Pa. "Big Sister, meet your new little brother. I need you to hold the baby while I help your mother clean up."

Fannie took the baby and looked at him, "Oh, Pa, ain't he cute?" Fannie loved little babies. Clemmie wanted to hold him too, but Fannie said, "Wait till Pa or Ma say it's alright."

After Elmos had finished helping Cornelia, he left her to rest for a while. He and the children sat on the blanket, each taking turns holding the baby. After a while, Elmos took Cornelia some food. After supper, Elmos started helping the children get bedded down for the night. When all was settled and quiet, Elmos asked Cornelia, "Have you decided on a name for him, yet?"

"Yes, I like the name John Lee. He's not going to be named after anyone. I have a feeling this baby is going to be somebody. He needs a name of his own, because someday, John Lee Whittenburg is going to make it on his own."

1890

John grew to be a healthy, strong boy and well-mannered for his age. By the time he was ten years old two of his sisters, Fannie and Clemmie had married and moved away. Just he and his sister Ida and brother Charlie lived at home now, helping Elmos and Cornelia with the farm. Elmos was a good, honest man and hard worker, but just never could make a farm pay off and barely kept the family fed. As the years went by, he sold the farm near Stephenville and bought one closer to Dublin. John couldn't understand why, as that farm wasn't any better than the others, except it was closer to his grandparents.

1891

John about age 10.

One time John went to visit his grandparents. He and grandpa had just finished checking on the animals for the night and were heading back to the house when Grandma came out on the porch and called to them, "Ya'll wash up for supper, now."

"Grandpa," John tugged at Grandpa's sleeve. "Look, there's somebody on horse back riding up this way."

"Hum-m-m, sure is. Don't look like anybody I know."

They stopped and waited for the rider to come to them. John was intrigued with the stranger who wore a gun on his hip and had a rifle in a holster on the side of his saddle.

"Howdy, stranger, what can I do for you?" Grandpa asked.

"Have you got a place I can bed down for the night?" asked the stranger.

"As you can see my house is small, but you're welcome to bed down in the barn."

Grandpa told him. "We were 'bout to go in for supper. Would you care to join us? Or I can bring you some food out here."

"Thank you, Sir. I'll take it out here, if you don't mind. I ain't much for socializing." The stranger rode on toward the barn and started taking the saddle off his horse.

"Who is he, Grandpa?" John quietly asked as they headed on to the house.

"Don't know and it don't matter, Son. The Lord says do unto others as we would have them do to us." Grandpa opened the door, "Divide the vittles, Ma and fix another plate. Got a stranger bedding down in the barn for the night."

John, curious for another look at the stranger, asked, "Want me to take his food out to him, Grandpa?"

"No, you stay away from people like him. I'll take him the food."

John knew better than to disobey his grandpa.

The next morning when they went out to the barn, the stranger had left his dirty plate beside where he had bedded down and had already left. Grandpa and John hitched up the horses to the wagon and they all road into town. While Grandma went in the General Store, John went with Grandpa to the post office. While Grandpa was getting their mail and talking with the clerk, John looked at the portrait drawings posted on the wall. One of the pictures, of a wanted criminal looked just like the man that had slept in the barn. The poster read, "Wanted, John Wesley Harding, for Train Robbery."

"Grandpa, look," John pointed out. "That's the man that slept in the barn last night."

Grandpa looked at the poster. "Well, it sure could be. Anyways, best not to get involved. He didn't do us no harm, so let it be."

1892

By early spring, Elmos heard there was good money to be made making railroad ties and barrel staves. John, almost twelve years old now, and his brother Charlie nearly fourteen were big enough to help. They got up one morning and while eating breakfast Elmos told them, "Boys, you and I are going to East Texas. There are lots of trees over there we can cut for nothing. We'll cut a wagon load and come back through Ft. Worth and sell 'um to the railroad company. We'll be gone maybe a month or so. We are going to be getting the wagon ready today. I traded the horses for a pair of Oxen. We go get them soon as we have breakfast and we'll be pulling out in the morning."

"But what about school, Pa?" John asked.

"You know how to read and write don't ya?" Pa asked.

"Yeah, but...."

"A man don't need to know more than that to work hard and make a living."

"Yes, Pa." John, although disappointed, obeyed his Pa. He had completed the fourth grade, but there were eight grades of school and surely more to learn. He could not only read and write, but add, subtract and divided. The rest of his education would come from hands-on experience and he would have plenty of that.

Elmos and the boys loaded up the wagon with only the basic needs: a couple of quilts and one or two changes of clothes, besides their tools. Food items included dried beans, salt, pepper, coffee and cornmeal. They basically would live off the land, camping by a river for water.

John shot a mess of squirrels with his Pa's muzzle loading, double

8

barrel shotgun. Sometimes, a deer, rabbit or if the hunting was lean they took what they could get, like frog legs or opossum. Opossum stew was greasy, but when you're hungry, it sure tastes good. The Trinity River had plenty of alligators. Once in a while, he and Charlie would catch a two or three foot long 'gater and cook the tail. John thought they tasted a little like chicken. John also cut a straight thin limb off a small tree and tied a long piece of cotton string on one end and a hook on the end of the string for a fishing pole. Bait was primarily grasshoppers or other bugs, or minnows if he was lucky enough to catch some. It didn't matter what kind of bait, as long as the fish were biting and he caught supper.

On one trip they camped out beside the river. Across the river from them was a nice clearing with tall grass. "John," Elmos said. "I want you to take the oxen up the bank to that bridge we saw a mile or so back. Take them cross the river to the other side over there and let them graze that good grass for a while, then bring them back."

"Yes, Sir." John said. As he walked he thought, *"It's at least a mile or more up to that bridge, then another mile or two back down the other side to that grass. Oxen can swim and so can I. Why walk all that way?"*

As soon as he was out of sight of his father, he mounted the biggest ox, held the reins of the other one and started swimming across the river. But John didn't think about the currant being strong enough to carry them down stream. They floated down the river faster than they crossed. He began to get scared. But the ox finally made it across to the other side, out of the water and 'to a grassy clearing'. John turned around slowly and sure enough they had been washed down stream, right across from their camp. There stood his father with his hands on his hips looking mad. *"Oh! No!"* John thought. *"I'll be getting a whipping tonight."* John let the ox graze as long as he could. He didn't know how long it would take to walk all the way to the bridge and back to camp, but he would have to do it sooner or later, like he should have done in the first place.

John, Charlie and Elmos made a couple of trips a year for two years; once in the spring and once in the fall. It was coming up spring and John already dreaded making the trip. But, to his surprise his dad traded the oxen for a pair of horses and was looking for some other dream to follow.

1894

One Saturday, when John was fourteen years old, he drove the horses and wagon into Dublin with Elmos for supplies. On the town bulletin board, outside the general store was a notice, *'Hiring Workers, Thurber Brick Factory, fifty-cents a day.'* John thought about that as they headed back to their farm. He was tired of being a poor, dirt farmer. He wanted to make some money of his own and make something of himself.

"Pa, I'm going over to Thurber and see about getting a job at the brick factory."

"Why?" Elmos asked. "I got plenty of work for you here, boy. Besides, you don't know anybody in Thurber. Who you going to stay with?"

John was pleased his Pa hadn't come right out and said no. "I don't know, yet. But I gotta' give it a try. You still got Charlie to help you and he likes farming. Mr. Taylor takes a load of supplies over to Thurber every Monday to sell. He spends the night and comes back next day. I could hitch a ride with him. If I can't find work when we get there, I'll come back with Mr. Taylor the next day. Pa, you're a farmer. I'm not. I gotta' find what I want to do and I know it ain't farming or making railroad ties."

After a long pause, Elmos said slowly, "Well, Son, I guess you've thought it out and you got a right to do what you want to do."

The next day Elmos, Cornelia, Ida, Charlie and John road to town to attend church. Grandpa retired from being an itinerant preacher because of his health. But, he still preached once in a while at the Dublin Methodist Church. John hated going to church and listening to all the shouting and hollering about going to hell and burning in hell. Hell, he couldn't move to shoo a fly off his nose that he didn't get a dirty look or scolding when he got home. If a person had any hell in him, Grandpa could certainly scare it out of him. Besides that, hell couldn't be much hotter than August in Texas. If he ever got out on his own, he'd never set foot in another church, ever again. He would meet God someplace else, but not in a church.

After church, John talked to Mr. Taylor about riding over to Thurber with him in the morning.

"Sure, boy," said Mr. Taylor, "I'd enjoy the company. Tell you what, I'll give you ten cents if you'll come early and help me load the wagon."

"Sure thing, Mr. Taylor, I'll be there."

John's family always brought some food with them and after church they went to his grandparent's house for Sunday dinner together. While having dinner, John told them all about going with Mr. Taylor to Thurber the next day and helping him early in the morning. The men agreed to it, but his Ma and Grandma were a little reluctant. Even though John was tall, strong and mature for his age, he was still only fourteen years old. But they reasoned, no one would hire a fourteen year old to do a man's work any way and he would be back with Mr. Taylor the next day.

Before going to bed that night, John filled his canteen with water and his lunch pail with bread, cheese and beans left over from supper. Next morning, he jumped out of bed the minute he heard the old rooster crowing. He was at Mr. Taylor's store, waiting on the steps when Mr. Taylor came driving up in the empty wagon.

"Good to see you're on time, boy." Mr. Taylor commented.

"Thank you, Sir." John replied.

"Well, let's get started."

They were loaded and on the way within the hour. As they traveled, Mr. Taylor told John, "Boy, don't buy anything from the company store, lest you're starving to death for three days in a row. And don't let them talk you into putting it on credit and paying it back come pay day. I sell to the store for a fair price. Then they more than double the price to sell to the minors and factory workers. You go buying on credit and next thing you know, it takes all your paycheck just to pay the bill, then you have nothing to live on till next pay day."

"Thank ya' for the warning, Sir."

"Now another thing, if you get the job when we get there, you come on over to Mrs. Mazzano's Boarding House. I stay there every time I come to town. She places an order and I sell some of these goods to her, then I go sell the rest to the company store. I'll tell her you're coming. If you get the job that's the best place for a boy like you to stay. She runs a nice place and don't allow no drinking, cussin' or wild women."

"Oh, don't have to worry about that, Mr. Taylor."

Now, another thing," Mr. Taylor continued, "If you don't get the job, you come on over there anyway and get you some supper and you can bunk in with me tonight and ride back with me tomorrow. And don't get your hopes to high on getting a job. If this don't work out there'll be another job come along later."

"Yes, Sir, thank ya'. I just want to get a job and save up my money, so I can go into Fort Worth and get a really good job with steady pay."

"Well, good for you, Boy. Sounds like you got a good head on your shoulders. I hope your plans all work out."

They stopped to eat lunch and let the horses rest a spell then headed out again. It wasn't long before the two big smoke stacks of the Thurber Brick Factory came into view. From then on John's excitement and anticipation grew.

Mr. Taylor guided the horses to pull up in front of the main building of the brick factory. "This is it, Boy. Good luck. When you leave here, Mrs. Mazzano's is straight down this street, just past the company store, the big white house with big front porch."

"Thanks, Mr. Taylor." John said, jumping down from the wagon. He walked over to the steps of the big building. Mounting each step, he kept repeating to himself what to say. He wanted this job so bad, he would do or say most anything to get it. Well, except lie. His Pa and Ma and grandparents had instilled honesty into his upbringing.

Walking up to the big, wide door, he tried to act calm, as he took off his hat and opened the door. He walked in shutting the door behind him. He calmly walked over to the desk where a gentleman appeared to be working.

"Excuse me, Sir. Could I speak to the head foreman? I'd like to ask about getting a job here."

The man looked at him, peering over the top of his horn-rimmed glasses, as though trying to decide how old he was or maybe how strong he might be. "Wait here."

He walked over to the door that had 'President' painted on the white glass. He knocked and walked in shutting the door behind him.

John stood nervously turning his hat between his fingers.

A few minutes later, the man came back out and told John, "You can come in now. This is Mr. Marston. You can talk to him."

"Thank you, Sir," John said as he walked into the office. "Mr. Marston, glad to meet you, Sir" and stuck out his hand to shake Mr. Marston's.

Mr. Marston slowly extended his hand across the desk to shake John's.

John continued talking, "I'm John Whittenburg. I saw your sign in Dublin that you wanted workers. I need a job, Sir. I'm a hard worker and I learn fast. Just show me what to do and I can do it."

After what seemed like an eternity of being stared at, Mr. Marston asked, "How much schooling you got?"

John looked down at his hat, a little embarrassed about his lack of schooling, but he could read and write, so he was about like most folks in that regard. "Fourth grade, Sir, but I got lots of learning at cutting lumber, making and repairing wagons and I helped my Pa build a barn and I'm good with handling horses."

Mr. Marston asked, "How old are you? Did you run away from home?"

"I'm fourteen years and no, Sir, I didn't run away. My Pa said I could try it on my own and if it didn't work out I could come back home. But, Sir, I don't like dirt farming. I want to work and earn some steady money."

Mr. Marston continued to stare at John, "What did you say your name was?"

"John Whittenburg, Sir."

"Hum, I think I've heard that name before." Mr. Marston paused. "Are you any kin to Reverend Whittenburg that used to come through here preaching once in a while?"

John wasn't sure if it was going to be a good or bad thing to claim kin to his 'hell fire and damnation' grandpa or not, but he truthfully answered, "Yes, Sir, he's my grandpa."

"Well, John, I don't normally hire somebody your age." Mr.

Marston rubbed his chin whiskers, "But, you seem like an honest young man. Tell me, do you like beer?"

John, slightly confused, thought *"what did beer have to do with making bricks?"* "I never tasted it, Sir and don't really have a hankering to from what I hear and seen how it makes a man act."

"Good answer, John. Now, I'll tell you what I been thinking. Most of this community is Italian, Polish and a few other kinds that like beer. The company furnishes each man one cup of beer with their lunch everyday. The men I've hired before to do the job drink too much and get drunk on the job before the other men get their share. I need someone who won't get drunk and will be fair at seeing the men get their share at lunch break. Now, before and after serving the men, you will stack the finished bricks in the yard, in stacks of one hundred. I'll pay you fifty cents a day, starting tomorrow. But, if you get to playing and messing around on the job, I'll fire you quicker than I am hiring you right now."

With a big smile, John replied, "You can count on me, Sir. Thank you, Sir. I won't let you down."

"Now, let's go get you on the payroll." Mr. Marston stood and walked around his desk to the door, opened it and called, "Goldstein, get the information from John here and put him on the payroll starting tomorrow. Then show him where to report to Ben in the morning."

Those were the best sounding words John had ever heard. He held his composure and tried to act mature, till Mr. Goldstein finished asking all the questions and told him where to go and what time to report in the morning. Then he ran down the steps, two at a time, anxious to tell his friend Mr. Taylor the good news. Mr. Taylor would get word back to his folks tomorrow.

John ran till he spied Mr. Taylor's wagon in front of the general store. Mr. Taylor was just coming out of the store and starting to unload some merchandise. "Mr. Taylor, I got the job; fifty cents a day, just for counting and stacking brick." He thought it best not to tell him the 'serving beer' part for fear it would get back to his Pa and Grandpa and they would not approve.

"That's great news, Boy." Mr. Taylor extended his right hand to shake John's and patted him on the back with the other. "Your folks will be proud to hear the good news."

"Thank ya', Sir. I best be finding a place to stay now. Ya' want me to help you unload first?"

"I told Mrs. Mazzano you'd be coming at least for supper tonight. She's expecting you. You go talk to her first. You can come help unload later."

"Yes, Sir," John excitedly ran on down the street to the big white house and knocked on the door.

Mrs. Mazzano came to the door. She was the same height as he was, about five foot or so and with black hair slightly graying, black eyes and eyelashes. She looked about the same age as his ma. She spoke with a strong Italian accent. "Oh, you must be Giovanni Mr. Taylor telling me 'bout."

"Yes, Ma'am. John Whittenburg."

"An' a handsome Giovanni, too. Did you getta' the job?"

John blushing proudly said, "Yes, Ma'am."

"Then you be needin' place to stay. Mr. Taylor and I talked. I keep his room for him every Monday night. The rest of the week, I getta' somebody once in while, when hotel is full. I charge forty cents a day for room, two meals and packed lunch bucket, and laundry, seven days week."

John was thinking, while Mrs. Mazzano talked, *"if I make fifty cents a day and pay forty, I could still save ten cents a day."*

Mrs. Mazzano continued, "Now, I hav'a no room 'cept for Mr. Taylor's, so he and I work out d'accordo. You tak'a his room, iffa you let him sleep there on Monday nights. And iffa you want, you help with chores on Sundays and I charge you thirty-five cents day."

John, surprised at the offer, realized he could save more money. "That sounds good, Mrs. Mazzano." John reached into his pocket to get the thirty-five cents. "I don't mind sleeping on the floor one day a week or helping you on Sundays."

"Who talk 'bout sleeping on'na floor? There two cots and Mr. Taylor already pay me for tonight. Come, I show you." Mrs. Mazzano motioned for him to follow, leading the way down the hall past the sitting room and dining room, to the second door on the right. She opened the door. "This'a you and Mr.Taylor's room."

John walked into the small room and saw two cots made up with nice bed linens. There was a small table and chair and a cabinet for clothes and even had curtains hanging on the windows. Much nicer than anything he had ever seen or expected. "This is really nice, Mrs. Mazzano. Does it matter which bed I take?"

"You ask Mr. Taylor. I getta' back to my pasta, now."

"Oh, I better hurry. I told Mr. Taylor I'd help him unload at the company store. Thank ya, Ma'am, I'll be back later."

John hurried out of the bedroom behind Mrs. Mazzano, down the hall and out the door. He ran down to the general store and helped Mr. Taylor finish unloading. They rode the wagon back to Mrs. Mazzano's barn and removed the harnesses and put the horses in the stalls. Picking up their bags from under the seat of the wagon, they went in the back door. Entering into a closed-in porch, there was a wash bowl and pitcher of water and towel. Mr. Taylor smiled at John as he poured some water in the bowl, "Be sure and wash your hands and face before you sit down at the supper table. Mrs. Mazzano's rule; cleanliness is next to Godliness."

"That's what my Ma and Grandma always say." John said, just as Mrs. Mazzano called out "Ora dicena."

Mr. Taylor pointed down the hall toward the dining room, "That means, 'dinner is served' in Italian," and he motioned for John to follow.

As they took their seats, four other men came from upstairs. Mr. Taylor introduced John. They all welcomed him and included him in their conversation. He felt like a man now, not a little boy.

The next morning, they all ate breakfast together. Mr. Taylor would be leaving at the same time John and the men went to work. Mr. Taylor promised John he would get word to his folks about his job and where he was staying. They shook hands and John walked with shoulders back and head held high toward his first job and the beginning of a life on his own.

2

On His Own

1896

John found stacking brick a little more physical exertion than he thought, but still better than plowing, hoeing, picking cotton or making railroad ties for sure. He cleaned Mrs. Mazzano's barn every Sunday as part of his chores. The barn didn't get that dirty as Mr. Taylor and an occasionally traveler were the only ones using it for their horses.   Thurber had its own power plant and every building and house had the new electric lights. And all the houses had water running into the house, just pump the handle and it flowed right into the kitchen sink. He didn't have to haul water from the outside well. Wow, if Thurber had all this, wonder what all the big city of Fort Worth had? How he wished he could have talked his Pa into moving to Fort Worth. His sister Ida had married and moved there, as well as his two older sisters. John was determined to make it to the big city as soon as he could.

During the year, John grew to his full height of six foot, two inches and about one hundred and eighty pounds of muscle. As soon as he had saved enough money he asked Mr. Taylor to bring him a new pair of pants next time he came. As he saved more, he bought a new shirt and later a new pair of high-top, lace-up boots. One day he walked over to the depot and asked the ticket agent, "How much does it cost for a one way ticket into Fort Worth?"

The ticket agent looked at his chart, "Fifty-eight cents. There's one train a day, leaving at six in the morning and arrives in Fort Worth at nine, fifty-five. Want ticket?"

"Not yet, Sir. I have to save some more money."

John had been able to save enough for train fare, besides buying him some city clothes, but he needed enough to live on till he could find a good job and a place to stay. Besides, one of the men at the boarding house, a school teacher, had been teaching him at night how to read and write better. He wanted to learn more before leaving.

A couple of months later, on a Monday, John walked home from work. Mr. Taylor's empty wagon was in front of the general store. Just as he got even with the wagon, Mr. Taylor came out of the store.

"Howdy, Mr. Taylor."

"Howdy, John. How are ya'? I just finished here. Want to ride up to the barn with me?"

"Sure." John climbed on the wagon.

"I got some news from your folks." Mr. Taylor continued, "They moved into Fort Worth last week. Your Pa heard about a job hauling gravel on the north side of the river. Apparently, they left the farm for Charlie and came through town last Monday as they were leaving and stopped by the store long enough to tell my wife. Sorry, I'm just now getting word to you."

John was angry at first as he thought, *how many times did I try to get Pa to move to Fort Worth and he waits till after I leave home to finally do it.* He turned to Mr. Taylor, "Thanks for bringing me the news." He hoped his disappointment with his Pa didn't show.

January 1902

It was mid winter and a cold front had blown in one Sunday morning. Everybody at the boarding house huddled around the fireplace in Mrs. Mazzano's sitting room. They were talking about how cold it was going to be working in the brickyard the next day. John had outgrown his old coat this past year and had to buy a new one, which cut into his savings even more. But, he kept saving ten or fifteen cents a day and it was adding up. He lay on the floor watching the flicking flames of the fire and day dreaming about his plans.

He decided to work two or three more months to make sure he had enough money. He wasn't telling anyone of his plans to leave or how much money he carried in his pockets.

The next day when he got off work and started walking home, he saw Mr. Taylor's empty wagon in front of the general store. He could ride with him up to Mrs. Mazzano's barn. Mr. Taylor was inside the store watching out the window. When he saw John he came out and waved. John waved back and walked over and they both climbed on the wagon at the same time.

"Glad to see you, Mr. Taylor."

"Good to see you, too, John. But I got some bad news for you, Son." Mr. Taylor continued, "Your Pa broke his leg in an accident. I heard a wagon load of gravel fell over on him. Doc says he can't walk on it for six weeks, at least, which means he can't work."

"Oh, me." John said, as he was thinking fast, *what can be done?*

Mr. Taylor added, "That's not all. Your Ma is too sick to take care of him. They are living in what's called 'tent city' on the north side of the river. Your sister Ida sent word to your grandpa. Both your grandpa and grandma can't go, they are barely able to take care of each other. Ida did what she could the first week, but then she had a miscarriage and doctor put her to bed. Charlie ain't got the money to go. Your grandpa asked me to get word to you."

They were both silent till Mr. Taylor guided the horses and wagon into the barn. John had to think for a minute about what to do. "Thanks for letting me know, Mr. Taylor. I guess I better catch the morning train. I had planned to work another month or two and make sure I had enough money. But I need to go now. Do you think it would be alright if I went to Mr. Marston's house tonight to tell him what's happened and apologize for not giving him more notice that I have to quit?"

"I think it would be very thoughtful, John. I think Mr. Marston would appreciate that."

John started to get off the wagon.

"Here, just take the wagon." Mr. Taylor offered, as he handed John the reins. "The horses are still hitched and it will be faster getting up New York Hill. I'll tell Mrs. Mazzano to hold your supper and when you get back we can unhitch the horses."

"Thanks, Mr. Taylor." John slide over to the middle of the wagon seat when Mr. Taylor got down. He went to Mr. Marston's and told him he had to quit to go look after his folks.

Mr. Marston told him, "I appreciate you coming to tell me John and I certainly understand. You are one of my best workers and I hate to loose you. If you ever need a job, you come back to see me, you hear?"

Next morning, John and Mr. Taylor were up and dressed early. They were going to slip out the backdoor, hitch the horses and Mr. Taylor was going to take John to the depot and then be on his way back to Dublin. They were surprised to find Mrs. Mazzano had already cooked hot biscuits, stuffed with scrambled eggs and had packed John's lunch bucket with crackers, cheese and summer sausage and ice tea in his canteen.

"You no getta food on train, you need to eat. I tak'a care of my boys, like'a you mama. I'm a gonn'a miss you, Giovannie." Mrs. Mazzano had tears in her eyes. Wiping them with her apron, she gave him a hug. "You always have casa here iffa you need one. Now, go 'fore you missa you train. Saluta."

"Thanks, Mrs. Mazzano." And teasingly adding an accent like hers said, "I'ma gonn'a miss'a you, too."

"Oh, Mr. Taylor, you take'a John to depot, then come back and get you good breakfast before you leave town." Mrs. Mazzano added.

"Yes, ma'am."

John said goodbye to Mr. Taylor, bought his ticket and sat in the waiting room of the depot eating his biscuits while waiting on the train. He had waited a long time for this day...*his first train ride and going to the big city of Fort Worth.* But his excitement was diminished a little, as his reason to go now was more urgent.

Arriving in Fort Worth, he got off the train and asked the conductor, "Can you tell me how to get to a place called 'tent city'?"

"Ya, Sir. Ya just goes in the depo' and out the front door and go right over to Main Street. Go left and go all the way ta the river. Cross the river about a mile and ya can't miss it."

John thanked the man and started walking. It turned out to

be a longer walk than he had anticipated....about 3 or 4 miles he guessed, not counting the flat barge ferry crossing the river. When he saw all the tents, he realized why they called it 'tent city'. There must have been fifty or more tents. How in the world was he going to find which tent was his folks? Well, he would just have to start asking everybody he saw or every other tent.

"Sir, do you know of Elmos Whittenburg?"

"Never heard of him."

"Ma'am, I'm looking for my folks, Cornelia and Elmos Whittenburg. Have you heard of them?"

"No, sorry."

In between inquires, he kept looking to see if he recognized his Pa's wagon or horses. Coming to yet another tent, a man stepped out.

"Sir, I'm looking for my folks Elmos and Cornelia Whittenburg." This time John thought to add, "I heard he broke his leg when a wagon fell over on him."

"Ummm, there was an accident about a week or so ago. I think it was the man down at the last tent in this next row. Never caught the man's name, so can't be sure he's the one you're looking for."

"Thank you, Sir," John said as he hurried on. He had seen several horses but very few wagon and none so far looked familiar. As he neared the tent at the end of the row, a wagon was next to it and a few yards out in the field, he thought he recognized one of the horses. *I hope this is it,* he thought as he approached the tent. "Hello, inside. I'm looking for the Whittenburg's."

"In here, who's there?" Elmos called back.

John pulled back the flap of canvas covering the entrance, "Pa, its me, John."

"John? Son, what're you doing here? Boy, it's good to see ya."

Cornelia raised her head up off the pillow, "John!" she said in a weak voice and started crying.

John dropped his bag and lunch pail and went to kneel at her side and hug her. "It's alright, Ma. I came soon as I heard." She felt feverish. "What's going on Pa?"

Elmos brought him up to date. He broke his leg when a wagon load of gravel fell over on him. The same leg he broke during the

Civil War. He hadn't been able to work for two weeks. Cornelia got sick about a week ago. Some neighbors had been looking out for them, since Ida hadn't been able to come, but they had run out of money and couldn't afford to get a doctor.

John asked, "Where can I find a doctor and where's the general store?"

"Back on Main Street about four blocks north," Elmos said. "But ain't no use, we ain't got the money and ain't got no credit at the store."

"I got money, Pa. I'll be back soon as I can. Those your horses outside?"

Elmos nodded, yes.

"I'm going to ride one of the horses, it'll be faster." John headed out. He recognized Clyde as one of the horses they had when he lived at home. John talked to Clyde and petted him as he put the reins on him to make sure the horse remembered him. Clyde did as he nudged John playfully. "Atta' boy, Clyde, but we got work to do right now." John swung up on the horse's bareback and guided him in a fast trot toward Main Street.

Finding the doctor's office first, he went in and arranged for the doctor to come see about his Ma. Next he went to the general store and bought some bacon, eggs and bread and headed back to his folks. The doctor was just leaving his office in his horse drawn buggy. John guided him to his folk's tent.

As the doctor left he told John, "Your mother has pneumonia. Here's some medicine to give her, but I can't promise it will do any good, unless you can get her out of this cold, damp tent and into a warm place. Call me if there is any change."

John thanked the doctor, telling him he was going to see what he could do.

After he had fixed his folks something to eat, he asked where his sister Ida lived and how to get to her house. He mounted Clyde again and rode to her house. Between all of his siblings, he was closest to Ida, even though he and Charlie had gotten along good together. Ida had married a good man, who made a living raising, training and selling horses. They were living in a nice two bedroom house in North Fort Worth. Ida came to the door in her long flannel robe. She was pale, with dark circles under her eyes and her hair tied back with a ribbon. Not the pig-tailed sister he remembered, but he was so glad to see her he didn't care what she looked like. She looked up at him now, no longer her height and didn't recognized him at first. She used to call him little brother, now he looked down at her and smiling said, "Howdy, little sister."

Ida, realizing who he was, jumped into his big hug. "John! Oh, thank goodness, you must have gotten my message. I am so glad you're here. Oh, it is so good to see you and look at you all grown up and dressed up in city clothes. Have you seen the folks? I haven't been able to get down there to check on them. I had a miscarriage a week ago and I'm just now able to be up and ..."

"Whoa, little sister, one thing at a time. Are you okay?"

"Yes, I am fine, especially since you are here."

John filled her in on what the doctor said about Ma. "So, is it alright if I bring them here, till Ma gets well?"

"Oh, by all means, if you can get them to come. I tried to when pa first got hurt and he wouldn't hear of it. Maybe you can get them to come now. James is out of town on his annual horse buying trip or he would help."

"That's okay, I can handle it. We just need to get Ma someplace warmer than that tent, so she'll have a chance to get well. I'll go back and load 'um up now and see you after while."

John rode back to tent city and hitched both horses to the wagon. He told Pa, "I'm taking Ma to Ida's so she can get well. You can be stubborn and sit here and fin for yourself or you can let Ida and me help you till you get back on your feet." Pa finally gave in and John helped him get in the back of the wagon, and then carried his Ma out. He could come back later for their belongings.

After getting his Ma and Pa settled in at Ida's house, he helped Ida with some chores. When he had finished he sat down with the others. "Pa, I've been thinking," John said. "Where do I go and who do I talk to about possibly taking over your job till you get back on your feet. Meanwhile, that will give me time to find a job and a place to stay."

"That's mighty generous of you, son. That would be alright with me. You can talk to Mr. Price down at the gravel pit, along the river bank, just east of where we were camped. See if it's alright with him."

"I'd need to use your wagon and horses and if you don't mind, I'll stay in y'all's tent till I find a place to live."

Ma spoke up, "But, John, it's so cold in the tent. You sure you want to do that?"

John tried to reassure her, "Ma, I have stacked bricks in weather colder than this. I'm used to it."

Ida spoke up, "John, you'll do no such thing. We have a bed on the screened in back porch, with the awning fasted down for the winter. We just use it in the summer time to sleep out there where it's cooler. It would be a lot drier than that tent. And you could help me out with James being gone."

"You sure?" John questioned. "Do you think James would mind putting up with all of us for a month or so?"

"Of course, I'm sure. Just wait till you meet him, John, you'll like him and I'm sure James will like you. Now, go on and pull into the barn and unhitch the horses. You can go back after the rest of their things tomorrow."

John left early next morning and headed back to tent city. He noticed a trail of wagons heading east out of camp. Assuming they were heading to the gravel pit, he followed. Sure enough, there was a little building with a sign, 'Office' over the door. He pulled the wagon over and stopped the horses and set the brake on the wagon. Entering the building he found one man sitting at a desk.

"Mr. Price?" John inquired.

"Yes, what can I do for you?"

John told him who he was and what he wanted to do.

Mr. Price replied, "That sounds fine to me. A lad your age, willing to help out his father like that, is bound to be a good man and a good worker. Now, here's what you do. You go down to the river bank here," he pointed east, "and load up with gravel and take it up Main to where they are laying the bricks to pave the street. They tell you where to dump it. You check in with the foreman when you go in and when you come out with a load. I pay two dollars a load. Most men do two loads a day, unless you have a partner and then maybe three loads a day and you split the money."

"No partner, Sir, just me, but I think I can handle it."

"Well, if you decide to get some help, there's usually a few negro men hanging out at the pit, willing to help for a coin or two."

"Thanks, I'll think about it." That irritated John. He could never understand how anybody could expect a man to work just as hard but get a fourth of the pay, just because they had different colored skin. If he did decide to hire a helper, he would split the money he made and one day he did.

A month into the job, it was an unusually warm spring day. He had turned down help before, but that day this same Negro man came walking by again asking for work. John said, "I believe I do. You help me load this last wagon full and I'll give you a dollar."

"But, Mass'a, you's only makes two dollars a wagon," the negro man replied in surprise.

"You load half of it, you get half the money. Deal?" And John stuck out his hand to shake on the deal.

"Yas, Sir, deal!" The man shook hands with John.

"What's your name?" John asked.

"Samson, Sir, but ev' body calls me Sam."

"Well, Sam," John looked up at the man, a few inches taller and about thirty pounds heavier, "I bet your Mama got that name from the strong man in the bible."

"Yas, Sir, she sho' did." Sam's grin broadened and they began shoveling.

1902

By June, Elmos had recovered and returned to work, even though he still walked with a bit of a limp. The weather had warmed and he and Cornelia moved back into their tent at tent city. John, James and Ida all protested, but their pa could be stubborn at times; this being one of those times. John had been asking and looking around for another job. The new stockyards on the North Side were being built to handle the growing live stock business. He and Elmos were able to get a job as carpenters building cattle pens. Then John learned the electric company was hiring men to dig holes for the poles to be set to string the electric wires. He went to inquire. Standing in line, he looked thin and lean compared to the other men beside him, even though he was tall and strong. The man doing the hiring, looked at John and said, "Boy, I don't think you're strong enough to dig ten holes a day, even in a two man team."

Before, John could answer, the Negro man, Sam, spoke up from behind, "Mass'a, you make him and me a team and we out dig all them other teams. We's worked together 'fore." The man looked at Sam and back at John and said, "Okay, you're both hired." John shook Sam's hand again. They made a good team and did out dig the others for one dollar a day.

A couple of young men working as a team worked beside Sam and John almost daily. The two men talked about "soon as they saved up enough money they were going to hop a train to New Orleans, Louisiana. There they were going to get on a mule boat bound for Spain." They tried to talk John into going with them. Although strongly tempted, the feeling of being right where he was supposed to be, out weighed the excitement of unknown adventures.

1902 – 1903 - 1904

By the end of summer, John heard he could make more money working for the city and laying bricks to make streets. He applied for the job, was hired and got the foreman to hire Sam as well. They laid bricks for the last part of North Main Street. The bricks were all imprinted with the word 'Thurber.' John couldn't help but wonder if it was the same bricks he had counted and stacked when he worked at the brick factory.

With that job finished the crew moved to laying bricks for Camp Bowie Boulevard.

By September 1904, they were laying brick for Commerce Street, close to Second Avenue, in downtown Fort Worth. As they worked closer and closer to the fire station, every time the fire wagon went out on a call, John watched with envy. To handle those big, strong horses, drive that wagon at full speed with bells ringing would be a dream come true. Little did he know, his life was about to change and he would find his vocation.

3

Job with a Future

September 12, 1904

It had rained the night before, but John reported to work anyway. A layer of gravel helped to make it possible to work around the mud to lay the brick street. By now, they were working across the street from Central Fire Station, in downtown Fort Worth.

Shortly after their lunch break, they heard the fire alarm go off. Their foreman yelled, "Everybody get over to the side of the street. Move that wheelbarrow out of the way."

As the bricklayers and John stood at the side, they watched the firemen open the big doors of the station. The horses were anxious to run. The driver signaled for them to go. The horses came out in a fast trot pulling the wagon behind them into the muddy street. Just as they got even with where John was standing the wagon got stuck in the mud. The driver grabbed a whip and started beating the horses. The horses were frightened of the whip, hurt and confused. On top of that the driver was yelling cuss words the horses couldn't understand. John couldn't either. He hated to see a horse or any animal being mistreated. It made him mad and the longer he stood there watching the madder he became. John couldn't stand it anymore and walked over to the wagon, looked up at the fire chief and said, "If you'll make that SOB quit beating those horses I'll get your wagon out of the mud for you."

The chief looked over at the driver and said, "get down" and motioned for John to come around and take over.

As John walked to the front of the horses he asked the chief, "What are their names?"

Chief replied, "Abe on right, George on the left."

John patted the horses on the side, walked around checking the bits on their harnesses to make sure it wasn't cutting the sides of their mouths, while talking to Abe and George, so they would know the sound of his voice, "No beatings, boy's. But we got work to do. You can do it, I know you can. I helped you, now you help me." John walked on around and as he started to climb on the wagon, he noticed the firemen still standing on the back of the wagon. "You men get off the back and when I signal the horses, you start pushing. It ain't right to expect these horses to do everything for you."

The chief yelled back, "Do as he says."

John climbed into the driver's seat and flipped the reins. "All set, boy's lets go."

He kept flipping the reins, "Come on Abe, pull. Atta' boy, Come on George, you can do it. Come on PULL, PULL! Come on, GO, GO, GO!"

John's father always said he had a way with horses. These horses were no different as they responded to John's voice, signals and encouragement and pulled together, soon pulling the wagon out of the mud hole. John called, "Whoa, boy's that's enough" as he pulled back on the reins. He was going to get off and let the driver take over, as the other firemen got back on the wagon.

To John's surprise the chief yelled, "Don't stop now. We got a fire to go to. You want this job? It's yours!"

John's excitement grew. Driving a wagon and taking care of horses was something he could easily do and enjoy. He didn't even ask how much the job paid. He just flicked the reins and kept on going, as the previous driver ran to jump on the back of the wagon with the others.

"What's your name?" Chief asked.

"John Whittenburg, Sir."

"John, turn left at the fork in the road. We should be able to see the fire and smoke from there. Head for it. When you get there hold the horses as they will get scared if the fire is really big. Under the seat here are burlap bags. Put them over the horse's heads.

They aren't afraid if they can't see the fire. When you get the horses calmed down, relieve one of the men on the pump."

John could see the fire now, as they crossed over the river on the wood bridge, leading to the red light district, and then headed south toward the flames and smoke. When the chief yelled stop, John pulled the horses reins with one hand, "Whoa, Abe, Whoa, George" and pulled on the wagon's brake with the other hand. He stopped the horses and wagon across the street from the wood frame house; totally engulfed in flames. Setting the brake, he looped the reins around the hook, grabbed the burlap bags and jumped down to tend to the horses. He calmly talked to them as he placed the bags over their heads. They responded to his touch and voice.

John went to the back of the wagon where two of the firemen were pushing the pump up and down, one on one side, one on the other. He relieved the first one he came to. Standing there pumping he could now look around and observe what was going on. He remembered the first thing the chief did was ask the bystanders if everybody got out of the burning house. They all said yes. All the firemen could do was try to keep the fire from spreading and get it out as fast as possible. John watched and learned as he stood there pumping.

He had heard about the red light district, sometimes referred to as "Hell's Half Acre." This was his first time to observe the saloons, gambling halls and the scantly clad ladies with painted faces. John wondered, *why would anyone want to live this way? No wonder it's called Hell's half acre.* He chuckled as he thought *they need to hear my grandpa preach. He'd scare the hell out of the whole acre.*

After the fire was completely out and John could quit pumping, he took the bags off the horse's heads and prepared to drive the wagon back. The chief told John where to pull around to the back of the station and come in the back door. This put the horses and wagon in line to go straight out the front door next time.

Soon as he stopped the wagon inside, the chief said, "John, you're the best driver I've ever had. Are you married or fixing to get married?"

"No, Sir.'"

"Good cause this job's for single men. What do ya' say? You want the job?"

John grinned, "As soon as I can walk across the street, pick up my lunch bucket and tell Mr. Pruitt I quit."

Chief grinned, too. "You haven't even asked how much the job pays."

"I like the job and I already guessed it pays more than a dollar a day."

"How 'bout forty-five dollars a month?" Chief asked.

"Sounds good to me."

Chief stuck his hand out to shake John's, "By the way, I'm Jim Maddox, but everybody calls me Chief."

"Nice to meet you, Chief. I'll be back soon as I talk to Mr. Pruitt, Sir."

John hadn't been this excited since the day he got the job at the Thurber brick factory. He walked over to where he had left his lunch bucket, picked it up and walked over to his previous foreman. "Sorry, Mr. Pruitt, I didn't mean to leave like that, but Chief said keep on going he had a fire to go to."

"That's understandable, John. You did a service to your community. Now, better get back to work," Mr. Pruitt said.

"Well, Sir, the chief offered me the job of driving the fire wagon for him, starting right now. I hate to give you such short notice but handling horses and driving the wagon is something I'm good at and it sounds like the kind of job security I've been looking for, so I'm going to have to quit, Mr. Pruitt."

"I hate to loose you, John, but I understand. Good luck to you." Mr. Pruitt reached to shake John's hand.

John walked back across the street to the fire station. For the first time, he felt confident this was going to be the job in which he could excel and give him the financial security he wanted.

John returned to find the chief sitting at his desk. "Let's get all the paperwork done and get you on the payroll, since you've already been working. Where you living?"

"In North Fort Worth with my sister and her husband."

"Well, you can go home tonight and bring your things when you come on duty in the morning. You'll be living here, now. You'll be on duty 144 hours and off 24 hours a week. You can trade days off with one of the other men, if you need to. You'll be in training for three months. Then you'll be assigned as a regular at whatever station needs a man."

After they finished the paper work, the chief started introducing him to the other firemen. "Boy's, this is John Whittenburg, our new driver. John, this is J.R., he's going to station #3 tomorrow."

John shook the man's hand while thinking, "*I hope I didn't cause him to loose his Job, but on the other hand if he beat those horses more than once, he deserved it.*"

Chief continued walking around where all the firemen were still washing the wagon and equipment. "This is Bill Bideker, my second in command."

"Nice job driving." Bill said as he shook hands with John.

"Thank you."

Chief pointed, "That's Joe and Homer over there."

The men nodded a greeting and continued cleaning up. Chief started leading John to the back of the station. "I better warn you I run a tight ship. Any man gets drunk, out of line with a lady or rude to any tax payer that pays our salary, gets fined and it comes out of your pay." They were near the horse stall now. "And you have already met Abe and George."

Abe and George walked over toward John and he reached out and patted them. "Good job, Boy's. You and I are going to make a good team." They raised their heads up and down as though they understood and agreed with what he said.

Chief said, "You seem to have a way with horses."

"Yes, Sir, that's what my Pa says."

"Well, let's get you acquainted with how things work around here. Your job will be to take care of the horses. Make sure they have food and water of course and clean out their stalls every morning, sometimes every evening too. As you can see, there is only a chain across the front of their stall and the horse collars hanging from the ceiling on this 'L' hook. When the alarm sounds, that chain will fall and the horses know to put their heads through the horse collars as they come out of their stalls and to run get in front of the wagon to be hitched. You and Joe are assigned to strap down their harnesses, while Will and Homer hitch them to the wagon. When you get in the drivers seat, they go open the doors. The horses are going to be anxious to run the minute the doors open, so you have to hold them back till the men can jump onto the back of the wagon." Chief motioned for John to follow and continued giving him instructions. "You have to be sure the back of the wagon is clear out the door, before directing the horses which way to turn." They stopped by the big map on the wall. Chief pointed, "Meanwhile, I will be getting the information through this new electrical system that tells me what alarm box has been set off or sometimes people call us on the telephone to tell us there is a fire."

As John looked at all the equipment, he thought, "*My goodness, they have all this new electricity stuff and telephones I've been hearing about.*"

Chief continued, "These red lights are the alarm boxes. Also, see the red dots on the map? That marks where the fireplugs are. It will be good if you get familiar with their locations. You need to stop the wagon at the nearest fire plug. When the men get off the back they have the hose in hand, drag it and wrap it around the fireplug. You then run the wagon down closer to the fire and this pulls the hose off the wagon, rather than the men dragging it all the way. When the wagon stops or the hose is all off the wagon, then they connect it to the plug. Otherwise, the hose might tear loose from the connection. Also, study the street names, so between the two of us, we know where we're going."

The fire station was all one big room downstairs, except for the half wall around the horses, forming their stall. Chief showed John the kitchen area. "We all put in a dollar a week to buy food. We take turns being in charge of buying groceries and helping with the cooking and cleanup. Whoever is in charge of cooking at the time the alarm goes off, is responsible for taking the food off the stove or out of the oven. Don't want to burn the firehouse down while we put out another one."

John nodded a yes to that.

"Well, now let me show you the sleeping quarters." Chief led the way over to and up the stairs. "Each man has his own cot, bed linens and one blanket. No laundry service, you do your own. Each man gets a locker and a small trunk at the foot of the bed, for extra clothes, extra blanket or whatever personal items you might have."

John surveyed the one big room, filled with six iron frame cots, like he had at Mrs. Mazzano's. Each bed made up nice and neat but, one was bare except for the mattress. In the middle of the room was a large round hole in the floor, with a brass pole in the middle. John had to ask, "What in the world is that for?"

Chief smiled, "When we are all up here sleeping and the alarm goes off, all five of us can get down this pole faster than going down steps. It's actually safer than falling down the stairs. What you do is jump toward the pole, wrapping your arms and legs around the pole at the same time and you slide right down like this." Chief jumped and slid down, landing on his feet. Looking back up he hollered at John, "Now you try it."

John, always ready to try anything at least once, jumped, wrapping his arms and legs around the pole at the same time and down he went. "That was more fun than swinging on a rope from a hay loft."

"A little awkward, but you'll get the hang of it after a time or two." Chief replied.

"The rest of the things you need to know will come from working on the job, common sense and good judgment. Tomorrow we'll all tell you about some of our experiences in some of the fires we have fought. You will be in training for next three months. Which means you'll handle the horses and the pump, till you've been to enough fires to learn more. You don't do anything unless I tell you. Understood?"

"Yes, Sir." John replied, while holding in his excitement.

"Good," Chief said. "Now, it's time for me to go off duty and I'm going home and get some clean clothes. I'll see you here in the morning, say.... eight o'clock."

"I'll be here."

John walked part of the way home, too full of anticipation to sit still and wait for the trolley. This also gave him more time to rethink the events of the day and everything the chief had told him. The trolley came along so he rode the rest of the way to North Fort Worth.

John had been staying with Ida and James and paying them room and board. He hadn't found a good boarding house and besides his work had taken him all over town. He and James liked each other and when James went off on his horse buying trips, John helped Ida with the chores. It had been a good arrangement, but now he would be leaving.

John could hardly wait to get there to tell them the good news. He got off at the trolley stop and practically ran the last three blocks to their house. "I'm home." He yelled as he came in the front door.

James and Ida were just sitting down to supper. Ida said, "It's about time. Where have you been?"

John excitedly started to sit down at the table. "I can't wait to tell you."

Ida interrupted, "Whoa, young man. You go wash up first."

"I'm sorry, Ida, but I have had the best day of my life and I am starving." John went to the sink and washed his hands and splashed water on his face.

Ida said, "You smell like smoke. Did they have a fire close to where you were working?"

"No, it was in the red light district."

Ida was shocked and scolding like the protective big sister she had always been.

"John Lee Whittenburg, don't tell me you have been to the red light district! Uh-Uh, Shame on you." She gasped.

John, drying his hands and grinning, said, "I sure was." He let her rave another minute, while he looked at James and winked. "Ida, calm down, it's not what you think." Then he told them what happened and about his job with the fire department, except, he didn't tell Ida about seeing the scantly clad ladies in the crowd of onlookers.

4

Basic Training

September 13, 1904

John went to work the next morning, carrying a bag of clothes, with shaving mug, razor and razor strap. That was about all he had and all he needed. He wore his nice city clothes and boots and rode the electric streetcar into town. Getting off near the fire station, he walked the other two blocks, arriving at the same time as Chief Maddox.

"Howdy, Chief."

"Howdy, John. Glad to see you're on time."

They went inside and Chief said, "John, you get the vacant bed and put your things up. I'll put up my laundry and get you some bedding out of the store room."

"Yes, Sir."

Returning from the storeroom Chief said, "Now, besides your pay, you get an allowance each month to help pay for your uniforms. I'll give you your first allowance now so you can walk over to Monning's or Stripling's Department Store and get you a set of Khakis. Two would be better, if you have the money. If not, you can wait till pay day next month and buy more. But after a couple of months you're expected to be in uniform at all times."

"Yes, Sir," John replied, as he took the money.

As soon as he had made his bed, he started to the stairs, and then remembered the pole. *Might as well get used to it,* he thought and slid down. Chief was right, it was easier that time. John walked over to the department store. He had saved a little money since he arrived in Ft. Worth, even with helping his folks and paying his keep at Ida's. So he bought two shirts and two pair pants and a belt to go with them. He also bought a pair of BVD's and socks. (BVD stood for bottom vented design underwear.) He was all fixed up now. When he got back to the station he hung up his city clothes and put on one of his uniforms. He thought the navy blue pants and light blue shirt looked pretty good. He had a uniform, good job and good pay. He was only 24 years old and felt on top of the world. He slid down the pole to join his fellow firemen.

"Now fellows, how much do I need to put in the pot for food?"

Homer spoke up, "Nothing. It's just a couple more days till the first of the month. You can eat J.R.'s portion since he's gone. Do you know how to cook?"

"I can cook bacon, eggs, oatmeal and pancakes. Lunch if you like cold cuts, cheese, crackers or sandwich. Dinner I can make a pot of stew and corn dodgers. But I'm willing to learn."

Will said, "Good. How about we start with you making pancakes in the morning? Homer here makes pancakes so tough you could wear them for shoe soles." They all laughed.

Electricity had been connected in most businesses downtown and this cut down on the number of fires in that area. But a lot of homes in the red light district and the other poor neighborhoods still used oil lamps, easily knocked over, causing fires. So far, John experienced only a few small fires. He made it past his three months training period and felt more confident now. Little did he know he would experience one of the biggest fires in the history of Fort Worth.

October 15, 1904

Pa Whittenburg started receiving a Confederated Pension. It helped with their poor situation and relieved John's mind from having to take care of them financially.

December 3, 1904

No longer a Rookie, John became a regular fireman at Station Number One.

Three days later, the alarm went off early afternoon. Chief Maddox looked at the board and saw the light flashing indicating someone had triggered the alarm at the box near the depot. The phone rang and he answered. The voice on the other end excitedly proclaimed, "The T and P Depot's on fire. Hurry!"

After hitching the horses, they put on their coats and helmets and climbed on the wagon ready to go. Chief put on his boots while still on the telephone. He hung up the phone and as he ran to the wagon he yelled, "Big one, boys. The T & P depot. This high wind blowing, it's going to spread fast. I called station two to come help. They'll hit the east side; we'll hit the west wall." Chief grabbed his coat and helmet and climbed in the seat beside John. As soon as the wagon cleared the door and made the turn into the street, John gave Abe and George the signal to run full speed; the bells on their harnesses ringing loudly.

When close enough to see the whole roof was in flames, Chief yelled at John, "Stop at the first hydrant, let two men off with one hose. Then pull the wagon down to second hydrant. Take care of the horses; find a couple of volunteers from the onlookers to work the pump. We are going to need all the help we can get. Turn the water on full force. Joe and I'll get the other hose out and get ready. You get behind me and Joe."

"Will do!" John said as he slowed the skittish horses.

At the second stop, he put the hoods over their heads. Before he could get to the crowd of people, Chief yelled at him, "Get somebody to call station three and four."

John waved acknowledgement, turned to the crowd and asked, "We need volunteers, two to work the pump, two to relieve them and rotate." Four men in railroad uniforms came forward. "Now, I need someone to call station three and station four to respond under Chief Maddox's orders."

Two men dressed in suits waved and headed toward the Collins Company across the street to find telephones. John ran over to find Chief and Joe struggling to hold the hose and nozzle, trying to keep a steady stream of water aimed at the roof. John grabbed hold, too. When station three and four arrived, Chief went to direct them, station three to the front of the building and four to the rear. The strong wind some times blew the water away from where they directed it. Using their ladders, station four climbed on top of the shed roof covering the railroad tracks next to the building. They could then get water inside the second story windows. John and Joe, both young and daring, dragged their hose and climbed hastily upward through the smoke filled clock tower full of musty railway records. There they stuck their heads out the openings left by the collapse of the huge, clock faces, broken by expansion from the heat. They overlooked the fire now and directed the fire hose down on top of the flames. It took a while for the firemen to get the fire under control; still the building was gutted. All that remained was the outside walls and the tower. The firemen stirred the ashes looking for embers left smoldering, not wanting the high wind to reignite the fire. All the onlookers felt sure everyone was out of the building. They were glad they didn't have to look for bodies after a long, tiring day.   Little did they realize they made history and not just because of the biggest fire in Fort Worth, so far. Pioneer photographer Charles Swartz rode his bicycle to the location and made numerous pictures of the fire, proving cameras are invaluable for recording news events. Many copies were made and glued on the back of cardboard and sold for souvenirs.

After returning to the firehouse, John and Joe started thinking. Climbing that tower wasn't the smartest thing to do. One spark at the bottom could have spread the fire to all those old paper records, right up to the top and there would have been no place for them to go. Not to mention the fact the fire would have destroyed their fire hose along the way. They learned from experience; on the job training.

April 1905

Fort Worth hadn't rebuilt the depot, yet, so the city official's hired a banner company to decorate the outside of the burned out building with red, white and blue bunting. President Theodore

Roosevelt came to town in his private train. John had the day off. He rode downtown with Ida and James in their horse drawn buggy. They saw the train pull in, and the president being met by the city officials, but they were too far back in the crowd to hear any of his speech. Afterwards, the presidential party rode up Main Street in carriages. James, Ida and John got a closer look at the President as his carriage went by. The president supposedly planted a tree in front of the library and then returned to his train and left.

Ida said, "Wasn't that exciting to get to see the President of the United States?"

"About as exciting as the depot fire, huh, John?" James asked.

"Yeah, but not near as exciting as a fire in the red light district," John teased Ida.

"Oh, You!" Ida rolled her eyes. "I'm glad I didn't know you were fighting the depot fire. I would have been worried to death."

James guided the horse to a slow walk in all the crowd of people and headed in the direction of the fire station to drop John off. "You be careful, John."

"Will do. Thanks for the ride to work."

October 8, 1905

John got along with Chief Maddox alright, but he and Bill Bideker seemed to see eye to eye on more things. They enjoyed their conversations and working together. A year after John joined the fire department, Maddox resigned and went back to being police chief. Bill Bidaker became City Fire Chief. John was promoted to Hook and Ladder #1.

January 1906

The alarm sounded early one morning. The horses ran to take their place in front of the wagon. The men hurried through their routine and soon headed down Throckmorton Street. John signaled Abe and George into a full run with all the bells ringing. Suddenly, at the intersection of Tenth Street, coming from the right, the trolley pulled in front of them. The conductor panicked, froze and kept going. John pulled hard on the left reins, "Left, Abe, Left George.

LEFT, LEFT, LEFT," he kept yelling and pulling on the reins. Abe and George pulled a hard left turn and brought the side of the fire wagon along side the trolley with only inches in between. A row of horrified faces shown in each window of the trolley as the fire wagon rolled beside. All the firemen breathed a sigh of relief, especially those hanging on the back of the wagon. John kept the horses straight and in full run till the trolley came to a stop and the wagon moved ahead. John guided them back to the center of the street and on to the fire.

March 1906

Station two received a new pair of horses, so big all the men shied away from them. They also had a new, longer hook and ladder wagon. Every time they went out the door on a call, the end of the ladder hit the row of windows in the door, breaking every single pane. Bideker transferred John to station two for a while to teach the drivers how to get the wagon out of the station without breaking a window. John had them to practice waiting a little longer and come out a little further before signaling the horses to turn. After getting acquainted with the horses, John found them to be very gentle and playful. But when the alarm sounded, the horses focused on their work. John's ability to handle horses and earn the respect of his fellow workers, quickly led him into promotions and more pay.

January 1907

John was among the first to be trained, when #2 station received a new aerial truck.

He became excited the minute he heard about the truck. To climb a ladder without the ladder leaning against the side of a building sounded a little far fetched. But, it also had possibilities. You wouldn't have to worry about a wall collapsing while you were on a ladder leaning against a burning building. John watched the demonstration, anticipating being able to reach a second story window to rescue someone or getting a hose up higher over a fire. The lower end of the ladder stayed attached to the top of the truck, while the rest of the ladder rose into the air at a slant. John immediately volunteered for the training. It reminded him of the times he climbed up a ladder to help his pa put a roof on a barn.

Fifth Ward Station

February 1907

Chief Bideker called John into his office one afternoon and asked, "John, would you do me a favor?"

"Of course. If I can."

Chief began to explain, "There's a problem over at station six, at Petersmith and Fulton Streets. The men are complaining about these two bullies, who want to run things their way and not do their jobs. I've already had three men to quit just because of them. I'd like to send you over there to see what's going on. I want to know for sure who is causing havoc between the men and them calling me wanting to quit or be transferred to another station." Chief tossed a letter to John, "This is the fourth letter I've received."

John glanced over the letter, noticing the signature. He never started a fight but he readily would fight for the underdog if the opportunity arose. "I'll be glad to, when do you want me to go?"

"Next few days, if that's alright with you?"

John thought for a minute, "How about me going just after they go off duty? That will give me a chance to talk to the other men and be ready for the bullies when they come back to work."

"Good, let me look it up for you. Just a minute." Chief looked through his papers. "Marcus Mathews, supposedly the meanest, gets off duty at five pm Wednesday, comes back at five pm Thursday. Francis Foust or Frank as he is called, goes off….hum-m..he has the same time off. That would give you from Wednesday night till Thursday afternoon at five. Is that enough time?"

"I think so, you take care of the paper work, I'll take off Wednesday afternoon for station six and plan to stay there till things are taken care of or you call me back here."

"Thanks, John, I appreciate you doing this. I know I can count on you. Oh and by the way, you'll be going as the new Captain of station six with a raise in pay."

John, surprised and pleased, reached his hand out to Bideker, "Thank you, Chief. I appreciate that very much."

"You deserve it, John. Congratulations."

John started out the door, stopped and asked, "Could you not send word to six just yet. Let them think I am just another replacement till I have time to see what's going on. They might be more honest with a fellow worker than an officer."

"Good thinking, John. Will do."

*****

Wednesday afternoon, John packed up his belongings and caught the trolley. The trolley stopped on the corner next to station six. John walked into the station, arriving just after Marcus and Frank had left. "Howdy, fellows, Chief Bideker sent me to replace Jones that quit. I'm John Whittenburg."

The other firemen introduced themselves with the usual, "Glad to meet you" and "Good to have you" and "Welcome." After a little small talk John picked out the man who wrote the letter to Bideker. "Floyd, I know the stations are all about the same, but how about you show me around. I'll get acquainted with the horses first. In case, we get a call, I want them to know my voice."

"Sure thing, John, set your gear over there for now," Floyd said as they headed back to the horse stalls. "We have Storm and Thunder. How long you been handling horses?"

"Since I was knee high to a duck and I've been a driver since I joined the fire department." John stroked the horses as he talked to them. Thunder, solid black as coal and Storm, a dark brown with a white mark down the center of his face; easy to tell them apart. While he was petting the horses, John asked Floyd, "So, why did Jones quit?"

Floyd, silent at first, slowly began to explain. "Well, you might as well know we got a couple of men that are always causing trouble. Nobody likes them. They won't do their chores and me and the others are tired of being bullied into doing things for them or things don't get done. You being new, you might as well get ready cause they'll be coming after you."

John asked, "So how do they perform when you're out on a call?"

"They holler out orders to the rest of us like we don't know what we're doing, even if we are doing it at the time. They go talk to the crowd of people gathering or they 'disappear', like if the fire is in the front of the building they go around to the back and we don't see them till the fires out. They say they are looking to see if the fire has spread, but their boots aren't pulled up, their coat not hooked and they never carry a hose. I'm just thankful we haven't had to rescue somebody yet or have a fire get ahead of us."

John thought for a minute before answering. "Thanks for an honest answer and the warning, Floyd." Knowing Floyd would follow, John started walking back to where the others sat around a table playing cards. "Can I interrupt your card game for a minute or two, fellow?"

They stopped playing and looked up at John.

"I'm here because Bideker sent me to see first hand what the problem is with Marcus and Frank. Sounds like they want to get paid for doing nothing."

The men all looked at each other with disbelief, till they realized what he had said. Then Floyd spoke up, "Thank, God, Bideker's finally taking us seriously."

Earnest asked, "What are you going to do?"

"I'm not sure, yet. That's why I came on duty while they were gone, so I could talk to you fellows first and get up on everything going on."

One by one, John asked their opinions and thoughts. Now, time to think about how to handle things. "Let's start by taking a look at the chore assignments for this week." John led the way, as the others followed over to the big chalkboard on the wall. "Now, whose turn is it to do what jobs?"

"Well, Marcus will want....."

John interrupted. "No, that's not what I asked. Whose TURN is it to do what?"

The men seemed a little hesitant to speak up, but Floyd took the lead. "It's Marcus's turn to clean the kitchen floor and Frank's turn to wash dishes after Ernest and I get through cooking tomorrow night."

John printed all their names beside the tasks to be done. "Now, I can't do it all, but when I stand up to these fellows, you men be ready to stand behind me. I have an idea those blowhards, if backed into a corner, will back down. There are more of us than the two of them and we got Bideker behind us. The worst that can happen is one of us may get a black eye. Are you with me?"

"We're with you," they all said in unison.

The next day, after lunch, the alarm rang. Floyd and Harry grabbed lunchmeat, milk and cheese and put in the cooler. John got in the driver's seat and talked to the horses while holding back on the reins. "Whoa, Boys, calm down." Floyd and Harry opened the big doors. Floyd climbed on the wagon beside John and Harry got on the back with Ernest and Tucker. John lightly flipped the reins, holding them taunt till the wagon cleared the doors, then signaled Thunder and Storm to go right. After completing the turn, he flipped the reins hard, "GO! GO!" The horses took off in a full run.

The fire, a barn full of hay, flamed at one end. Floyd and Harry took one hose to the right and Ernest and Tucker took a hose to the left. John wanted to take a hose, but for now, he had to pretend he was just a driver, take care of the horses and work the pump. The fire was too far ahead of them to save the barn. They could only try to keep it from spreading and get it out. They had to move the remains of every bale of hay and water everything down to make sure nothing was left smoldering. It was a long seven hour ordeal.

Returning to the station about seven o'clock; hot, tired, hungry and shedding coats, helmets and boots, they unhitched the horses. After putting them in their stall and making sure they had water, the men headed to the kitchen for some ice tea. They found their dirty lunch dishes still on the table and no sign of supper on cooking. Marcus and Frank sat at the card table. The men looked at John. He motioned for them to follow. They all walked over to Marcus and Frank.

Without looking up from their card game, Marcus said, "You fellows have fun today? What's for supper, Harry?"

John spoke up, "Whatever you two want to fix."

Marcus looked up to see who was talking. "Who in the hell are you?"

"My name's John and from what I've heard about you, you must be Marcus."

"Well, John, you're new here and in case you didn't know, I run things around here. You do as I say."

"Not any more," John said.

"You want to bet?" Looking at the others, Marcus said, "Ya'll get back to work. Get that kitchen cleaned up and fix supper or I'll call Bideker and get you all fired."

John spoke up, "Go ahead, and call Bideker. You know his number. And be sure to tell him John is threatening to beat the tar out of you."

"Huh! You and who else?" Marcus stood up, surprised to find himself looking up at John who was at least a head taller and twenty pounds heavier.

The others spoke up, "All of us!"

Marcus's eyes grew big with surprise when the others sided with this new man. "It's against regulations to fight in the station."

John said, "We aren't fighting, are we boys?

The other men said, "No, not at all."

"But, if you want to," John said, "we can step outside to finish this discussion."

Marcus didn't know what to do. He looked over at Frank, but Frank was waiting for instructions from Marcus. After giving it some thought Marcus plopped down in his chair. Frank, with a look of disbelief that Marcus had backed down, took a seat too.

Marcus said, "Well, since you're new here, I'll let it pass this time. Ya'll go on and get to work and get supper."

John leaned over, grabbed Marcus by the collar and said, "We have been working for the last seven hours. You two just came on duty and been playing cards. Now, we are going to finish our jobs and get cleaned up and you two are going to get your sorry butts out of those chairs and into the kitchen and fix supper and it better be good. Because if you don't, I'm calling Bideker with my report he is waiting for and I am going to recommend he fire you both for not doing your share of the work. Do you understand me or do you want to go outside where I can pound it into your head?"

Nobody was saying a word as John let go of Marcus's collar and straightened up.

"You'll be sorry for this." Marcus retorted.

"Go ahead; call Bideker if you want to." John replied and turned to go. "Oh, by the way," he stopped and turned back toward the men, "I never properly introduced myself. I'm John Whittenburg, your new Captain."

Marcus and Frank sat there with their mouth open. When the other men realized what he said, snickering spread across the room. Ernest and Tucker went back to clean the wagon, while the others wiped down the horses. As they finished and went upstairs to clean up, Marcus and Frank had cleared the kitchen table and started cooking supper.

"I think Marcus must have called Bideker." Floyd said, "I heard him say something, then the rest of the time, he kept saying, "Yes, Sir, Yes, Sir, Yes, Sir."

John replied, "Now, we'll see what they do when we go out on a call."

They had a nice supper and a quiet evening, while Frank washed dishes, Floyd dried and Harry put them up, then Marcus mopped the floor. John made sure he entered the fire call in the Captain's log and went back to pet the horses. Earnest came up to John and said, "Captain, You're a really good driver, but shouldn't I take over driving for you and caring for the horses? I mean, you being Captain, are you supposed to drive the wagon, or just what?"

"Ernest, my job is to make sure we all work together as a team. I don't care if it's fighting a fire or cleaning the horse stalls. If I'm delayed, getting information over the telephone, or it's my day off, you drive. If I happen to get in the drivers seat before you finish hooking up the horses, I'll drive. It really doesn't matter as long as we do the best job we can."

"Thank ya', Cap."

The first couple of fires they made, John had to remind Marcus or Frank, "Fold those boot tops up", "button that coat", "Grab that nozzle before turning the water on."

John reported in each week to Chief Bideker. Within a few months, John had them all working together and getting along.

No. 6 Station

5

Courting Days

Early May 1907

Chief Bideker, one of the finest chiefs the city of Ft. Worth had, now supervised thirty-eight paid firemen in seven stations and all fully horse drawn. He worked with city officials to change the rules to allow married men to be firemen.

Some of the men were anxious to propose to their girlfriends. Others immediately took their days off to find a girlfriend. John always felt shy and had a hard time carrying on a conversation around women. He tried to convince Ida to quit inviting single ladies over to her house when he would be there on his days off. Even though he enjoyed looking at pretty girls, he hadn't met one yet who wasn't giggly, whiney or otherwise didn't strike his fancy. He was too busy working, saving money for the future. He helped his parents find a room to rent at 1508 Weatherford St. and get out of the tent. Up till now, he couldn't get married and still stay on the fire department.

During warm weather, the firemen put their chairs outside under a shade tree, in front of the station. John noticed a cute young, dark haired, girl walking down the street once a week to the house across the street. After a while she left and walked back to the trolley stop. John thought, *"Now there's a girl I would like to meet, but how do I get properly introduced?"*

*****

One day, his friend, J.W. said, "John, I got a girlfriend, Mable, but she won't go out with me unless we double date. She is very prim and proper. She's the chambermaid for the Moore's, up on 8th Avenue & Pennsylvania. Mrs. Moore has a personal maid, Jennie. Mable wants me to find a date for Jennie or she won't go out with me. All the other men have girlfriends. I can't find anybody else. Will you please help me out and go with me to take these ladies for a Sunday buggy ride? Mable said they would pack a picnic lunch and we could drive through the park."

John first responded by shaking his head no, "J.W., I'm really not interested."

J.W. pleaded, "Please, just help me out this one time. It won't take long and if it turns out a bad situation, we can always say we have to go back on duty sooner. We have to get them back home before dark anyway. If you'll do this for me, just this one time, I'll owe you a big favor and pay you back."

"Well, okay, just this once," John gave in.

J.W. called Mabel, "I got a date for Jennie with my Captain. He's a really nice fellow. If that's all right, we'll be by Sunday morning at eleven to pick you ladies up."

Mabel replied, "Oh, how lovely. We'll pack a lunch and be ready. Oh, be sure to come around to the back door, so as not to disturb the Moore's in the sitting room."

"Sure thing. See you Sunday."

*****

Sunday rolled around and the two young men bathed and put on a fresh uniform before going off duty. J.W. arranged to borrow a two seated surrey from his folks. They rode the streetcar to his parent's house, hitched up the horses and trotted over to Pennsylvania Avenue, the elite neighborhood of Ft.Worth. It was called Quality Hill because the wealthy railroad and cattle barons lived there. J.W. guided the surrey around to the back door of the Moore's mansion at 1326 Pennsylvania Avenue. The men walked to the door and J.W. tapped lightly.

Mabel a cute, little, young blond-headed girl opened the door. "Hello, J.W. it's nice to see you again. Won't you come in?"

"It's nice to see you again, Miss Mabel. This is my friend, John. John, I'd like you to meet Miss Mabel Johnson."

"Pleased to meet you, Miss Johnson." John nodded.

"Nice to meet you, John. You may call me Mabel."

"Miss Mabel," John said with a smile.

"Ya'll have a seat at the table. I'll go up stairs and get Jennie. J.W., no peeking in the picnic basket," Mabel smiled at J.W. and walked out the kitchen door.

As soon as she was gone, J.W. bumped elbows with John, "What do you think? Ain't she a cutie?"

John saw another side of J.W. he hadn't seen before, like a puppy panting wanting to play with another puppy. "Yes, she is a cute little lady."

John grew more nervous by the minute. Glancing up at the kitchen clock, he reasoned it took two hours to get here, which meant they needed to have the ladies back by six, so they could get back to the fire station on time tonight. His palms were sweating as he wondered *what in the world am I going to talk about to this strange woman? What if we don't get along?*

The kitchen door swung open and Mabel entered, followed by a pretty, five foot tall young girl, full bodied but not plump or fat, with black hair, dark eyes and long black eye lashes. Her eyes sparkled with laughter even though she just smiled. John thought *she looks like the girl that walks to the house across the street from the fire station.* His eyes refused to move, they seem glued to her. *What? Oh, Mabel is introducing us.* He stuttered, "How do you do, Miss Campbell?"

"Nice to meet you, John." Her voice floated through his ears.

Everything seemed to move in slow motion. Mabel handed J.W. a quilt and he put it in the back of the Surry. John picked up the picnic basket and set it beside the quilt, and the men helped the ladies into the Surry. As J.W. guided the horses out to the street, Mabel said, "Jennie is from Michigan. The Moore's go there every summer and that's where they met Jennie and hired her."

"You came all the way from Michigan?" John asked. "Did you come on the train? How long did it take?"

"Yes, we came by train and it took us three days to get here."

"How did you come to start working for the Moore's?" John

could have spent the time just silently looking at Jennie, but he was curious to learn more about her.

"I was a waitress in the hotel dining room at Wenona Beach. I was assigned the Moore's table. After the guests left and we had cleaned up the dining room and kitchen, all the employees were allowed to dance." Jennie didn't seem shy as she asked, "Do you dance, John?"

"No, I've never been anyplace where folks danced." John didn't say it but he thought, *Pa and Grandpa would have beaten me to death if I had.*

"It's fun, you should try it." Jennie continued, "Anyway, one night Mr. and Mrs. Moore asked me if it would be all right if they stayed and watched. 'Sure, I says'. Afterwards, Mr. Moore asked if I would teach his wife to dance and he even offered to pay me extra. I taught her to dance and just before they were to leave Mr. Moore asked me to come to Texas. He wanted to hire me as Mrs. Moore's personal maid. So, I asked Ma, but she wanted to meet them first."

"That's understandable," John said.

"But, I didn't want them to meet my pa, 'less it was the night before payday when he was sober. But, listen to me chattering like a clucking hen. You don't want to hear all that." Jennie stopped.

John was so enthralled, looking and listening to her, "No, don't stop. I want to hear more about you."

"I don't want to bore you with my chattering."

"You're not a bit boring," John encouraged her. "I'm enjoying listening to you."

"There's not much more to tell. I told Mr. Moore about my family and he was very understanding and kind. Ma runs a boarding house to make a living for all of us children. That's why I was anxious to get my own job."

"I understand," John assured her. "I felt the same way. So what does your father do?"

"He works in the coal mine by day and drinks at night till his whiskey and his money plays out. He saves just enough to pay the priest on Sunday to pray for him, another waste of money in my opinion."

"Sorry to hear that. I guess your folks approved of the Moore's, or you wouldn't be here."

"Not until my pa said they would be deprived of my income. Mr. Moore bribed my pa with $200 to let me go. I hated pa for taking the money. The Moore's are the nicest people I've ever known. I offered to pay Mr. Moore back out of my salary a little each week, but he wouldn't hear of it. They treat me more like a daughter than a hired servant. Know what I mean?"

"I understand." John said. "It's good that you like your work and the people you work for."

John, so engrossed with listening to Jennie, couldn't believe they were at the park already. They found a nice shady place and J.W. set the brake on the wagon and tied the reins to the hook. John got the quilt, handed it to Jennie and picked up the basket. The girls spread the quilt on the ground. They sat down and the girls began to hand out napkins, pieces of fried chicken, buttered homemade bread and cookies, apples and glasses of iced tea from a large canteen.

"Umm, umm, I haven't had homemade cookies like these, since I left Thurber to come to Fort Worth," John admitted. "Ladies, this is a wonderful lunch. Much better than J.W. and I make at the fire station."

"You're right about that," J.W. agreed.

The girls laughed. Jennie confessed, "You can thank Mabel. She's a good cook. I don't cook very much."

Mable spoke up, "But, you can cook and you help a lot."

"I just learned some from helping my mother."

"Miss Jennie," J.W. asked, "how do you like coming to Texas?"

"I like coming here for the winter. Michigan is so cold and the snow is terrible at times. I was born and raised in Indian Territory and when the coal mine closed there, pa heard about a mine opening in Frontenac, Kansas and we moved there for a while. Then we moved to Bay City several years ago."

Jennie continued. "Nobody visits Michigan in the winter. The Moore's like spending the summers there. They say it is cooler than Texas. But they come back here for the winter, 'cause you don't have much snow here. I loved it this winter. That one day we just had snow flurries, the cook didn't want to get out and go to the market. I didn't think anything of it, so I went shopping for her."

John had not looked forward to today, now the afternoon passed far too quickly. He tried not to stare at Jennie but when he looked away, his eyes seemed drawn back to her. His thought's drifted. *Her face is not painted like some girls I've seen. She has a plain, natural beauty with pale pink, thin lips. Her lips and my thin lips would come together so perfectly. But I dare not think of that now. It wouldn't be proper with us having just met.*

"John." Suddenly, he was jolted back to reality. Jennie spoke to him. "You haven't told me a thing about yourself. Have you lived here long? Do you like being a fireman?"

"Oh, not much to tell. Lived in Stephenville and Dublin most of my life, till I went to Thurber for a couple of years, then came to Fort Worth. I've cut timber, stacked bricks, hauled gravel, dug post holes and layed bricks. Then I got hired on the fire department 'cause I can handle horses purty good."

"Purty good is right." J.W. spoke up. "You should have seen how he guided those horses to keep from colliding with a trolley one day."

The girls both gasped. "Oh, my goodness! Do tell us about it , John."

"I didn't do anything. The horses did it all." John mumbled a little embarrassed.

J.W. continued telling them, "We were in full run down Throckmorton Street when a trolley pulled into the intersection right in front of us. John yelled at the horses to turn left and pulled on the reins. Joe and I hung on to the back of the wagon, ready to jump off. But, John brought the horses 'round and pulled the wagon right along side the streetcar with only a few inches between. Everybody on the trolley had a scared look on their faces. All of us thought sure we'd go 'slap-dab'," J.W. slapped his hands together, "up against the side of that trolley car."

"Heavenly days!" Mabel exclaimed, putting her hand to her cheek.

"Surely things like that don't happen often," Jennie questioned with concern.

"Nah," John said, "most times things are pretty dull, sitting around the fire hall with a bunch of fellows."

J.W. spoke up, "John, look-see what time it is. We gotta' get these horses and rig back in time to catch the last trolley. I don't like to think about walking those three miles back to the station."

John reached for his pocket watch he had recently bought at a pawn shop, "Oh, my, it's almost five-thirty."

"Oh, goodness," the girls exclaimed as they began picking things up. The fellows stood up and offered a hand to the ladies. John delighted in having an excuse to hold Jennie's hand again; helping her up and again helping her into the surrey. He couldn't believe the time passed so quickly.

J.W. put the horses in a fast trot.

Curious, John asked, "Miss Jennie, if you don't mind my asking do you visit someone over on the corner of Peter Smith and Fulton, every Wednesday?

"Why, yes, how did you know?"

"I've watched you walking back and forth to the trolley stop for last 5 or 6 weeks. J.W. and I work at the fire station across the street."

"You work at that Station? Oh, my! You have been watching me?" Jennie put her hands on both sides of her eyes, like a horses blinders. "I was trying not to look that way. I didn't want any of you men to think I was flirting like a hussy."

John smiled, "I have been thinking of how we could get properly introduced."

They both laughed and Jennie explained. "The daughter of one of Mrs. Moore's friend's, is bedridden. She is my age so Mrs. Moore lets me off on Wednesdays long enough to go visit with her."

As they arrived at the Moore's mansion, John spoke up, "If you ladies have next Sunday off, could we come pick you up and take you to dinner. Mrs. Simpson's dining room serves some good food."

"Oh, that would be lovely," Jennie exclaimed.

"Oh, my yes," Mabel agreed.

"Then we will see you next Sunday. Is eleven o'clock all right with you?"

The men left the ladies at the backdoor of the Moore's residence and headed out to return the horses and surrey. J.W. looked over at John, "Look who wasn't interested in going on a date, but was the first to ask for another." They smiled at each other and this time John nudged J.W. with his elbow.

Come Wednesday afternoon, John sat out under the shade tree with the other men, waiting for Jennie to come by. But, they had a fire call. By the time they got back, he saw Jennie walking toward the trolley stop in the next block.

The rest of the week passed slowly. John woke early Sunday morning, excited and anxious for the morning to pass. He put on his uniform he wore yesterday and slid down the pole, ready to start cleaning the horse stalls. Since being the first one up, he put the coffee pot on to brew. Opening the back door, an unusually cool spring morning breeze greeted him. *Perfect day for a buggy ride,* he thought.

J.W. broke the silence, "What are you doing up so early?"

John turned around, "Just couldn't go back to sleep. Coffee pot's on."

Looking to see, J.W. said, "It's not even perking yet."

"Might as well check the stalls." John said, as he walked toward the horses.

The stalls weren't very dirty and didn't take long to clean. The men got a cup of coffee and just as they sat down at the table, the alarm went off. They jumped up, John reached to cut the gas burner off under the coffee pot. The other men began sliding down the pole, the horses took their places, Chief took the call for the box number and they were soon ready to go. "Twelfth and Henderson" Chief instructed, as John led the horses out of the station.

When they arrived, they found a wagon accident, not a fire. Something spooked the farmer's horses while bringing a load of potatoes to market. The horses pulled the wagon into the electrical pole, setting off the fire alarm box. The jolt caused a lot of potatoes to roll off the wagon. The farmer apologized and for their trouble he offered them some of the potatoes. The firemen picked up some and put back in the farmers wagon. The farmer insisted they take the rest. Taking the two burlap bags, they normally put over the horses heads at a fire, they filled them with potatoes. They would be eating a lot of potatoes for the next few weeks.

As soon as they were back at the station and unhitched the horses, John looked at his watch. He and J.W. would have to hurry to bathe, dress, pick up the surrey and get the girls by eleven o'clock.

They made it only fifteen minutes late. The girls laughed when they told them what happened.

Mrs. Simpson ran a hotel on Fifth Avenue, off Henderson Street. During the week her dining room served guests only, but on Sunday she opened to the public. The room had nothing fancy, as far as furnishings, but the food was excellent.

"It is a rare occasion when ever I get to go out to eat." Mabel exclaimed.

Jennie said, "When I worked for the hotel, after we cleaned up at night, we could eat the leftovers for free. Then, when I came to Texas on the train with the Moore's, most times when the train stops you don't have time to get off. We started out with a picnic basket and we bought extra food when we did stop. I was always afraid the train would leave before we got back."

As they left the dining room, the big grandfather clock in the lobby was striking two-fifteen. "My goodness, we spent two and a half hours talking and eating and having coffee. Time sure passed in a hurry." John remarked. "But I can't remember when I have enjoyed anything any better than today."

"Me, too," the others all spoke at the same time.

J.W. kept the horses at a slow walk and took the long way back to Quality Hill and to the Moore's Mansion. As they neared the house, J.W. said, "What would you like to do next Sunday, Ladies?"

Mabel spoke up, "We aren't for sure if we have next Sunday off or not. Why don't ya'll call us mid-week?"

"Will do," J.W. said.

Jennie said, "All the house staff is expecting the Moore's to announce any day now, when they want to leave for Michigan." There was a sound of disappointment in her voice.

"Oh, no, we just met and now you'll be leaving," John said, definitely with disappointment.

"The Moores usually give the staff a week's notice when they plan to leave. I'm the only one who will be going with them."

"How long will you be gone?" John asked.

"Probably till sometime in September," Jennie answered.

They pulled around to the back of the house and J.W. stopped the horses, tied the reins and set the brake. The men got off the surrey first and helped the ladies. John held on to Jennie's hand to stop her for a minute while the others walked toward the door. "Miss Jennie, I hope I get to see you again. But, if not, would you be so kind as to write to me while you are away this summer?"

"Yes, John, I would like that very much. But, I have to warn you, I only went through third grade and you may not be able to read my handwriting."

"That's okay. I only went through fourth grade and you may not be able to read my handwriting either."

They smiled and John walked Jennie to the door and reluctantly let go of her hand.

*****

Wednesday morning, John did his chores. By then, Joe had breakfast about ready. After eating and helping to clean up the kitchen, John looked around for something else to do. Everybody had finished their assigned tasks. John went up stairs, bathed and put on a clean uniform. He felt restless. It was getting close to ten o'clock. "J.W. don't you think," John tried to sound casual, "it's about time to call the girls, so we know whether to plan anything for Sunday?"

"Getting a little anxious?" J.W. asked.

"Well," John said, "I'm just wondering when Jennie's going back to Michigan."

J.W. walked over to the phone, "I'll call Mabel and see if they know, yet."

Mabel answered the phone, "Moore's residence."

"Mabel, is that you?" J.W. asked.

"Hello, J.W.," Mabel said quietly.

"John and I were just wondering if you ladies were going to be off this Sunday."

"No, I am so sorry. The Moores are leaving Monday on the eleven o'clock train. We have to get last minute preparing and packing done. I can take off anytime after they leave. But, of course, Jennie will be leaving with the Moores."

"John is going to be disappointed to hear that."

"I have to go J.W.," Mabel said softly. "Call me back Monday afternoon."

"Will do, bye."

J.W. hung up the phone and told John the news. John immediately started trying to figure out how he could see Jennie at least one more time. *Maybe she will come visit her friend across the street this afternoon.*

After lunch, John pulled his chair out under the shade tree in front of the station. But Jennie never came.

*****

John arranged to trade days off with Ernest. Come Monday morning, he dressed in fresh uniform and caught the nine-fifteen trolley into town. Arriving at the depot he looked at his pocket watch. It showed ten o'clock. *The Moores and Jenny should be arriving soon*, he thought, as he paced back and forth in front of the train station. In a few minutes, a two-seated carriage with driver on front came up the street. His heart skipped a beat when he saw Jennie in the carriage. He couldn't wait for the driver to get down and open the carriage door. John walked over to open it. "Mr. Moore, Sir. I'm John Whittenburg. I hope it's all right with you, Sir. I came to say goodbye to Jennie."

"Yes, John, by all means. Jennie has told us about you." Mr. Moore stepped down out of the carriage and reached to shake John's hand.

"Thank you, Sir," John said as he shook Mr. Moore's hand. "Glad to meet you. Jennie's told me how nice you folks have treated her."

"Nice to meet you, John. We care a lot about Jennie." Mr. Moore turned to help Mrs. Moore out of the carriage. After she had stepped down, John offered to shake her hand and Mrs. Moore extended hers.

"Pleased to meet you, Ma'am."

"It's a pleasure to meet you, John." Then turning to Jennie she smiled as she said, "We will go on inside, dear, take your time."

"Thank you, Ma'am." Jennie replied.

John thought he detected a little blush on Jennie's face. He reached to take the picnic basket she carried and with the other hand he took Jennie's to help her out of the carriage. "I just couldn't let you go off without seeing you one more time and saying goodbye. I hope you don't mind my coming, Miss Jennie."

"Of course not, I think it's very thoughtful of you to come see me off, but aren't you supposed to be at work?"

"I traded days with another fellow when Mabel told J.W. you couldn't get off yesterday."

"I'm so glad you could do that. It was a nice surprise to see you here."

The Moore's driver and a porter had taken care of their trunks and other bags. John carried their basket and extended his arm to escort Jennie into the depot. It felt wonderful as Jennie held his arm. Oh, how he wished she didn't have to go.

"Miss Jennie, you promised to write to me, remember. Just address it to me, Number Six Fire Station, Fort Worth, Texas." He reached into his pocket and pulled out a piece of paper. "Here I wrote it down, in case you didn't know how to spell my last name. I hope you'll let me know you got there all right and how to address a letter to you."

"I will. I promise. You be careful and don't run anymore races with a trolley," she teased.

John liked her sense of humor. He smiled, "I'll try to keep those horses in line."

They were in the depot now and sat down on the bench seat across from the Moore's. Mr. Moore spoke to John. "Jennie tells us you handle the horses and the fire wagon."

"Yes, Sir, my pa always said I had a way with horses and I like driving the wagon. I like the security of the job and the steady pay."

"That's a very honorable job and a service to your community." Mr. Moore complimented.

"Thank you, Sir. I was raised on honesty and integrity and not much else. I'm trying to do better than my pa."

All too soon the conductor was calling, "All aboard for Kansas City and points beyond, track number three."

"There's our train, ladies," Mr. Moore said as he rose from his seat and flagged a porter to help with their overnight bags. Again John carried their basket and escorted Jennie. Before stepping on the train, Mr. & Mrs. Moore said their "nice to meet you" and "good-byes".

John shook hands with them, "Nice to meet you, too, Ma'am, Sir." Then turning to Jennie said, "Miss Jennie, you take care and don't miss the train coming back."

"I will try my best," she smiled. "John, you can drop the Miss now and just call me Jennie, if you would like." This was a sign she liked him well enough for their relationship to progress.

"I would like that, Jennie." He took her hand, kissed it, handed her the basket and helped her up the train steps before reluctantly letting go of her hand. John watched through the windows as she went down the isle and took her seat across from the Moores. He watched as she removed her hat pin and hat. Mr. Moore rose to put it on the shelf for her, as she was too short to reach that high. He wished he could have done that for her, but seeing Mr. Moore helping he was confident Jennie was in good hands.

Late May 1907

John hadn't been too anxious, knowing it would take awhile to get to Michigan and for a letter to get back to Texas. But a week later, he anxiously waited for Turner to go to post office and pick up the mail. *Still no word from Jennie. Had she forgotten about him? He hoped she like him as much as he liked her. Had something happened on the way? He wouldn't allow himself to think of that.*

Wednesday, Turner returned from the post office. "John, you got a letter." John tried not to act too excited in front of the other men. But, J.W. heard and began teasing, "Hey fellows, John got a letter and I bet it's from Miss Jennie. All the way from Michigan." The others started teasing, too. "Wow, read it to us, John." "What does she say?"

"I'm not telling," John grinned and walked upstairs to have some privacy. He could hardly wait to open the first letter he ever received in his whole life, and it was from Jennie. He hoped it contained good news.

> Dear John,   May 31, 1907
>
> We got here all right. Mrs. Moore feeling poorly for a few days. I took care of her. She got better, so now I am sending word, we are all doing well. My ma was happy to see me. Pa too, once he got sober and new who I was. My friends at hotel were happy to see me to. I hope you are well. You can write me at Wenona Beach Hotel in Bay City, Michigan.
>
> Regards, Jennie Campbell

John opened his trunk and got out paper and pencils to answer her letter.

> Dear Jennie,   June 6, 1907
>
> I got your letter today. I'm glad to here from you and no you got there all right. Sorry Mrs. Moore was poorly. Glad she is al right now. She and Mr. Moore are good people. I was glad to meet them and no you are in good hands. We only had 2 fires this week. Both grass fires as it's been dry and no rain. So, not much news here. Best regards, John

*****

John and Jennie wrote back and forth all summer. It was a long summer. Come September he waited anxiously to receive the letter telling him when she was coming home. *Listen to me,* he thought, *saying she's coming home. She is home, but I want her back here in Texas.* A few days later, her letter arrived.

Dear John,   September 10, 1907

Mr. Moore said we leave on the 14th and get into
Fort Worth on 16th. We had lots of rain and Mrs.
Moore feels poorly in wet weather so she ready to go
home. I will be happy to get back to Texas too. I got
letter from Mabel and she said she and J.W. are still
dating. The four of us have good times together. I am
looking forward to us getting together again. I will
let you no when we get home. Yours truly, Jennie

John looked on the calendar; not his day off. He asked every man
on the roster and no one could trade days with him. Guess he would
just have to wait till his regular day off. But then he didn't know
when Jennie would have time off. Oh, the frustration.

Turner heard why John wanted to trade days. "John, just between
you and me, how about on the 16th, you go get the mail. The post
office is next to the train station. If you can time it just right," Turner
paused, "it might take you a little longer than me, to get the mail,
since you haven't been to the post office before. And there might be a
long line of people at the post office that day. Know what I mean?"

John grinned, "That's not being dishonest is it?"

"Not at all," Turner said and gave John a slight salute.

"Thanks, Pal, I'll return the favor."

September 16, 1907

John called the train station yesterday and again this morning
checking the train's schedule. Turner told John the quickest way to
the post office. John carefully planned out his time. Turner said it
took him twenty minutes to walk to the post office, about five minutes to get the mail and twenty to walk back. That gave him forty-five
minutes. If he only walked two blocks and took the trolley to the post
office and back, he could save another five minutes both ways. He
anxiously waited to go, like the horses when the alarm goes off. John
called again about an hour before the train's arrival. The agent assured him, "The train should arrive here at 3:55 p.m. as scheduled."

John finished his chore of cleaning the kitchen floor after lunch, went upstairs, bathed and put on clean uniform. Sliding down the pole, he took a seat with the other men in the sitting area, as through finished for the day. He made sure he could see the big clock on the wall. At three-thirty, he got out his pocket watch to make sure he had the same time as the fire station clock. This also signaled Turner, it was time.

"John, why don't you run over to the post office and pick up the mail for me?" Turner said. "I'm kind'a tired today."

"Sure, be glad to. I need to get a little fresh air anyway." John tried not to sound too enthused or hurried. He strolled out the door and when out of sight, he walked faster. The trolley came along just as he reached the corner. He dropped a nickel in the change box, took a seat and looked at his watch every few minutes. At the post office stop, he got off and ran inside. He, not too patiently, waited in line as he kept looking at the clock on the post office wall ticking away the seconds. Finally, it came his turn. "Fire Department mail, please Sir."

The postmaster asked, "Where's Turner, today?"

"He said he was tired, but I think he's just being lazy. He asked me to come get the mail today." Just then John heard the train whistle.

The postmaster turned and walked over to the sorting bins, reached in one of the slots, and retrieved three envelopes. Walking back to the counter, he handed them to John.

"Thank you, Sir." John took the envelopes and put them in his shirt pocket and walked out. Seeing the train just coming to a stop, he ran across the street and into the depot and out the back to the tracks.

Mr. Moore, having stepped off the train, turned to help Mrs. Moore. John caught their attention and motioned he wanted to help Jennie off the train. Mr. Moore smiled as he moved back from the steps. John stepped up and held out his hand.

"John!" Jennie yelled, "Oh, my goodness, you surprised me. I thought you'd be working."

Helping her down the steps he said, "I am working. I traded places with Turner, so I could come to the post office to get the fire department mail. I can't stay, but I had to see you. I'll call you tomorrow after you've had time to rest and see if we can schedule our days off at the same time."

"That will be good. I am a mess after three days on the train. I hate for you to see me this way. But it was wonderful seeing you here."

"Jennie," Mr. Moore called, "Moses is here with our carriage. If you'll see after Mrs. Moore, I'll see after our luggage."

"Yes, Sir," Jennie replied.

"John, can we give you a ride?" Mr. Moore asked.

"No thank you, Sir. I appreciate the offer, but I have to get back to work. It's nice to see you again." Turning to Mrs. Moore he said, "Nice to see you again, Ma'am."

Taking Jennie's hand he kissed it. "I'm glad your back. I'll call later."

"Bye John. It was so nice of you to come meet me. Thank you."

"You're welcome." John trotted off inside the station, glancing at the big clock on the wall as he ran out the door; he had twelve minutes to get back to the fire hall. He trotted a little faster. When the trolley came along, he rode it as far as he could and ran the two remaining blocks. When he came in sight of the station, he stopped to catch his breath, then walked into the station and took the mail to the Chief's office. When he sat down with the others, he gave a slight nod to Turner. "Whew! It's hot out today. I worked up a sweat coming back from the post office."

*****

John and Jennie continued to court each other the rest of the year.

John about age 24

Jenny age 18

6

Taking Care of Family

1908

January eighteenth started like any other day. John just finished cleaning the horse stall when he heard the telephone ring. Wondering if it might be a fire call, John moved out of the way of the horses.

"John, you got a phone call," one of the men called out.

John halfway cringed. He received very few calls at the fire hall, and it usually meant bad news or at least very important news. Pa couldn't earn enough money, so his folks were back living in a tent, northeast of the stock yards, which worried John.

"Coming!" he called out as he hurried to the phone. "Hello, this is John," he answered.

His sister Ida said, "John, Ma sent a rider to tell me something's wrong with Pa. I went there as soon as I could. He was feverish and out of his head. I came to get Doctor Hayes. I'm calling from his office. We are on the way to Ma and Pa's now. I'll call you back after while."

"Please do that," John replied and hung up the phone. He went to the office. "Chief, I just got a phone call, my Pa's bad off. I think I better call in a sub to take my place the rest of the day."

"Sorry to hear that, John. You do what you need to do."

John called a fellow fireman to come in and work for him and went upstairs to freshen up. Just as he slid down the pole, the phone rang again. "I'll get it," John called. "Number Six Fire Station, John speaking."

"John, Pa's gone." Ida cried. "Doc says he died from blood poisoning. Pa had a badly infected sore on his swollen left hand. Ma said Pa had cut off a wart with his pocket knife." Ida pulled herself together to finish saying, "I brought Ma home with me to get her out of the cold. Pa's…….. Pa's body is in their tent. I didn't know what else to do. James is out of town and won't be home till tonight."

"Ida, honey, you did the right thing. Just take care of Ma. I'm leaving in just a few minutes and I'll go take care of Pa. I've arranged for a sub so I can take the rest of the day off. I'll go ahead and arrange for tomorrow too. Is it all right if I stay at your house tonight?"

"Oh, yes, of course."

"Now, don't you worry, I'll take care of everything and then see you later."

"All right."

John waited a few more minutes for his sub to get there and arranged for him to work tomorrow, also. Putting on his coat, he walked two blocks to catch the streetcar to the North Side. Getting off at Twentieth Street, he walked a few blocks east to his folk's tent. Lifting the flap door, he saw what appeared to be a body covered with a quilt. The well worn quilt had covered his parent's bed for as long as he could remember. He hesitated at first, but as tears began to flow, he knew he had to look and say his final goodbye. Pulling back the quilt, he saw his Pa's pale face. According to what his Pa and Grandpa used to say, John spoke the first words that came to his mind. "Well, Pa, I hope you have gone on to a better place." And he wept.

John had remembered seeing an undertaker parlor back on North Main Street. He wrapped the quilt around his father's body. Getting his father's two horses, he tied the body over the back of one horse and rode the other horse bareback, walking the horses up the street. Arriving in front of the North Fort Worth Funeral Home, he tied the horses to the hitching post and went in.

A middle-aged gentleman greeted him. "Hello, I'm Mr. Shannon, the owner. May I be of service to you?"

"Yes, Sir. I got my pa's body outside. I need to bury him, as cheap as possible and soon as possible?"

"I believe the soonest would be tomorrow. The cheapest would be a pine box. Will you want to buy a burial plot in Oakwood Cemetery? Or bury him in North Exchange Avenue Paupers Grave?"

"Paupers will be good enough."

Mr. Shannon asked, "Will you be bringing a suit for him to be buried in?"

John almost chuckled. Pa never bought a suit in his whole life. "He was doing good to have a change of work clothes. How much for the funeral and a suit?

After adding some numbers on paper, Mr. Shannon replied, "That would come to $102.75."

"That's reasonable. Can I leave the body here while I go to the bank and get the money?"

John, wearing his fireman's uniform, looked trustworthy enough, so Mr. Shannon agreed, "Yes, Sir. Can you bring the body around to the back door? I'll meet you there, and I need to write down some information about the deceased."

"Much obliged for your help, Sir." John shook the man's hand, then walked out and guided the horses to the back door.

After answering all of Mr. Shannon's questions and setting the time for the funeral, John said, "I'll be back with the money as soon as I can. Thank you, Sir."

"You're welcome. If there's anything else I can do for you let me know."

John led the horses straight to the bank and back and paid Mr. Shannon. Then he guided the horses to Ida's. As he rode along he began to think, *Well, Pa, I just spent more money on you, than you probably spent on me my whole life. But, that's all right. I know you did the best you could. But you just wouldn't leave the farm. You weren't a farmer and never could get a farm to pay off. Well, let's see…. Ida said she would notify the rest of the family. She would call the general store in Dublin and hoped somebody would ride out to the farm to tell their brother Charlie. Everything else has been taken care of now, except for Ma. I can sell the horses and wagon and that will give her a little income for a while. On second thought, I'll buy the horses and wagon from her, give her some income and I'll have a wagon for Jennie and me to date without having to depend on J.W. Hum-m I'll need a place to board the horses and store the wagon until Jennie and I….* His thoughts startled him. He hadn't admitted it before, but suddenly, *I just surprised myself. I want to marry her. Oh, that reminds me, I have a date with Jennie and Mabel and J.W. tomorrow. I'll have to call and cancel. That means another whole week before I see Jennie again.*

Arriving back at Ida's, he tied the horses to the hitching post, went in and told his ma what he had done. Ma didn't have five dollars to her name, but John told her not to worry, he had taken care of every thing.

James, Ida's husband, had come home from his trip sooner than expected. On hearing the news of Pa, he offered to help. He and John rode the horses back to Ma and Pa's tent. James hitched both horses to Elmos's wagon, while John loaded all their possessions into the back, including the tent. John wasn't sure what to do, yet, but one thing for sure; his Ma was not going to stay in that tent ever again.

After getting the wagon into James and Ida's barn and putting the horses in the corral, they went inside. Ida poured them a cup of coffee and they gathered around the pot bellied stove to get warm.

"John did you ever get any lunch today?"

"No, I didn't. I was too busy to think about it till now."

"Will a piece of pie do, till suppertime?"

"That would be great, Ida. I'm starved." John turned to his Ma. "Now, Ma, I thought of something I want to talk to you about."

"What's that, Son?"

"I want to buy your horses and wagon. That will give you some money at least for a while. We can find you a room at a boarding house but you're not going to live in a tent any more."

"No boarding house." Ida said, as she handed John a piece of pie. "Ma, James and I have already discussed it. She's going to live with us."

"Oh, well, if you're sure, that will take a load off my mind. So, can I buy your horses and wagon, Ma?"

"You don't have to do that, Son. You can have them. You done paid for your daddy's funeral. I can manage."

"I know I don't have to, but I want to. I need a way to get around without depending on the trolley all the time." He didn't mention the real reason; to take his girl for a ride. "James, what do you think that wagon and the two horses are worth?"

James thought a minute. "I'd say about a hundred dollars. I doubt you'd get any more than that on the auction block."

"Sounds reasonable. Is that okay with you, Ma?" John asked.

"Anything you want to do, John. Are you sure that's not too much? I would have sold them for less and you don't have to pay me all at one time."

"No, Ma. That's not too much. Next week, I'll bring you the money. Meanwhile, James, can I work out a deal with you to take care of my horses and store my wagon?"

"I've got the space, if you'll just buy their food." James bargained.

"Sounds great to me," John said. "Now, can I use your phone? I've got one more thing to take care of."

"Of course," James and Ida spoke at the same time.

John finished the last bit of pie. "Thanks, Ida. That was delicious. We don't get good stuff like that at the fire hall."

"Well, I'll have to teach you how to make a pie, so you can." Ida said.

John got up, took his plate and coffee cup to the kitchen and went to the hall where the telephone sat on a small table. He picked up the phone and dialed the number for the Fire Station.

"Station Six, Floyd speaking."

"Floyd, this is John."

"Yes, Captain. Is everything all right?"

"Yes, I was just checking in. William is working for me again tomorrow. Pa's funeral is at two o'clock, so I'll be back at work by six."

"That's fine, Captain. You do what you have to do and if you need more time, just call me. I can work for you tomorrow night, if you need me."

"Thanks, Floyd. Could you let me talk to J.W., please? There's something I need him to do."

"Sure, just a minute." Floyd called out, "J.W., John's on the phone."

"Yes, John." J.W. answered.

"J.W., my Pa's funeral is at two o'clock tomorrow. Would you call Mabel to tell Jennie I can't make it? Ya'll go on to lunch without me. Tell Mabel to tell Jennie I'm sorry and I'll see her next week."

"Will do, John. I'm sure they'll understand. Is there anything else I can do for you?" J.W. asked.

"No, thanks. I'll see you tomorrow evening."

Morning arrived and so did John's two older sisters, their families, a few friends and other distant relatives. Everybody brought a dish or two of food. After lunch they all climbed in their wagons and trailed one after the other to the cemetery about two miles away. The cold, windy, January day had everyone bundled up in heavy coats and scarves and some with quilts wrapped around themselves. James drove their buggy with Ida in front and John in back with Ma. As they neared the burial plot, John thought he saw a familiar looking surrey, but with canvas sides tied down, he couldn't be sure. As James stopped the horses at the site, John helped his Ma out of the buggy. Then he turned and saw J.W. helping Mabel out of the surrey. *"I'm glad to see them, but,"* As if wishes come true, he saw J.W. turn back and help Jennie out.

"James, Ida, help Ma here a minute. I have some friends to greet."

John was so happy to see Jennie he wanted to wrap his arms around her and swing her around. But that wouldn't be proper. The most he could do would be to take her hands in his. "I don't know what to say. This means a lot to me. Surely ya'll had better things to do than come to a funeral on a cold day like today."

Jennie looked up at John as she held his hands, "Oh, John, I'm so sorry to hear the news of your father. I wanted to be with you. We all did. Friends share in bad times as well as good."

J.W. reached over and put his hand on John's shoulder. Mabel reached out to touch his arm.

"Thanks. Come, meet my family." They walked toward the family gathering. "Ma, I want you to meet my friends, Jennie, Mabel and J.W."

Jennie greeted her, taking both of Ma's hands in hers. "Mrs. Whittenburg, my sincere sympathy in your loss. I'm sorry we are meeting under these circumstances, but I am so glad to meet you."

Ma seemed to set aside her grief for a moment, as she accepted Jennie's warm respects and meaningful greeting. "Thank you, dear. That's very kind of you to come today and I am happy to make your acquaintance. You must come and visit me sometime."

Jennie smiled, "I would like that very much."

Mabel and J.W. stepped forward and shook Ma's hand. "Pleased to meet you Ma'am. So sorry for your loss."

John pointed out as he spoke, "This is my sister Ida and her husband James. Ida, James, my friends Jennie, Mabel and J.W."

After the "pleased to meet" and handshakes all around, James said, "I believe everyone is here and the preacher is ready. Shall we proceed?"

John took Jennie's hand, intending to keep her by his side, but she pulled back.

"John, you go with your Ma. She needs you right now. Everyone else has their spouse or someone to lean on and I'm not family. Your Ma needs your strength."

He hesitated, but she whispered, "Shoo, go on now," gestured with her hand. He wanted to say, "But I want you to be a part of my family." This was not the time. Jennie was right. He let her hand slowly slide out of his. The look on her face assured him he had to be with his ma for a while, so he walked on to lead Ma to the front of the crowd.

The preacher spoke of Pa as being a good man, even though he was poor. Then he started saying things like, we need to live a good life, so we won't burn in hell's fire.

John thought, "*I could use a good fire beside me right now. Here I am daydreaming, like I used to do in church.*" John was just about ready to tell the preacher "that's enough" when the sound of a horse trotting up caught everyone's attention including the preacher's.

Charlie, their brother, had received the message and rode all night to get here. Dismounting, he ran up to hug Ma. Nodding to the rest of his siblings, he stood beside Ma till the preacher finished. John walked over to the preacher and paid him his fee. Everyone, anxious to get out of the cold weather, began climbing into their wagons. They wanted to go back to Ida's house to visit with Charlie, whom they hadn't seen in a long time. The only family member who hadn't moved away from Dublin, Charlie still tried to make a go of the farm Ma and Pa had left to him when they came to Fort Worth.

John saw J.W., Mabel and Jennie walking to their surrey. He ran over to say goodbye. He took Jennie's hands in his. "I wish I could see you home, but I trust J.W. to do that. I have to go back to Ida's and get my things and be back to work at six. Can we plan on next week, as usual?"

"Of course, John. I'll look forward to next week."

"I'll have a surprise for you then." John caressed and kissed her gloved hands. "Thanks for coming today. It meant a lot to me." He leaned over and whispered in her ear, "You mean a lot to me."

They looked at each other. Jennie smiled, her eyes seemed to dance. "You mean a lot to me, too." She whispered. "Now, you have to go with your family and get to work. I'll see you later."

John helped her into the back of the surrey. J.W. and Mabel were in the front.

"See you later, John," J.W. said, as he flicked the reins, guiding the horses into trotting off.

John returned to his Ma's side, helping her into the buggy with Ida and James. Charlie rode his horse beside their buggy. Arriving back at Ida's house, the whole family visited with Charlie, gathered their empty dishes and began leaving for their respective homes. John had gathered his things and went to find James. "James, here's some money to feed my horses till next week. I'll buy some feed and see you next Tuesday."

"Sure thing, John."

"James, I sure appreciate you and Ida taking Ma in."

"Glad to do it, John. I think it will be good for Ida. It will take her mind off us not having any children."

"It might be good for both of them. Well, I best be saying goodbye to Ma and Charlie. I have to catch the streetcar and be back at the station at six."

"See you later, John."

John walked into the sitting room where he saw Charlie had pulled up a foot stool and sat facing Ma. He walked up behind Charlie just in time to hear him ask "Ma, since you ain't going to be need'n the wagon and horses anymore, can I have the horses?"

Before Ma could speak, John spoke up, "You got the farm, what more do you want? Ma ain't got five dollars to her name and you're already asking her for more. What kind of man are you?"

"But, John, I need......"

"You need to sell the farm and get a job. You're never going to make that farm pay off any more than Pa did. Besides, Ma done sold the horses and wagon to have money to live on. The buyer will be bringing her the money in a couple of days, so don't go asking her for the money 'cause she hasn't got it."

"But, John, my oxen died. I need the horses to get my spring plowing done. It's the dead of winter and I gotta keep my family fed till the spring crops come in. I don't suppose you could loan me the money? I'll pay you back soon as my crops are sold."

John had a pang of soft heartedness for a woman, who like his ma, would never have anything but kids to feed. "Tell you what," John said slowly, then paused. "James," he called out and motioned for James to join them. "James, am I right in thinking oxen are cheaper than horses or mules?"

"Considerably, I believe."

"How much would a pair of oxen cost?" John asked.

"Hum-m," James though a minute, "I'd guess about fifty or sixty dollars a pair."

"That would be my guess, too," John said as he turned back to Charlie. "How long you planning to stay, Charlie?"

"Well, I was hoping to borrow some money and as soon as I can buy some animals, I'd head out for home. That is if Ida and James or somebody can put me up for a night or two."

"You're welcome to stay here." James offered. "You can sleep on the closed-in porch where John usually stays."

"Thanks."

"Then, Charlie," John said, "You meet me at the Fort Worth bank in the morning at nine o'clock and I'll get the money and loan it to you. You'll have the rest of the day to go to the stock yards and buy your oxen."

"Thank ya, brother. I'll pay you back soon as my spring crops come in." Charlie held out his hand to shake on it. "I give you my word on it."

John reluctantly shook his hand while thinking, *I'll believe it when I see the money in my hand.* But John added, "If I'm late, it will be because I'm out on a fire call. So you just wait for me and I'll get there as soon as I can."

"That's fine, John."

John turned to Ma, "I gotta go, Ma. If you need anything you get Ida to call me. Otherwise, I'll see you next Tuesday morning on my regular day off." He leaned over and kissed her on the cheek.

"Thank you, Son. I don't know what I would do without you."

John started to leave and gave a slight upward movement of his head to signal James to follow. When they were out of hearing range, John asked James, "One day this week, when Ma feels up to it, could you and Ida unload the wagon? See what Ma wants to keep and store it for now. Next Tuesday, I want to come clean the wagon up and then go get Jennie for a ride if it's not too cold."

"Be glad to. My business is slow right now anyway and I can take some time off."

"Thanks, James. I'd appreciate it."

John headed out the door. The bitter cold of January hit his face. But the wind had quit blowing, so the brisk walk to the trolley stop gave him a chance to clear his head of all the emotions of the last couple of days and start planning for a future. A future he hoped would include Jennie.

John arrived back at the station a little early. He knew Chief would be going off duty at six, so he rushed to talk to him before he left.

"Chief, I'm back, but I need to take off in the morning; about an hour at the most. I have to go to the bank to get some money and settle a family matter."

"That's all right, John. You sure that's all the time you'll need?"

"Should be, the banks not crowded that time of the morning."

"If you need more time, it's okay. I know how it is taking care of family matters after a death."

"Thanks, Chief. See you later."

January 19, 1908

Next morning, John hurried through his chores, cleaned up and arrived at the bank at nine sharp. So did Charlie. John withdrew sixty dollars, giving the money to Charlie, who assured him he would pay him back. John thought he had just done a good deed for the day and would probably never see the money again.

7

His Own Horses and Wagon

January 28, 1908

Getting up early, John put on his clothes he worn the day before. He took a change of clothes with him, caught the trolley and went to James and Ida's house.

Ida and Ma were just cleaning up the kitchen from breakfast. "Get you a cup of coffee and warm up, Son," Ma said.

"There's some bacon and couple of biscuits left, under that cup towel," Ida offered as she pointed to the table. "I'll fry you a couple of eggs."

"Thanks, I didn't stay for breakfast with the men. I wanted to get here and get my wagon cleaned up and make sure it didn't need any repairs. Oh, here, Ma," John reached into his pocket. "Here's the first payment on the wagon."

"What's your hurry, Son? I don't need any money right now. If you need it, you can pay me later."

"No, Ma. I got the money and I want to pay you what we agreed on. I can pay you fifty dollars a month for two months and not have to get any more out of my savings account."

"But you paid for your Pa's funeral. Why don't you take the wagon, instead of paying me for it?"

"No, Ma. You're going to need the money to live on."

"Well, if you're sure you got the money. Thank ya, I appreciate it, Son."

James had finished feeding their horses and came in the back door. "I'll have another cup of coffee with you, John. Then I'll help you clean up the wagon."

"Thanks, James. I'd appreciate the help, since I'm in a bit of a hurry."

"So, you finally found a girlfriend," Ida chimed. "How did you meet her? She looks pretty young. How old is she? What do you know about her?"

James protested, "Ida, it's none of your business."

But, John didn't mind. "Ida she is a really nice girl, born and raised in Oklahoma Territory. Her pa moved to Michigan to work the coal mines. He moves every time a mine closes and a new one is started."

"How in the world did she end up here? Is any of her family here?"

John answered all of Ida's questions, including, "I haven't asked how old she is, but judging from the number of years she's been working, I'd guess nineteen or twenty."

Ida finally gave in, "She did seem like a really nice girl."

Ma spoke up, "I liked her, John. What kind of work does she do?"

"She's a companion to an elderly lady up on Pennsylvania Avenue."

Ma nodded, "An honorable profession. I bet she's got a tender, caring heart to be doing that kind of work."

John hadn't thought about it, but Ma was right. "I believe so," he replied.

Ida asked, "So how serious is this friendship?"

James again protested, "Ida, that's none of your business."

John finished his last bite of breakfast and answered her. "Big sister, you don't have to worry. I'm twenty-eight years old and Jennie is just as nice, or nicer, than any of those silly, giggly girls you been trying to match me up with." John got up, "Now, I gotta get to work."

James followed, getting their coats on the way, they headed to the barn.

"John, last week we were out in the barn when Charlie came back from the stockyards. The Oxen he bought were poor looking.

I doubt he paid over forty dollars for the pair. Then he saw the tent and wanted it. It wasn't my place to say anything, but we could have sold that tent for probably twenty dollars for Ma. Ma told him he could have it."

John just shook his head. "That's okay. It was Ma's to do whatever she wanted."

"If you don't mind my saying so," James said, "I think Charlie's a beggar. Always wanting a handout."

"You're thinking along the right track." John got a bucket of water, brush and broom and was scrubbing the wagon. James checked the wagon wheels, adding a little axle grease to two of them, as they continued to talk. "John, that pile of stuff over there is things your Ma don't want. I told her I'd get rid of it for her. Ida and I thought maybe you might go through it and see if there's anything you want to keep, especially if you and Jennie are thinking about getting married. There wasn't much Ma wanted to keep and we put that in her room."

"Thanks, James. Don't know as there's anything I want."

"Well, think about it. There's a good iron skillet, kettle and coffee pot. Not much else, but it'll save you a little money."

"Well, guess you're right. I'll take a look later. Maybe next week or so, if you're not in any hurry to throw it out."

"Not at all." James said, "Just whenever you get to it."

John looked over at the pile of things covered with one of Ma's old quilts. *Maybe later, not right now. He wanted to propose to Jennie, but she might not accept.* He looked at the quilt again. Picked it up and shook the dust out and folded it up to make a cushion for the wagon seat. He and Jennie could use it this summer to spread it on the ground for their picnics. There was still a chill in the air and John thought, *we can use it for a lap robe, too.*

On cold days, like today, he and J.W. would go see the girls and sit in the Moore's kitchen, drink coffee and the girls would fix a light lunch for them as well as the Moore's. Today, he planned something special. Looking at his watch, he told James, "I gotta get these horses hitched, get my bath, dress and head out of here."

"I'll hitch the horses for you, if you need to go get ready." James offered.

"I'd really appreciate that, James. I gotta go by the station and pick up J.W., then go out to Pennsylvania Avenue."

"Sure, go on, get ready."

When he left, he told Ida, James and Ma, "I'll be back before dark."

John drove the wagon and horses to the fire station, picked up J.W. and drove on to see the girls. Arriving at the Moore's, John pulled around to the back as usual.

Mabel answered their knock at the door, "Hello, come in out of the cold. I just started a fresh pot of coffee, it'll be ready soon."

J.W. sniffed the air, "What's smells so good?"

"Jennie and I made cinnamon bread this morning. She's gone to take a tray of bread and coffee to the Moore's."

Jennie came through the kitchen door. Her face lit up when she saw John had arrived. "Hello, fellows. How about some hot, buttered cinnamon bread to go with your coffee this morning?"

"Sounds good." John said. "Mabel said she just put a fresh pot of coffee on the stove, so while we wait on the coffee to brew, ya'll grab your coats. I got something outside to show you."

"Oh, I like surprises. This must be a big one if it's outside," Jennie exclaimed.

"Oh, how exciting." Mabel said, as they went to get their coats.

"Ready," they said as they came back in the kitchen with their coats on.

John reached for the door handle, "Let's go then."

Walking out the door, the girls saw the horses and wagon. "Where's the surrey, J.W.?" Mabel asked.

J.W. just shrugged his shoulders.

"Oh, my goodness! John, is this yours?" Jennie asked excitedly.

"Yep, it sure is." John said proudly. "You want to take a quick ride?"

"Oh, sure, but we'll have to hurry. The coffee pot is on and the Moore's will want me to pick up their tray." Jennie said.

Meanwhile, J.W. had taken Mabel aside and whispered to her, "We need to stay here."

Suspecting something, Mabel offered, "You two go on. J.W. and

I'll watch the coffee and if you're not back, I'll pick up the Moore's tray."

"Are you sure? We won't be gone long." Jennie, excited for John, could hardly wait for him to take her for a ride.

"I don't mind. Go on."

Jennie walked over to the horses. "What's their names?"

"Clyde and Max."

Jennie petted each one, "Hello, Clyde. Hello, Max."

John held out his hand. Jennie took it and climbed into the wagon seat. John told her, "You can sit on the quilt or unfold it for a lap robe, if you're cold."

"I'm not that cold, yet. We won't be gone long anyway."

John walked around and got in the seat beside her.

"How exciting to have your very own wagon!" She clapped her hands together, "I'm so happy for you, John."

John had hoped she would be. He flicked the reins and trotted the horses out into the road. It was too far and too cold to go to the park where they had their first date. So John chose the road heading south out in the country, away from houses. A few minutes later, John pulled back on the reins and put the horses into a slow walk.

"Miss Jennie, we have been dating over a year now. I come to realize I've never felt this way before about any lady I've ever met. I got some money saved up and in another month, I'll have these horses and wagon paid for. I got a good job and with my raise and promotion to Captain, I believe I can afford to support a wife better than my ma ever had. There would be one drawback though. I'd only be at home one day and one night a week. But I can take off in emergency. So under those conditions, Miss Jennie, would you consider marrying me?"

"Oh, my goodness." Jennie gasped. "Yes, John, Yes," she said sincerely.

John, elated, yelled, "Yah, Whoo!" Putting his arm around her, he said, "In that case, may I kiss you?"

"By all means," Jennie said.

On the way back to the Moore's, John said, "I think it is customary for the man to go to the father and ask permission to marry his daughter. Do you think I should ask Mr. Moore, since your father isn't here?

"I don't think that is necessary, since I am of age."

"Oh, good, I was a little worried there for a while, since I've never met your pa."

"I would like for you to go with me to tell the Moore's, soon as we get back. They like you, John. I know they will be happy for us."

"If you want me to," John said, "But can I have a cup of coffee and some cinnamon bread first? I've been thinking about that bread ever since I smelled it."

Jennie laughed, "You have not. You were thinking of how to sweet talk me out of a kiss." Her eyes danced and sparkled as she smiled at him.

"Well, and that too," he had to admit.

Jennie was sitting close and leaning his way and he quickly leaned over and stole another kiss.

They were nearing the neighborhood now, so she moved over a proper distance like a lady. "Have you thought about when we will get married?"

"I need some time to pay off the wagon and save up a little more money. We both need time to seriously think and let the butterflies settle in our stomachs. So, I'm thinking maybe six to eight months. Is that all right with you?"

"That's alright with me. That gives me time to make my trousseau and finish a quilt I am making for my hope chest."

"Oh, so you have a hope chest. Have your hopes come true?"

"They just did." Jennie admitted. "I'm surprised you know what a hope chest is."

"I have three sisters, remember? All three had hope chests, full of things they had made like cup towels, pot holders and fancy pillowcases and doilies. I guess they are using them now that they're married."

Arriving back at the house, they found J.W. and Mabelle sitting at the kitchen table having bread and coffee. Jennie could hardly contain her excitement as she told Mabel, "John, proposed and I said yes."

"So that's why it took you so long. Congratulations."

The servant's bell rang just then, Jennie quickly removed her coat and smoothed back her hair. "That will be the Moore's for me to pick up their tray. Come on John, you said you would be with me when I tell them."

"But, I haven't had my cinnamon bread and coffee, yet." John protested.

"You're not going to starve," Jennie held out her hand. "Come on."

"John quickly took off his coat and layed it on the back of his chair. He would hold her hand if he never got a bite of that delicious smelling bread. He took her hand and pretended to let her drag him into the sitting room.

"Mr. Moore, Mrs. Moore, there's someone here who would like to say hello."

Looking up from their reading, Mr. Moore spoke, while rising from his chair, "John, how nice to see you again. Jennie told us about your father's passing. Sorry to hear that."

"Thank you, Sir," John walked over to shake Mr. Moore's hand. Then he walked over to Mrs. Moore to take her hand. "How are you, Ma'am?"

"I'm fine, John. It's nice to see you again."

Jennie spoke up, "John had a nice surprise when he came this morning. He bought a wagon and two horses and he took me for a quick ride." Her excitement was plain to see and hear in her voice. "He is good with handling horses."

Mr. Moore said, "I can always use a man that's good with horses on my cattle drives. If you ever need a job you come see me."

"Thank you, Sir. I appreciated the offer, but I really like the fire department. Matter of fact, I was telling Jennie, since I got promoted to captain, I been able to save more money and now I can afford to…. Well, Sir, I asked Jennie to marry me."

Mr. and Mrs. Moore smiled and looked at Jennie. "And?"

Jennie blushed and smiled, "I said yes."

"Oh, my dear," Mrs. Moore held out her hand to Jennie and taking her hand said, "I am so happy for you, Jennie."

Mr. Moore held out his hand to John, "Congratulations, John.

I guess you know Jennie has been like a daughter to us. So as a substitute father, let me say, I whole heartedly approve."

John shook Mr. Moore's hand, "Thank you, Sir. I didn't know if I should come to you for permission or write to her father, but Jennie said neither since she was of age."

Mr. Moore offered, "Well, if you and Jennie need me to, I'll write a letter to her father. I've dealt with him before."

"Thank you, Mr. Moore," Jennie spoke up. "But, I don't think Pa will object."

"Thank you, Sir. I appreciate your offer." John said. "Well, we won't take up any more of your time, now. Jennie has been promising me a piece of cinnamon bread every since I got here."

Mrs. Moore laughingly spoke, "Young lady, get this man of yours some of that delicious bread."

"Yes, Ma'am." Jennie said, as she picked up the tray and headed out of the room.

Mr. Moore looked at John, "Her bread is well worth waiting for."

"Good day, Sir...Ma'am." John nodded.

When they went through the door into the kitchen, Jennie said, "See, I told you they liked you and would be happy for us."

"You were right, but I was still a little nervous. Can I have a piece of bread now and a cup of coffee to settle my nerves?"

"Only a small piece, lunch will be ready soon and you wouldn't want to spoil your appetite." Jennie teasingly chided.

"I promise I can eat both and clean my plate. I'm starving."

Late March 1908

John had paid his ma for the horses and wagon. Meanwhile, he learned she was eligible to draw a widow's pension, because his pa had served in the Confederate Army during the civil war. He took her to the court house to fill out all the papers. Things worked out well with ma staying with Ida and James. Ida and ma liked to sew and they began making a quilt. The future looked good.

The fire department usually had at least four trained horses at a time. That gave them a spare team to take to one of the other stations, if a horse became sick or injured. Everyday, he took the horses out for a run to keep them in shape. John arranged to keep one of his horses in the feed lot next door. He could ride Clyde back and forth to Ida's to get his wagon.

John looked at his pocket watch. It was time to saddle Clyde, clean up and change clothes. He and Jennie had the day off. They were trying to save money, so instead of going out, he would ride over to the Moore's house and they visited in the kitchen or they would take a walk. Sometimes, John put Jennie on Clyde and he walked the horse while she rode over to the market to do the shopping for the cook.

Today, when he arrived at the Moore's, Mabel answered the door. "Hello, John, come in. Get yourself a cup of coffee. Jennie's with Mrs. Moore. I'll go get her."

"How is the Mrs.'s?"

"The doctor just left. Maybe Jennie can tell us the latest report. She and Mr. Moore have been taking turns sitting with her the last couple of days." Mabel headed out the kitchen door to go upstairs.

In a little while, Jennie came through the door with Mabel behind her. She looked tired and not her usual bubbly self. When she saw John, tears came to her eyes. "Oh, John, the doctor's sending a nurse over this evening to sit with Mrs. Moore. Tomorrow, another nurse comes on duty. The doctor says she hasn't much time."

"Oh, Jennie, dear. I'm so sorry." He put his arms around her and held her while she cried.

Sitting down at the kitchen table, Mabel poured them all a cup of coffee. Getting a cup from the cupboard, she poured another cup and put it on a small tray, with a small muffin. "I'll take this up to Mr. Moore. Poor thing didn't eat much breakfast" and she left the kitchen.

John asked, "Should I go?"

"No, please stay." Jennie reached over and took his hand. "I know I'm not in much of a good mood, but it sure feels good to have you here beside me."

"Then I'll stay as long as you need me." Then, to maybe cheer her up, he added, "Well, at least till dark. Old Clyde can't see too well in the dark any more and he's liable to wonder off the road." John got a little smile out of her that time. "Now, how come you didn't offer me one of those little muffins, like Mabel just took up to Mr. Moore?"

"Oh, you, you're always hungry. Don't you ever get filled up?"

"Not when I eat 'fire hall food' all week. Come my day off, I want some good home cooking."

A few days later Jennie called John to tell him Mrs. Moore had passed away. The next day she called to tell him where and when the funeral would be. "John," Jennie added, "Mr. Moore asked me to ride in the carriage with him to the funeral. I told him you were coming. He asked if you would join us. I hope you don't mind, but I told him we would. I feel so sorry for him."

"Tell him it would be an honor. After all they have done for you, that's the least we can do. I've got all day since that's my day off, so I'll see you the usual time."

A lot of people attended the service. When they returned to the house, John and Jennie went to help in the kitchen, preparing the evening meal for all the relatives, some of whom were spending the night. Jennie and Mabel had prepared beds and rooms all day yesterday. Cookie had most of the preparation done, but it was time to finish cooking and get ready to serve. John offered to help and Jennie and Mabel gratefully put him to work…to work for his supper.

"Reach up on that top shelf and get those big serving bowls."

"Chop up that block of ice."

Mr. Moore and his overnight guest gathered in the sitting room. Mr. Moore rang the servant's bell three times meaning Jennie should answer the call.

Jennie said, "Oh, dear! Do I look okay?" She began smoothing wisps of hair back from her face, "I wonder what he wants me for?" She took off her apron and wiped her brow, tossing the apron aside as she went out the door."

Mabel went into the dining room to the buffet and took out the silver ware to set the table. The French doors between the two rooms gave access to conversations without it being obvious and still satisfy Mabel's curiosity. As Mabel laid out the silverware, she heard Mr. Moore say to his relatives, "I hired Jennie to be Alice's companion, to look after her while I was at the office or on business trips. Jennie has been like the daughter we never had. Alice and I grew very fond of Jennie. She was a great comfort to Alice in the end. Jennie, this is Alice's sister Nellie and her husband Samuel. And this is my sister Florence and her husband Joseph. And my sister Mary Ann and her husband George."

Jennie politely nodded to each introduction.

"Jennie, would you show the ladies to their rooms and the facilities for them to freshen up."

"I would be glad to, Sir. Right this way, Ladies." They followed Jennie.

Maybel came back into the kitchen and told the others what took place, as each continued with their assigned tasks.

About five minutes later, Jennie suddenly came busting through the kitchen door, so hard the door banged against the back wall. "Oh, I hate people like that. That old biddy. I told her off but I wanted to yank out her tongue." Jennie was pacing the floor. "She doesn't even know me and had the auda....the GALL to....." Jennie started crying.

John went to hold her. "Calm down. Tell me what happened."

"Don't tell me to calm down! I have every right to be mad and I am furious." She cried, "When I get boiling mad I have to cry and that makes me madder."

John had never seen Jennie like this before and Mabel shook her head at John indicating she hadn't either.

Jennie let out a big, 'Gr-r-r-r' as she clinched her fists and held her arms ridged to her sides, then began pulling herself together. "I'm sorry, ya'll. If there is anything or anybody I hate most is a jack-ass, excuse me, a narrow minded, busy body looking for something or someone to gossip about."

"Your right," John shook his head in agreement.

Mabel did to, "I agree."

John took her hands and said, 'Now, take a deep breath, relax and tell us what happened and who do I beat up for hurting you?"

Jennie gave a half smile as she wiped her tears. "I'm sorry. You don't have to beat up anybody. I can take care of myself." She pulled herself together. "I had shown Florence and Mary Ann to their rooms. Then I showed Miss Nellie to her room. She asked me to come in and thanked me for what I did for her sister. She is sweet just like Mrs. Moore. Well, Florence and Mary Ann must have thought I had gone back down stairs, cause Miss Nellie and I both overheard them talking. Florence was making dirty remarks about me chasing after Mr. Moore for his money and just biding my time taking care of Mrs. Moore. Well, I went right in there and called that old fart Florence every name I could think of and most of them not nice."

John almost laughed as he realized this spunky little lady could take care of her self and was no push over.

Again the servant's bell rang three times for the sitting room. Jennie headed to the sink to splash water on her face. "That old biddy is probably trying to get me fired."

"Just tell the truth." John advised.

Jennie held up her right hand, "So help me, God," and marched out of the room.

Mabel went into the dining room and began setting the plates and glasses on the table. John stood at the kitchen door with the door slightly ajar. They could barely hear the words being said.

Mr. Moore asked, "Jennie, I understand you had some disagreement with Florence and called her names. Is that true?"

"Yes, Sir."

"Would you like to tell me why you called her names?"

Jennie looked over at Florence who sat with a smug look on her face.

"I'm sorry to say it, Mr. Moore, but Miss Nellie and I both overheard her say she thought I was chasing after you for your money and biding my time taking care of Miz' Alice. She doesn't even know me and she said those things about me." Jennie was choking back tears and glaring at Florence.

"Florence," Mr. Moore said looking at his sister. "If Jennie has any faults, it's for telling the honest-to-God's truth. Now, you will apologize to my 'adopted' daughter or you are free to leave any time you wish."

Florence gasped and raised her chin a little higher than the smug. "Well, I didn't really mean anything by it."

Everyone stared at her, waiting to see if she would apologize. Finally, Florence said, "Well, all right. I'm sorry Jennie."

"Sorry for what?" Mr. Moore asked.

Florence looked at him as though to say, 'you are embarrassing your sister.' She was fluster, but finally said, "I'm sorry for insinuating you were chasing my brother."

"Now, Jenny, what do you say?" Mr. Moore asked.

"Apology accepted." Then turning to Mr. Moore, "May I be excused, now?"

"Yes, you may, but will you be my hostess at dinner tonight?"

"Thank you, Sir, but under the circumstances, I....You see John is here to be with me. He's helping us in the kitchen."

"Have we had a fire in the kitchen?" Mr. Moore gave a slight smile.

"No, Sir." Jennie smiled. "He offered to work for his supper."

"That's very kind of him. I didn't know he was still here. Please have him join us too. I want these people to meet him."

All the relatives sat silently listening, wondering if Mr. Moore had lost his mind, inviting what they considered to be hired help to eat at the same table with them.

"Yes, Sir." Jennie turned around to leave the room. Walking past Florence, Jennie couldn't resist sticking her tongue out at her.

Mabel and John quickly moved away from the doors and back to doing something. Jennie came in the door, with her shoulders back and a smug look on her face. "Well, that old biddy got her come-uppence. John, you and I are going to dine with the elite tonight." As she pranced with one arm out and the other on her hip, swinging back and forth.

"Jennie, I can't go into dinner like this. My shirt is sweaty and wrinkled."

Jennie thought quickly and ran to the laundry room. She came back out with a freshly laundered blue shirt, just like the one he had on. "Here wear this. You can change back before you leave. You and Mr. Moore look the same size. He has three or four blue shirts anyway. No one will ever know the difference. Now, go change in the servant's bathroom. I'm going to my room and change. Mabel, Cookie is there anything else I can do for you right now, before I change?"

"No, chil'. You go par-ty." Cookie laughingly replied in her southern drawl. "You go show off that handsome fe-ahn-say of yours to that old biddy."

John stood there wondering if he should do this or not.

Jennie insisted, "Go on now. Off to the bathroom and change so you can go slay the ugly dragon for me." She motioned him toward the bathroom and took off running to her bedroom.

When she came back to the kitchen, to get John, he stood amazed. She was beautiful, wearing a different and prettier, dark blue dress with a low neckline, but not too low. It made her black hair and dark eyes stand out against her pale skin. She had a black ribbon tied around her neck with a pearl pendant and matching pearl earrings. She had brushed out her braided bun and tied her hair up into loose curls with the ribbon hanging down among the curls. John stood speechless.

Cookie, Mabel and even Moses, the butler who had come in, began to clap their hands together.

Jennie, twirled around, "Do I look okay? Not too dressy I hope."

John found his voice, "Absolutely, out standing." He walked over to her, held out his bent arm and said, "Miss Jennie, may I have the honor of escorting you to the ball where the wicked witch awaits."

"You may, my good fellow," as she took his arm and they headed for the door.

"Wait!" Moses shouted softly. He ran and went out the door in front of them, then motioned for them to follow. He stopped at the wide doorway into the living room.

"Excuse me, Sir. Miss Jennie and her fiancé Mr. Whittenburg."

Jennie and John had to stifle a big laugh, but Jennie was still giggling when they walked into the room. Mr. Moore walked over to shake John's hand and introduced him to the other astonished guests. "John is not only Jennie's fiancé, whom by the way has my blessing; he is also a captain on the Fort Worth Fire Department, a very honorable position." Mr. Moore smiled at John and winked at Jennie as though he was also playing along with giving his sister her come-up-pence.

April 1908

In the days, following the funeral, Mr. Moore spent a lot of time just looking out the window. Jennie tried to cheer him up, but nothing helped. Meanwhile, Jennie and Mabel cleaned the guest rooms and set the house back in order. Mr. Moore asked the girls to clean out everything belonging to his wife. Jennie found some pictures she thought Mr. Moore would like to keep but he glanced through and said throw it all away. Jennie asked, "Sir, if you don't mind, I'd like to keep this one photograph of Mrs. Moore, to remember her by."

"That's fine. Keep anything you want. Give the rest to the poor people down in the Marine Creek area. Ask Moses to deliver it there."

One day, Mr. Moore called Jennie to the sitting room. "Jennie, I have given it some serious thought and I think we need to go back to Wenona Beach next month, just as in the past. Is that all right with you?"

Jennie had mixed emotions. She didn't want to leave John. On the other hand it would be good for Mr. Moore to get away and she could visit her family. After she married, she may not get a chance to make the trip. She and John were planning to wait till fall to get married anyway and she would be back by then. So, she told Mr. Moore, "I think that would be good for you, Sir. It will give you a fresh start. Do let me know as soon as you have made the arrangements. I would like a week or even two, to get ready."

"I will see about tickets for two weeks from today. Is that all right?"

"Yes, Sir."

Jennie had to get rid of some mixed feelings. She ran up the front stair case, down the long hall, looking in every room for Mabel, and down the back stairway to the kitchen. She paced the kitchen floor as she told Mabel the news.

Mabel said, "Calm down, Jennie. John and J.W. will be here tomorrow. You can talk it over with John and decided what to do.

It was a beautiful spring day and John and J.W. brought the wagon to take the girls out for a ride in the park. They had packed a picnic lunch and after they ate, Jennie urged John to go for a walk around the little duck pond. She had saved up some stale bread crusts and wanted to feed the ducks. As they strolled along, she told him about Mr. Moore wanting to go back to Michigan. She would be leaving again for the summer. They were both feeling disappointed. But, John reminded her they could still write like they did the previous summer. She could visit her friends and family because it might be a while before she could visit them again. They could survive the summer apart and would be married in the fall when she gets back; just like they had planned.

April 23, 1908

It was getting dark and cloudy about noon. The horses had been out grazing all morning. John didn't like the looks of the clouds rolling in and decided to bring the horses in to their stall. He walked out the big back doors, whistled and the horses came running. He walked them into their stall, secured the chain and soon heard thunder in the distance.

It grew darker, the thunder louder and huge, close strikes of lightning. The same thing had happened just a few days ago. So much rain the river had overflowed and flooded tent city. He was so glad his folks didn't live there anymore.

The horses usually weren't skittish with a little thundered or lightning, but this time they were pacing the stall. "Looks like we are in for another big one," John said. "The horses are nervous this time. I'll try to calm them, but some of ya'll better go upstairs and shut the windows."

"You really think those horses know when the weather is going to be bad?" asked one of the men.

"I'd trust a horse's instinct a lot more than a farmers arthritis. Animals can sense when to take cover or when to run to higher ground. Judging from the way Clyde, Sam, and Brown are acting right now, I'd say they're wanting to run to higher ground. So something big is about to happen."

The thunder and lightning grew closer and louder, then as if a dam broke, there was a heavy deluge of rain. John thought, "*Thank goodness we are on higher ground and everyone I know is too.*"

John stayed beside the horse stall, talking to them and trying to distract them with treats of apples and carrots, all the while thinking, *"It's a big one alright, worse than last weeks. Lord, I hope we don't get a fire call and have to get out in this weather."*

Just as it sounded like it was going to quit raining, it began hailing. For a total of forty minutes the rain and hail pounded on the roof and windows. Then just as quick as it came, it ended. Quarter size hail dotted the ground. But the worst was yet to come.

The phone rang and the alarm sounded. "Station Six, Floyd speaking."

The voice on the phone said, "This is Chief Bideker. Put John on the line."

Floyd yelled, "John, its Chief Bideker."

John came to the phone, "Yes, Chief."

"John, the West Fork of the Trinity River is out of its banks, again. Central station's been called out to help the police department with rescues and setting up road blocks on northwest side of town. Switchboard is calling in all off duty personnel. John, you take #6 supply wagon and report to the police on North Main at the viaduct. North Main is flooded with four feet of water, closing the trolley and street traffic. All electricity and telephone lines are down to North Fort Worth. Do what ever you need to do to save the most lives, but don't put your men in danger. Also check for fires or downed power lines."

As Captain of Station #6, John directed the men to the disaster scene. Arriving at the top of the cliff, they could see everything at the end of the viaduct below was underwater. "J.W., Marcus, come with me, Frank help the police with the barricades. Leave your coats under the wagon seat, but wear your boots. Marcus, when we get a wagon load of people, you take them to the Salvation Army shelter and return as soon as possible for another load. Let's load any sick or injured first, then come back for the women and children."

People were everywhere on the bridge and still wading out down below. As they made their way down, they told some injured people to sit down and stay there and they would be back. Arriving at the bottom, people were being knocked down by the current of the water and swimming to get footing on the pavement 4 feet below them. John, J.W. and Marcus took each others hands and waded out as far as they could, forming a human chain. John grabbed people and pulled them passed him to where they could get a hold of J.W. and then Marcus and work their way out. The employees at the electrical plant had shut everything down before the water got in the building, but many were still wading out. When all were out of the water, they loaded some injured and told Marcus to pick up the others on his way back up the viaduct. Then come back for others as soon as he could. Many were carrying what few belongings they were able to salvage. Women were carrying the smallest of the children with others hanging on to their mothers skirts. Dazed and not knowing what to do, many kept walking away from the water and up the viaduct. John told the women to wait and they would be taken by wagon to the shelter. The men from the gravel pit had loaded people into their wagons and made it to Main Street. But the water got too deep for the horses to pull the load through the water. All the men jumped off and waded, swam or helped push the wagons, loaded with women and children, as far as they could. Getting everyone to the bridge and unloaded, the horses could then pull the wagons out of the water. They loaded people back in those wagons and directed them to the shelters.

After several trips, they had everyone out of the water that they could find and everyone off the bridge. A special train on the Santa Fe, Ft. Worth and Denver line, rescued the employees from the Swift and Armour meat packing plants, bringing them into the city, before about 2 blocks of rails were washed up against the telegraph poles. The police could handle the barricade now, so the firemen headed back to the station.

John reported back to Chief Bideker, "nothing more could be done, till the water receded." At least 200 people had been driven from their homes and sheltered at the Salvation Army and United Charities by 7 p.m.

Newspapers reported this flood was equal to the one in 1889. It took three days for the river to get back within its banks. The task of helping with clean-up, started the next day. Every fire station in town was called out to help flush out the water lines and fire hydrants. They were instructed to connect a hose and use that water to wash out people's houses or what ever was needed. From daylight to dark for four days they worked where and when they could.

*****

Dearest John,   April 24, 1908

Just a note to tell you we got here today safely. Mr. Moore went to his room to rest. I wanted to write you and I will go mail it as soon as I finish writing. I hope it doesn't take to long to get there, so you won't be worried. When we go to lunch, I will see if any of my friends still work here. After lunch, I will go see Ma. We will decide about the best time to tell Pa about us getting married. When I looked out over the bay this morning, I had forgot how nice it is to see blue water, lots of water and not flooding. Are you still helping the poor people clean up the mess? I miss you all ready. I hope summer passes quick. Take care of yourself. Love, Jennie

*****

Dear Jennie,

I miss you too, sweetheart. Things seem dull round here, not getting to see you on my days off. With nothing else to do, I have been substituting for some of the men. Yes, we are still cleaning up the flooded areas. Not only from the flood we had before ya'll left, but the day after you left, we had a worse storm and flood. We are helping with that clean-up now.

Guess what? Ida called to tell me a vacant lot on the next street behind her was for sale. It is in good naborhood. I took time off to go see about it. It is nice big lot, plenty of room for barn and horses and a small garden and even a chicken house if you want one. I heard a doctor and his wife bought the lot next door. I am so sure you will like it too, I bought it. By the time you get back we can start building our house. It is getting hot here. Tell Mr. Moore hello for me.

Love, John

*****

Dear John,

I am so sad and mad. I don't know what to do. Mr. Moore said he don't need me anymore. It would not be proper for me to live in his house anymore, with Mrs. Moore not there. He said people like Florence (wicked witch) would start nasty rumors. No jobs at Wenona Beach and I had to move back home in Ma's boarding house and helping her. I told Ma about us getting married. She is happy for me. But when I told Pa, he got mad. He said he won't let me marry anybody he has not met. Mr. Moore came and talked to Pa, but it did no good. I haven't got enough money saved up to pay my own way back to Texas, since Mr. Moore will be going back by himself. Working for Ma, I get room and board and that's about all. Sometimes a boarder pays me to mend their clothes, but that ain't much. I just don't know what to do. Please tell me.

Love, Jennie

Mid May 1908

Dear Sweet Jennie,

Don't you worry your pretty head off. I got an idea. Is it alright if I come up there? Can you find me a place to stay? I will win your Pa over even if I have to pay him like Mr. Moore did. Now let me know if it is alright to come and where to find you once I get there. Then I will get on the next train headed that way. See you soon, Love, John

*****

Dearest John,

Oh, I knew you would think of something. You are my night in shining armor. Ma has a boarder moving out May 31st. She said you can stay in that room, but only for too days, then she has a lady moving in. Can you get here that soon? I will meet you.

Lovingly, Jennie

*****

A few days later

The door bell rings at the boarding house. Jennie opens the door. "Telegram for Miss Jennie Campbell." A young boy on a bicycle hands her a paper. "Sign here."

Jennie has never received a telegram before. She is worried it might be bad news and her hand is shaking as she signs her name. She rips open the envelope. "Arriving June 1st, 9:30 a.m. John"

Jennie can't contain herself and lets out a yell and jumps up and down.

8

The Devil Steps In

May 28, 1908

For weeks, John worked extra days, traded days off and lined up those who owed him a favor to work for him, so he could have 7 straight days off. That would cut down on his paycheck, but it would be worth it to go get Jennie and stay on good terms with her family. He had a place to stay, bought his ticket and made plans to leave the next day for Michigan, "Come Hell or High Water." He would help with the flood clean up when he got back.

Ida and Ma packed a sack of food for John and James took him to the depot. John left Fort Worth in a chair car, the cheapest ticket he could get. If he could sleep on a cot at the Fire Station with half the men snoring, he could sleep in a chair on a train. During the night the train stopped in Oklahoma City with only an hour lay over while more cars were added to the train. The next day, there was another lay over in Kansas City. He got off the train and asked the baggage handler where to get a good breakfast. Finding his way around the corner to a little café he filled up on bacon, eggs, hot biscuits and coffee. Then he bought a sandwich to take with him. He felt excited, since he had never been out of Texas, but he thought the scenery wasn't much different than Texas and big cities were still big cities. Getting back on the train, he settled down for a nap. Napping off and on day and night wasn't exactly a good nights sleep. As long as the train kept moving at a steady pace, he could sleep, but at every stop he woke up.

The next evening, the train pulled into Chicago. He had to change trains, with about two hours to wait. He would have a good supper and not need anything till he arrived in Bay City in the morning. As he got off the train, he saw a policeman and asked him where he could get a good cheap meal. He was directed to O'Reiley's saloon, across the street and down about a block. John had his doubts about a saloon, but trusting the policeman's judgment decided to take a look. He was surprised to find a large counter full of all kinds of meats, cheeses, breads and all the sandwich trimmings. He walked over to the counter and asked the bartender how much. The bartender handed him a fresh, drawn beer and said, "Five cents."

John asked, "I mean how much for a meal?"

The bartender said, "You buy the beer for five cents and the meal is free, all you can eat."

"Thanks." John said as he tossed a nickel on the counter. John figured he didn't have to drink the beer, except maybe enough to wash down the food.

After a good meal, John picked up his bag and headed back to the depot. He asked the ticket agent which train went to Bay City, Michigan. He boarded the train, put his bag on the rack and relaxed for the long nights ride. *"Just a few more hours and I will see my Jennie. I have her address, but I don't know how far it is from the depot to where she lives. I hope she got my telegram."*

As the train pulled out of Chicago he caught a glimpse of a big body of water. He asked the conductor where they were.

"That's Lake Michigan," said the conductor.

"Wow, I had no idea it was that big. I thought I had caught the wrong train and was looking at the Atlantic Ocean. Are we getting close to Bay City?"

"No, we have to go around the end of Lake Michigan, then across to the other side of the State. Bay City is on the south end of Saginaw Bay that comes off Lake Heron."

"Oh, thank you." John said as he thought, *I sure didn't remember my schooling when we studied maps.*

June 1, 1908

John woke several times during the night. The last time he woke it was getting daylight. He got up and stretched and looked at his watch. It was just 6:35. He had plenty of time, but before the restroom got busy, he decided to go freshen up. As he retrieved his bag off the shelf, he felt the train slowing down. The conductor came through the door. "Saginaw, in five minutes. Arriving on time at 7:05, leaving at 7:15."

John asked the conductor, "Will we be arriving in Bay City on time?"

"Yes, sir, at 9:30."

John thanked the conductor and made his way to the end of the car to the rest room. He got prepared and as soon as the train stopped, he quickly shaved. *"Now I know how Jennie and the Moore's got so dirty just riding in a train car for three days. The soot from the train engine sifted in between every crack. There's no showers or even a place to change clothes. There's barely room for me to get in here to turn around and I sure couldn't change clothes in here. Well, at least I can freshen up and have clean face and hands when I get there."*

John went back to his seat, getting more and more anxious to get there. *"Hurry, train, hurry. What am I going to say to her parents?"* He had brought each of Jennie's parents a gift to hopefully win them over. But he was still nervous about meeting them. *"What if he didn't like them or they didn't like him?"*

The conductor interrupted his thoughts, "Bay City, next stop. Arriving in five minutes, leaving at 9:45."

John stood, stretch and got his bag down. The train was slowing, so he stepped out the door and stood behind the conductor. When the train stopped, the conductor opened the gate and put a step stool down on the platform. Stepping onto the platform he heard, "JOHN!" Looking up, he saw Jennie running toward him, dodging between the people going in the opposite direction. "JOHN!"

"JENNIE!" He set down his bag, grabbed her in a big hug and whirled her around.

"Oh, John, I am so glad to see you."

"I am so glad to see you, too." He held her in a big hug, a good excuse to get to feel the soft warmth of her body and to drink in her beauty. "I can't believe I'm really here with you. But then I would go to hell and back to get you."

"When you meet my pa, you'll think you are in hell and meeting the devil."

John picked up his bag, "We'll see about that. Based on what I have heard, I came bearing gifts to win them over and allow me to take you home with me."

Jennie was leading the way out of the depot, "And just what are your plans, if I may ask?"

"You may ask, but I'm not telling. If I am to rescue my damsel-in-distress, I must have secret, well-made plans," John teased.

"Uoooo, my knight in shining armor sounds serious."

Giggling, Jenny motioned to the four storied building down at the end of the street. "That's the hotel at Wenona Beach. We turn here," she said, pointing left. "We are just a couple of blocks from the depot."

"Is Mr. Moore still at the hotel?"

"Yes, he said since he was here he might as well stay. John, he just wasn't thinking clearly. He said he asked around and couldn't find another job for me. He thought the best thing to do was to see that I got back home to my parents. I wish he had talked it over with me, or with us, before deciding to do that."

"That would have been a lot better for us, that's for sure. But like you said, he wasn't thinking clearly and wanted only the best for you."

"I left a lot of my things there, thinking I would be going back. So I wrote Mabel and asked her to store them for me, until I could let her know where to send them."

"Well, don't worry, we'll work things out. For now, all I can think about is getting a bath and putting on clean clothes. I feel like I've been fighting fires for 3 days."

"How 'bout some breakfast?" Jennie asked.

"That sounds good, too."

"Well, here we are." Jennie started cutting across the small lawn to the big front steps, leading up to the small front porch of a three story, brick building. Judging from the number of steps there looked like a cellar below the first floor. All the houses on the block seemed to almost be the same, but different painted trim and decorations or flower pots on the front porches. The houses were built so close together, you couldn't have driven a fire wagon between them.

John followed Jennie into the foyer of sparse furnishings, but adequate. A little run down but neat and clean.

"Ma, we're here." Jennie called out. No answer, so Jennie said, "Well, come on I'll show you to your room. After you get cleaned up, come on back down to the kitchen....down the hall there.....I'll have your breakfast ready." Jennie led the way up the stairs to the 3rd floor and second door on the right. "It's a real step down from the Moore's mansion, huh? The bath is down the hall, last door on the left. Ma's probably already out back doing laundry, so bring your dirty clothes when you come for breakfast. Don't take too long. I have big plans for us today." She smiled as she backed out of the room, shutting the door behind her.

John took some clothes out of his bag and hung them on the wooden pegs hanging around the room, to let the wrinkles fall out. He took one set of clothes with him to the bathroom. After a good hot bath and clean clothes he felt one hundred per cent better, although still looking forward to a good nights sleep. He carried his dirty clothes with him and went down to the kitchen.

Jennie had fried some bacon and when she saw him coming, started pouring pancake batter into a huge skillet. "Have a seat and I'll get you some coffee."

"Umm, sure looks good. I haven't eaten since last night."

"I knew you'd be hungry. We'll be having a late lunch, so this should hold you till then. While you eat, I'll take your dirty clothes to the cellar and wash them."

"You don't have to do that. I'm used to doing my own laundry. Just show me to the wash tubs."

"No, No! You're our guest." Jennie handed him the plate of pancakes and bacon. "You eat your breakfast and help yourself to more coffee and rest a while. I'll be back in no time." And she was out the backdoor in a flash.

When he had finished eating he carried his dirty dishes to the sink. Looking around he found the soap and washed and dried his dishes. Then he walked out the backdoor. It was a beautiful day with a nice and cool breeze for June. He heard voices and saw Jennie and her Ma struggling to carry a huge basket of clothes out of the cellar. He hurried down the steps, intercepted and offered, "Here, let me carry this for you."

Jennie said, "It's alright, Ma. Let John and I carry it to the clothes line for you."

Mrs. Campbell reluctantly let go of her end of the basket. She seemed a little confused as she followed them. After they set the basket down, Jennie said, "Ma, this is my John. John, my mother."

"Glad to meet you, Ma'am."

Mrs. Campbell looked a little confused or something, as she looked up at him and muttered, "Nice to meet you too, John. Jennie has spoken so highly of you."

Jennie caught on and smiled, "She's a little surprised at a man helping with woman's work. She didn't believe me when I told her how nice and helpful Southern gentlemen were."

"I hope I didn't offend you, Ma'am. That basket looked awful heavy and I just wanted to help you ladies."

Mrs. Campbell seemed to come out of her daze. "Oh, my, no. I've just never had a man do that for me before. How very thoughtful of you. Did you have a nice trip?" She began hanging the clothes on the line.

"Yes, ma'am, it's a long way from Texas up here to Michigan."

Jennie started helping her Ma hang the clothes. "We'll be through here in just a minute, and then we can go."

John got a handful of clothes and clothespins and followed Jennie to the next clothesline. As she hung a piece, he handed her another and soon they were through. "Don't look now, but you have every woman in the neighborhood peeking out a window, watching you."

"Why? What have I done?"

"You're out here helping us with women's work." Jennie smiled. "You're my gentleman from Texas and every young lady in the neighborhood is jealous of me."

John was surprised at what he heard. He had been raised to be helpful to women and polite. "Is that all?" he asked.

"For now." Jennie turned to Ma. "Is that all you need me for, Ma?"

"Yes. I'm just going to get the bread made, so it will have time to rise. You young folks go have some fun, while you can."

"Oh, before we go, I have to get something out of my bag. I'll meet you back in the kitchen in just a minute." John said, as he headed up the stairs ahead of them.

Returning in a few minutes he handed Jennie a little box, then walked over to Mrs. Campbell and handed her a little bigger but flatter package. "Just a little something to say thank you, for having me here."

Jennie said, "Oh, John, you are so thoughtful."

Mrs. Campbell was so surprised she held the package, just looking at it for a while. "I don't know what to say, besides Thank You. It's so seldom anyone gives me a gift. You open yours first, Jennie."

Jennie excitedly, opened the little box. "Oh, John, it's beautiful." She lifted out a little cameo locket.

John began to explain, "The lady in the store said you run a ribbon through the top there and tie it around your neck. It reminded me of the pearl pendant you wore the night we had dinner with the wicked witch, Florence."

"Oh, John, I love it. I really do. I'll be right back. I'm going to wear it today. Oh, wait, Ma, open your package. What did you get?"

"I....I don't know. I'm just so surprised." Mrs. Campbell ran her hand over the package, as if opening it would break the contents. She untied it slowly, as though wanting to savory the moment of unwrapping the treasure. A beautiful, hand embroidered dresser scarf. "Oh, John, it's beautiful. I don't know what to say." She began to cry. "I haven't had anything this nice in so long. Thank you, thank you, thank you. I can't tell you how much I appreciate this."

"Your welcome. My Ma made it. I paid her for it. She makes things like this and sells them where ever she can for extra spending money." John told her.

"Oh, how wonderful. That makes it even more meaningful to know who made it. Thank you so much." She kept fingering the material and the delicate stitches. "Just wait till I show the girls at coffee today."

"Ma, you'll be the talk of the neighborhood." Jennie laughed and looked at John, "I'll be back in just a minute." She darted off to her room and came back tying the ribbon and locket around her neck.

Mrs. Campbell encouraged, "You young folks run on now and have some fun."

"If you're sure I can't help you with anything else." Jennie said to her Ma.

"No, you go on now and have a good time."

"All right, we'll be back about four." Jennie said.

"Come on, John, let's go."

"Where're we going?" John asked.

"Sightseeing!"

"Sounds good to me."

They started walking down the street. Jennie would wave at each neighbor as they walked by. John nodded politely. John took Jennie's hand. "I don't suppose it has occurred to you that suddenly there is a lady on every porch, either sweeping or watering flowers or something."

"You noticed?" Jennie giggled. "I forgot to mention you're the sight everybody's seeing. Wait till Ma gets to the neighborhood coffee this morning and shows off her new dresser scarf. That's the only entertainment or fun these women get, is having coffee together every morning. That, and as soon as the children leave home they rent a room to a traveler or boarder."

"So what else is there to do in this town?"

"If you're a man you work in the coal mine. Unless you're lucky like my brother Peter and get a job on the road and bridge crew or the younger ones like William, bell hop at the hotel. A few are school teachers or shop keepers. It's not bad during the summer when tourists are here, but come winter it's like everything and everybody hibernates like a bear, except for the mine, school and general store."

"So, show me the town, the mine and all."

"You've seen the neighborhood. From the end of the street here, you'll see the mine. Then we'll walk over to the hotel." They were walking by a school house and Jennie said, "This is where all us kids went to school. We'll pass the general store on the way back from the hotel. It doesn't take long to see the whole town."

"It reminds me of Dublin, where I grew up. A general store, school, church and that's about it."

"But we only have one church here, a Catholic. I bet Dublin has more than that."

"Yeah, we had the Methodist where Grandpa sometimes preaches and a Baptist."

By then they had walked to the top of the hill. "Oh, wow, would you look at that view." John exclaimed. They stood looking out over the Bay to the right. You couldn't see the shore on the other side. To the left was the big mining operation, similar to the one in Thurber.

After a few minutes of silence Jennie said, "I like to come here sometimes and just daydream."

"What do you dream about?" John asked.

"That my knight in shining armor would come and rescue me and take me away to his castle and we'd live happily ever after. I'd miss Ma, but nothing or nobody else." Jennie confessed. "Oh, John, I have tried not to get my hopes up, so I wouldn't be disappointed, but I am so afraid that Pa is going to come up with some excuse as to why I can't go back to Texas with you."

"Well, we will face that tonight, I guess. I talked to all the men at the fire hall for advice on how best to handle your Pa. Do you have any suggestions?"

"Wait till after supper. Ma always says he's in a better mood when he's rested a while and had a good meal. Then catch him before he's had too much to drink."

"Sounds like a good plan. I'll give him his gift after supper then I'll ask his permission to marry you and then ask to take you home with me."

"Did you bring gifts to butter everybody up?"

"I didn't think I needed to butter you up. But it never hurts to cover all my options." John teased.

"You think of everything. I feel so safe and cared for when I am with you."

"You are safe with me Jennie." He put his arm around her. "Just how safe are we from prying eyes up here?" he whispered.

'Safe enough for what you're thinking about." Jennie smiled up at him.

John leaned over and gave her a kiss and she kissed him back. "Miss Jennie Campbell, sooner or later, one way or another, I'm going to marry you."

"I certainly hope so, Mr. John Whittenburg."

"Is this part of the big plans you said you had for us today?"

"Oh, my goodness! What time is it?"

John pulled out his pocket watch, "It's 1:45 already."

"Oh, good. We have plenty of time, but can't tarry too long. Come on." With that she started leading the way down hill toward the hotel at Wenona Beach. But instead of leading the way to the front entrance, she led John to the back door and into the kitchen. The dining room closed at two and the employees were allowed to eat the leftovers for their lunch. Her friends had told Jennie to bring John by at that time for them to meet him. As soon as they entered, one of the cook's helpers saw them and ran over yelling to everyone else, "Jennie's here!"

"Hello, you must be John. I'm Thomas. Nice to meet you."

By then, the others were gathering around Jennie and John and introducing themselves. Then the head waiter came up and with formality said, "Miss Jennie, may I escort you and your fiancé to your table?" Jennie wondered what her friends were up to. They usually just gathered around the center of the kitchen work area to eat the left-overs, but this time she played along.

Jennie took John's arm and said, "By all means, my good fellow."

She and John followed to a corner of the kitchen, where Jennie's friends had set up a table for two, complete with tablecloth, napkins, silverware and a small centerpiece. Then, one by one, each friend served them water, hors d'oeuvre's, salad, a little bit of two different main courses, a vegetable and for desert, a choice of plain cake or lemon pie. As always, the meal ended with the check. John wondered how much all this was going to cost him. He turned the check over to find the bill read, "Our very best wishes, your friends at Wenona Beach." Jennie and John thanked them for going to all that trouble to make lunch so special for them.

They left the hotel and walked down the beach a ways, then headed back to Jennie's place. The day had passed all too quickly. It was time for Jennie to get back and help her Ma with the evening meal.

John offered to help, but Mrs. Campbell wouldn't hear of it. Jennie got John a cup of coffee and he sat at the kitchen table talking to them while they worked. "The other day, Floyd put a roast in the oven. About an hour later, the alarm went off and he forgot to turn the oven off before we left. We got back from the fire and that roast was burned so crisp, even the horses wouldn't eat it. Floyd was so mad at himself. But we scrounged up some cold cuts and cheese and made do for supper."

He had Jennie and her Ma laughing while they worked. Jennie's little sister, Emma, age 12, came in from school. John won her over quickly by showing an interest in what she had learned at school that day. Emma thought sure he would be wearing cowboy boots and hat and have a gun strapped to his hip. He explained he was a fireman, not a cowboy. Jennie's brother William, age 14 had just got his first job, as bell boy at the hotel. John won him over by telling William he had also got his first job at age 14. Then Jennie's older brother Peter, age 17 came in from work. John asked him what he did as a bridge attendant. John had never seen a bridge raise up for boats to pass from one side of the road to the other and Peter was glad to explain to him how it worked.

Then everyone heard Pa Campbell coming in the door and everyone's mood changed. Little sister Emma went to her room, as did William. Peter asked John to go to the sitting room with him, leading the way through the dining room. Pa Campbell could be heard trudging down the hall toward the kitchen. John never heard a word of greeting but heard him set his lunch bucket down and then came back down the hall with a cup of coffee. He trudged off to his room, John supposed probably to get cleaned up from the black smudges from the coal mine. The other two boarders came in from their days work and went to their rooms.

After they talked for a while, Peter suggested they go to their rooms and get washed up for supper. He walked out of the sitting room leaving his coffee cup on the table. John picked up both cups and carried them to the kitchen. "Umm, something smells really good in here," he said, as he came in the door.

"John," Jennie seemed alarmed as she took the cups from him, "You shouldn't be in here. You go get washed up and be back in the sitting room or dining room before seven."

"Alright, see ya, later."

Jennie acted rather nervous or something. John couldn't quite figure out what was wrong. She just didn't act like her usual happy self. He went upstairs and freshened up and came back to the sitting room, bringing his gift for Mr. Campbell and putting it on the side table. John introduced himself to the other two boarders who were sitting there. They weren't exactly friendly, but they weren't rude. Peter came back to the room and said, "Did you guys meet John? He's Jennie's fiancé from Texas."

It seemed as though Peter woke everybody up from a trance, as they smiled and said 'nice to meet you' this time.

"How very strange," John thought. *"As though I was nobody till somebody connected him to somebody else."*

On the dot of seven p.m., Mr. Campbell came into the dinning room and sat down at the head of the table. It must have been the signal for everyone else to follow, as they began filing into the dining room and taking a seat. Peter directed John to sit next to him. Peter sat between Pa Campbell and John, "Pa, this here's John Whittenburg. Jennie's friend from Texas."

John reached his hand across the table. "Glad to make your acquaintance, Sir."

Pa Campbell glared at John and without saying a word reluctantly shook John's hand, then picked up his knife and began pounding on the table.

The kitchen door flew open and Jennie and her Ma came carrying in bowls of stew, setting the first bowl in front of Mr. Campbell and then serving the rest. Platters of fresh made bread were at each end of the table. John suddenly realized there was no place for Jennie or Emma or Mrs. Campbell to sit at the table. This might be a custom of theirs, so out of respect, he didn't say anything. But he sure planned to talk to Jennie about it later. Right now he wanted to 'observe' Mr. Campbell and so far John didn't see anything to like about the man.

Following the meal, Jennie and her Ma brought out pieces of still warm apple pie. No one spoke during the meal and as each finished eating; they left and headed up stairs. When Mr. Campbell finished he got up and went into the sitting room and started getting a glass out of a cabinet. John followed and picked up the wrapped gift and handed it to Mr. Campbell. "Sir, I understand you are from Scotland. I think you will like this."

"Wha' tis this?" Mr. Campbell asked in his Scottish accent.

"When two men need to talk some serious business, they need to understand each other. What better way than to share a drink and specially a drink from the old country."

By then Mr. Campbell had the wrapper off and could see it was one hundred proof, pure, Scottish Whiskey, imported from Scotland. "My, God, lad, whar' tha hell did ye git this? I naught seen this grand stuff since I lef' Scotland."

"I bought it in Texas, Sir."

"Git ye glass an we'll hav' a wee dram," he remarked greedily.

"If you don't mind, Sir, I like to put some in my coffee for an after dinner drink."

"In Coffee? Never heard tha' likes. Hell, might be good. Jennie," he yelled, "brin' us more coffee."

Jennie and her Ma were cleaning off the table. Jennie gave John a dirty look before quickly retrieving the coffee pot from the kitchen. *Hum, wonder what that was all about?"* John thought as Jennie poured their coffee without saying a word.

John offered to do the 'honors' by pouring some whiskey in Pa Campbell's cup and then with his back turned to Pa, who had already headed for his chair, John pretended to pour some in his cup. Turning around to face Pa, John held up his cup as to give a toast, "To the old country where they know how to make the good stuff."

"Here! Here!" Pa said and could hardly wait to taste this new drink. "Be gory, tis good." He took another sip and said, "Dam, good. Now wha' wis ye saying 'bout serious talk?"

So far, so good, it's working, John thought. "Sir, I have a very good job and good prospect for promotion in the future. I have been acquainted with Jennie now for almost two years. I would like your permission to marry your daughter, Sir, either here or in Texas. I will give her a good home and take care of her and be good to her, Sir. If you have any questions or anything you want to know about me I will give you an honest answer."

Pa Campbell was quiet for a minute before he spoke. " 'at Mr. Moore, wha hired Jennie, he says ye're a good man."

"That's good to hear." John said.

"Whit's Jennie worth tae ye?" Pa asked, as he poured more whiskey into his cup.

John thought fast for the answer that would please Pa. "Honestly, Mr. Campbell, I can tell you Jennie is worth a lot more to me than to you."

"How da ye figure 'at?"

"Well, to be honest, you haven't spoken a decent word to Jennie or any body else for that matter, since you walked in the door. That tells me, you don't care about anybody but yourself. So let's look at it this way. I'll take Jennie off your hands and that is one less mouth for you to feed."

Pa looked at John in silence and then said, "I like a man wha's honest 'nough tae speak his mind. Let's hav' 'nother drink."

John got up and said, "Let me do the honors, Sir. You want yours straight or more coffee?"

"'Tis dam good in coffee, laddy. Hell let's hav' 'nother."

"I'll go get some fresh, hot coffee and be right back, Sir." John said as he picked up both cups and headed to the kitchen.

Speaking softly to Jennie, he said, "Quick give me some more coffee. I've about got your old man to agree to let me marry you."

"John, are you out of your mind? You brought whiskey to an already drunkard. Well, you get him drunk, you can help get him to bed tonight. I'm not. I have to do it too many times. I'm sick and tired of it and that goes for you, too." Jennie spoke in anger.

"Jennie, what better way to get a drunk on your side than to butter him up by drinking with him? Only he just thinks I'm drinking with him. I'm having my coffee straight. And besides who cares how I get his permission, as long as I get it."

Jennie calmed down. "Well, maybe you're right. I sure hope so."

Jennie had poured the last of the coffee from the pot. "How much more coffee are you going to need tonight?"

"I think this will do it." John took the cups and headed back to the sitting room.

"Why ta hell didn't ye just yell at Jennie to brin' the coffee, 'stead of goin' after it?" Pa asked.

"Well, my pa always said, 'If you want something done right, do it yourself'."

Pa Campbell chuckled. That was the kind of answer he wanted to hear, but John hoped Jennie hadn't heard it. He poured whiskey in Pa's cup and handed it to him, then pretended to pour some into his own cup. "So what do you say, Mr. Campbell, do we have a deal?"

"Wha' deal ye talking 'bout?"

"I'll take Jennie off your hands."

"Oh, eye', well, like I wis saying," Pa continued, "how much tis she worth to ye? 'at Mr. Moore pay me two-hundard dollars to comp'n'sate for tha loss of Jennie."

"Sir, I will not buy Jennie like a common slave. My family has never bought or owned another human being and never will. I'm asking for her to be my wife, not buying a servant. Like I said, your compensation will be one less mouth to feed."

Pa reached over, picked up the bottle and poured more whiskey into his cup. He took a sip. "Hell, lad, ye got a point thar'. Ye drive a hard bar'ain."

Come on you old tyrant, say yes. John thought.

"Whit are ye plannin'?" Pa asked.

"Well, with your permission, we could get married here tomorrow or we can go back to Texas and get married there."

"Ye canna do neit'er wit'out me permission."

"Well, I believe we could since Jennie is of age, but we...."

"Eye, tis 'at whit ye thinkin' tis it? She winna be of age til' her nex' birt'day in August." Pa exclaimed.

John suspected Jennie of listening through a partially open kitchen door. He was right, when Jennie came busting through the door at hearing Pa say she wasn't of age. "You old drunkard, you don't know how old you are much less me. You're just saying that because you want everybody around you to live a miserable life because you're so miserable. You are lying because you to want to bribe John out of extra drinking money just like you bribed Mr. Moore. Well, it's not going to work this time. I'll...."

"Hush up, lassie. I'm ye Pa. I know when ye wis born an' ye winna be eighteen till August tent'."

"That can't be. You have to be sixteen before you can go to work and I been working for almost four years."

"Ye Ma lied 'bout ye age an' teld 'em ye wis sixteen so ye cou'd go ta wark, but ye wis only fourteen when ye got tha job."

"I don't believe you. I'm going to ask Ma." And with that she turned and practically ran from the room.

"Dam females, al'ays gettin' riled up 'bout some'in'. Jennie's tha only one wit 'nough spunk in'er ta talk back ta me."

"I have to admit, that surprised me too, about her age, as well as her talking back to you. She does have spunk to speak her mind." John, still trying to win Pa Campbell's approval, continued, "My apologies Sir. It seems we do need your permission. But since we are only looking at two months, perhaps you might consider giving us your consent a little early."

"No, Sar. Eighteen tis plenny young 'nough ta get mar'ied an' no' a day sooner. Ye can send fur her den."

John didn't know what to say, so he sat thinking.

Within a minute, Jennie and her Ma came back to the sitting room. "It's true! Ma did lie about my age. I'm really two years younger than I thought. Oh, John I hope you didn't think I was deceiving you. I really didn't know."

"No, no, everything's going to work out all right. It's just going to delay our plans, that's all."

Ma Campbell spoke up, "Peter Campbell, why are you always so difficult? It's just a couple of months, what difference can that hurt? Why don't you be nice for once and give in to these young folks?"

Pa Campbell retorted, "I rule dis house'old. Tis me decision an' she ain't marryin' til' she be eighteen yars old."

"Yes," Jennie said, "You rule this house all right. Like a tyrant, a dictator, a drunkard and all around jackass. Not one person is this house cares about you and all you care about is getting another drink for yourself." Jennie was mad and crying.

John walked over to her, "Come on, Jennie, let's take a walk. We both need some air and you've said enough."

Jennie was crying too much to resist John leading her outside. The cool of the evening breeze felt good against their hot faces. He put his arm around her. "Come on, sit down." They sat on the top step of the porch. "Stop crying now. We'll figure something out."

After a while, Jennie gathered herself together. "John, I hope this doesn't change your mind about me?"

"No, No, not a bit. You don't have to worry about something this minor coming between us. It's just that we both got hit with something totally unexpected and it caught us off guard."

"But, what are we going to do? I was so looking forward to going back to Texas with you and starting our life together."

"Well," John said, "let's back up a bit. Our original plans were, you would be coming back in the fall with Mr. Moore and we would be married then. So now, you won't be coming back the end of September with Mr. Moore, but you will be free to come on your own in mid August. When you think of it, that's not so bad is it? We have to wait two months now, not three like we originally planned. Now, I am dead tired and we've had a frustrating evening. Let's sleep on it tonight, think about it and tomorrow we'll talk about new plans."

Jennie nodded a yes.

"You sure that's all right with you?"

Jennie nodded yes again as she wiped her tears on her apron.

John got up and extended a hand to help her up. Then pulled her close and kissed her. "You know, I told you, I'd go to hell and back to get you. Well, I met the devil and he's put a stumbling block in our way. But he hasn't defeated us. Have a good nights rest and I'll see you in the morning." He held the door open for her and they went back in the house.

The next morning John woke with the sun shinning between the window frame and the shade and falling right across his face. He had slept hard and judging from the sunlight it was late morning. He quickly looked at his watch he had placed on the nightstand. Almost nine o'clock. Wow, he had over slept. Well, everybody else had left for work, so he had the bathroom to himself. After dressing, John went downstairs to the kitchen to find Jennie. Instead, he found a note on the table beside a plate of cooked bacon and two raw eggs.

"I hope you caught up on your sleep. Make yourself at home. I'm helping Ma with the washing. I'll be through in a little while and will fix your breakfast."

Looking out the window, he saw Jennie and her Ma hanging the clothes on the line. She wouldn't be much longer, but he might as well fry his eggs while he heated the coffee. He had just finished eating when Jennie and her Ma came up to the kitchen. "Good morning," they all said at once.

John said, "I'm sorry I slept so late. I guess I had some catching up to do after trying to sleep on a train for two nights."

"No reason for you to get up early. You needed the rest. I know, I've made that trip before." Jennie said.

John asked, "Are you feeling better this morning?"

Jennie gave a sigh, "I guess, but I'm still not happy about it."

Ma spoke up, "I'm sorry things didn't work out like you had hoped. I tried talking to him again last night."

"Oh, Ma, why do you continue to live with him like this, night after night? You're the one keeping a roof over our heads and keeping us fed. All his money goes for booze and paying the priest to keep praying him out of hell."

"Hush up, child. You have no idea what your Pa faces everyday going down in that mine."

"Then he could get another job someplace else, but meanwhile he is making life miserable for all of us."

John spoke up, "Jennie, your Ma is right. None of us know what you Pa faces everyday. He never sees daylight, works in darkness and besides that he has tons of rock that could come crashing down on him at any given time. He's probably afraid and he drinks at night to calm his nerves, so he can sleep and face the next day. He's not happy in his job, but maybe that's all he knows how to do and he may be afraid to try anything new. He can't quit, cause that would make your Ma the breadwinner and in his eyes that would be more of a disgrace than him hitting the bottle."

"How do you know that?" Jennie asked. "You just met him last night and I've lived with him for twenty......well, eighteen years."

"You have been too close to the problem and all you see is the hurts you've had as a child. Besides I lived with miners in Thurber."

"Thank you, John." Ma said. "I never thought of it in that way."

"Well, I've never had to live around a drunkard, but I've heard and seen a lot and try to learn what I can. Now to change the subject, Miss Jennie what have you got in mind for today?"

"Let's go walk along the beach first, then decide what to do next. You want us to get anything from the store for you, Ma?"

"No thanks, I need to go anyway and you young folks go have a good time. I'll see you this afternoon."

"All right then, I'll go freshen up a bit. Be right back, John."

"I'll meet you out on the porch. The weather is beautiful out today."

In a few minutes, Jennie came out and they walked down to the hotel and out to the beach. John broke the silence, "Have you thought about what we talked about last night?"

"Yes, and I guess your right. We'll just have to wait two more months."

"Now, there is one more option and that is to wait till September or when ever Mr. Moore decides to return to Texas, and let him escort you back, so you won't be traveling alone."

"No, I don't mind traveling alone. Unless you're afraid some traveling salesman might try to sweep me off my feet." Jennie teased.

"That had crossed my mind, but I have an idea you can take care of yourself."

"You're darn sure right. But, it would be nice to have someone along to talk to."

"Why don't you think about that? Then let me know when you want to come, either right after your birthday in August or when Mr. Moore can escort you. Then I'll send you the money for your ticket.

"Oh, John, I can hardly wait."

"We can write like we have done in the past. But this way, we will have your father's blessing and years from now, I think that will mean a lot to you. We have a lifetime to be together, to look forward to, so what's a couple of months. Meanwhile, I can be saving money to build us a house. It's going to be small, three rooms to start with but I can easily add on another room or two later. The quicker I get started the quicker it will be finished. I'd like to get at least the three rooms finished before you get there. We can live in it while I finish the rest. That would save us having to pay rent. So see, these next two months can be a preparation time."

"You're right. I was just too anxious to do what I wanted to do and I was disappointed," Jennie concluded.

"Now my train leaves at four this afternoon. Let's make the most of the rest of the day."

*****

All too soon the scene changes to two disappointed lovers, waving goodbye, but hanging onto hope for their future.

9

More Delays

June 6, 1908

Dear Jennie,

I arrived home yesterday and spent the night with Ida, James and Ma. I got a good night's sleep and went back to work this morning. We are still helping with the clean-up from all the flooding and flushing out the water lines and making sure the fire hydrants all work. The men were lucky and didn't have any fires last week while I was gone. I heard about several cases of typhoid fever caused from the dirty flood waters. Those were mainly in the poor sections of town where we helped wash mud out of people's houses. One of the guys opened a cabinet door and found a water moccasin. A blast from the fire hose stunned it till one of the others got an ax and killed it. It's been bad, very little salvageable. I am worn out just after a few days and just now have a chance to write to you. I can imagine how the other men feel who have been at it for 6 weeks now. All the people have been accounted for, but we ran across a dead horse covered in mud. Not a good thing to have to haul off to the dump and bury. It sure makes me think how lucky we are.

Love, John

*****

Dear John,   June 14, 1908

I was so glad to hear from you. The flood must have really been terrible. I'm so sorry you and the others are having to work so hard. I'm sure the flood victims appreciate all your help. Do be careful. Everything is normal and dull around here as usual. I go have lunch with my friends once or twice a week at the hotel. They all liked you and they are sad we are having to wait to get married. You saw my hill, so now you can picture in your mind, me sitting here as I write to you. The new boarder moved into the room where you stayed. Miss Davis is the new school teacher, but she is real nice. She found out I could sew and has hired me to do some mending and make a dress for her. I am going to use the money to buy some material to make me a nice dress for when we get married. She also helps me with my spelling. I miss you and please be careful.

Love, Jennie

*****

Jennie's letter arrived at the fire hall. John felt too tired to read it right then and stuck it in his shirt pocket. His shirt was sweaty, his body hot, but he shivered with a cold chill. As soon as he got a bite of supper, he would take a bath and go to bed. He...... so-o-o.... t-i-r-e-d....that's the last he remembered.

Unknown to him, his friend J.W. saw him collapse. The men carried John to the wagon and J.W. took him to Saint Joseph's hospital. J.W. called James and Ida. The doctor said, "It is typhoid fever." Ma, James and Ida took turns staying with John, keeping cool, wet rags on his chest and forehead to keep the fever down as much as possible. Doctor said it had to run its coarse and no telling how long that would take or what the outcome would be. John's personal stuff had been put in a drawer. It didn't occur to any of them to go through his things. They were too worried about him.

*****

------Three weeks later-----

Jennie climbed to the top of her hill. It had been three weeks since she mailed her last letter; plenty of time for John to have received it and to have written back. *Has he decided he doesn't want to marry me after all? Had something happened to him?*

*****

Another week past

It had been four weeks since John fell ill. At first there was no response, but the last couple of days, he had been twisting, moving his head side to side and speaking in muddled sounds. The doctor said, "That's a good sign."

James brought Ida to the hospital and took Ma home to rest. Ida changed the cool, wet rags on John's chest and forehead. "Come on little brother, you have been lazy long enough now. It's time to wake up and join the world again. You can't lay here and sleep your life away. What would I do without you?"

Ida turned to sit down, when suddenly John said, "What were you talking about?"

Ida turned back around, "Oh, John, you're awake. Thank God."

John muttered something and drifted back to sleep.

"Come on John, wake up. You're strong, you can pull through this." Ida wasn't giving up. She took the wet rag off his usually hot chest. That's when she noticed the dark pink spots were gone, and he didn't feel as feverish. She rung the wet rag out again and put it back on his chest, doing the same with the one on his forehead.

John opened his eyes for the first time in 4 weeks.

"Welcome back, little brother."

"Have I been gone?" John asked. "Oh, yes, I went to Michigan. Where's my Jennie?"

Ida didn't know what to say. She knew he was still not thinking straight. "She is home resting. Now, you go back to sleep and get some rest, too. We'll talk later."

"All right." John muttered and drifted off again.

In a few minutes the doctor, while making his rounds, came in the room. "Well, how is our patient today?"

Ida told him what had just happened.

"That's good to hear." The doctor said as he checked John over. "Still good strong heartbeat and his fever has broken. I expect he'll come out of it gradually, tomorrow or the next day. Just make sure he doesn't try to get out of bed. He's going to be weak. I'll check back in the morning."

"Thank you, doctor." Ida said. She sat down and began thinking about the words John had spoken. *'Where's my Jennie?' Oh, my goodness, that poor girl! She has no idea what has happened and I didn't even think to write and tell her. Well, I don't have her address anyway, so I couldn't write. Poor thing, I bet she is frantic with worry.*

*****

Jenny had checked their mail and again no letter from John. My birthday is in two weeks. *"I guess he changed his mind and doesn't want to marry me after all. Was it because he thought she was too young? Did he not want to have any more to do with her after meeting her family?"* Jennie walked up to her hill to be alone to cry. *"How could she forget him? How could he just stop writing with no explanation?"*

The next day every few minutes to an hour, all day long, John drifted in and out of consciousness. The doctor ordered potato soup for John's lunch and told Ida to try to get him to take a bite or two every time he was awake. By evening Ida had fed him at least a cup of the soup. James came to spend the night with John and let Ida go home to rest. Ida didn't want to leave, but James encouraged her to go tell Ma the good news, so she would quit worrying. She and Ma could come back in the morning.

Ida went home and that night she wrote Jennie a letter. She would have the letter ready to mail the minute John became alert enough to tell her where to send it.

*****

Ida and Ma, anxious to get to the hospital, were both up, dressed and had breakfast by dawn. Ma fed the chickens while Ida hitched the horse to the one seated buggy. They were on their way at day light. They arrived at the hospital to find James feeding John some soft boiled eggs. "He woke up hungry about four o'clock this morning. The doctor left word, if he was awake, he could have two eggs. He is having two more now," James explained.

"I'm so hungry, I feel like I haven't eaten in a month." John said.

They all laughed. "It has been a whole month," Ida exclaimed. "Has the doctor been in yet?"

"Not yet," James said.

"Oh, Son, we have been so worried about you. How do you feel?"

"I feel weak as a newborn calf, and hungry. James said I have been out of my head for four weeks now. What day is it?"

"It's the thirtieth of July, Son."

"You mean I really have been asleep all that time? Oh, my! Did anyone think to write Jennie?"

Ida spoke up, "I have written a letter but I didn't know where to send it. I was hoping you would be alert enough today to tell me."

"I got a letter from her. I don't remember where I put it. It has her return address on it. I don't remember her address. Why can't I remember? I've got to get word to her." John tried to get up, but was too weak to barely move.

James gently placed a hand on John's shoulder. "You are not going anywhere. Just lay back. Think about the letter you got from Jennie. What did you do with it?"

"Yeah, I got a letter from Jennie. I didn't answer it. I have to think....." and he drifted off to sleep.

James left to go home; Ida and Ma stayed. The doctor came in and they relayed what James had said and what had transpired after they arrived. The doctor, pleased to hear the good report, left further instructions. "I'm going to order light meals for today. His body is not used to food, so even if he feels hungry, I don't want him to overload his stomach too soon. And feed him slowly. Prop him up with pillows today while he eats. Tomorrow we'll see about letting him sit up. Now, that he is able to take food, he will start getting his strength back. I'll check with you again this evening."

"Thank you, doctor." Ida and Ma said.

A few minutes later, John woke again. "The letter....the letter is in my pocket, my shirt pocket."

Ida rushed to his side, "Don't try to get up. It's all right, John, we'll find it."

"I put her letter in my shirt pocket, but I never got to read it. Find my shirt. We have to write to Jennie."

To satisfy John and calm him down, Ida began going through every drawer of the night stand beside his bed. The bottom drawer contained his laundered clothes. Nothing was in the pocket of his shirt, but under his clothes was his pocket watch, a few dollar bills and a crumpled letter. "I found it!" Ida exclaimed.

*****

Jennie checked the mail again yesterday and went to her hill to cry. Ma had encouraged her to forget about John. She half heartedly went to get the mail today, expecting nothing, but found a letter from Ida Ross, John's sister. *Oh, God, please don't let this be what I think it is. Something has happened to my John. That's why I hadn't heard from him.* She didn't want to open the letter. She held it to her breast and ran up to her hill and fell to the ground. *She had to know, she had to read it sooner or later.* Fearing the worst, she tore open the letter.

Dear Jennie,   July 31, 1908

I am so sorry. I did not have your address to notify you sooner. John came down with typhoid fever and has been out of his head for the last 4 weeks. His fever finally broke and today he has drifted in and out of sleep. He is able to eat a little today. The doctor is pleased to report he expects full recovery in a couple more weeks.

When John woke yesterday, he asked where you

were. Today, he remembered putting your last letter in his shirt pocket. I found the letter for him and got your address. I will write again later and keep you informed of his progress, till he is able to do so. Again, I am so sorry I couldn't notify you sooner.

With Best Regards, Ida

*****

Jennie sat crying, hugging the letter, relieved to know he was alive and asking about her. She also worried that he was so sick. Oh, if only she could be there with him.

Dear Ida,   August 7, 1908

Thank you for letting me know about John. I have been so very worried when I did not hear from him. I wish I could be there to help take care of him. But, I know you and Ma Whittenburg will do a good job. It was good to know John thought of me even though he was so sick. Please do keep me informed of John's health.

Sincerely, Jennie

*****

Dear Jennie, my love,   September 3, 1908

I came home from hospital yesterday. I am staying with James, Ida and Ma for a while, till the doctor says I can go back to work. I am still trying to gain my strength back and I sleep a lot.

Jennie darling, this is going to put another postponement to our marriage. I had to pay my doctor and hospital bill and I have been off work almost five weeks now. Then I have to save up more money to send for you. I will get back to work as soon as I can and send for you as soon as I can. I am so sorry this came up. I miss you terribly. Please don't give up. We will get married. All my Love, John

*****

Dearest John,   September 11, 1908

It is so good to hear from you and know for sure you are all right. I'm so grateful to Ida for writing to tell me you were sick. I was so worried when I didn't hear from you. Summer is over. Mr. Moore left last week. The hotel guests are slowly checking out. Soon everything will be closing down for the winter, so no hope for me to get a job now. When I didn't hear from you for so long, I couldn't bring myself to sew on my new dress. Now, I am sewing again and I will look forward to the day when we can be married. I understand about you being off work and having bills to pay. I am just so glad that you are recovering. It is disappointing, but as you said, it's just another postponement. We have to keep up our hope. We'll make it. Love, always, Jennie

*****

Dear Jennie,   September 17, 1908

Chief let me come back to work, but it is with limited duty. He won't let me fight any fires, but I do all the cooking and cleaning up and take care of the horses. At least I am earning a paycheck again.

I found out Ma is entitled to a widow's pension, since Pa fought in the Civil War. I took her to the court house yesterday to fill out all the papers. She is getting twenty dollars a month, so I don't have to help support her anymore. I can start putting that money in savings. Keep sewing on that dress, you're going to need it.

Lovingly Yours, John

*****

Dearest John,   November 1, 1908

It has been snowing here all day today. Some old-timers are saying this is going to be a bad winter. Oh, how I wish I could be back staying with the Moores in Ft. Worth. It is so bitter cold here. Only the mine, general store, blacksmith and schools are open now. My brothers had to shovel six feet of snow off the sidewalk this morning, so they could walk the little ones to school. I can't even walk up to my hill, but I still look out the window and day dream of my prince charming. Three weeks ago, Ma and I cleaned out the attic and got everybody's winter clothing out to air. My old coat had moth holes all around the bottom. So I cut it off and took up the sleeves for my little sister. Ma bought me a new winter coat. With the pieces I cut off my old coat, I made me and Emma some mittens. So I am staying as warm as possible when I go to the store for Ma. It seems time is passing so slowly now that winter has set in. Maybe I'm just more and more anxious.

Love Always, Jennie

*****

Dearest Jennie,   November 15, 1908

It won't be long now. I got all my bills paid. I am back working steady. I have filled in some for fellows needing time off and picked up some extra money. By the first of next month, I will be able to send you the money to come to Texas.

My Sister Clemmie has a big house and her two oldest children have moved out. We can pay her room and board, till we can find a house to rent or till I get our house built. If that is alright with you? Otherwise, it will be spring before I get our house livable and I don't want to wait any longer for us to get married.

The weather has cooled off here and been very pleasant last few days. We didn't have any fires all last week, so we spent that time in painting and fixing up the fire hall. It looks real nice now.

J.W. was going over to the Moores to have lunch with Mabel. They invited me to join them. Cookie was there too and we laughed about the time you and I had dinner with the elite, wicked witch Florence. Mabel still has your things stored in the Moores attic. Mabel and J.W. said they would meet us at the court house and be our witnesses when we get married. Everything is looking good for us. It won't be long now, my darling. Loving you more, John

*****

Dearest John,   November 20, 1908

I am getting so excited and anxious, I can hardly sit still. I have all my summer clothes packed. Mr. O'Hare at the general store is saving me some boxes next shipment he gets in. I just told him Ma and I were packing some things away in the attic. I don't want word to get back to Pa that I am planning to leave.

That will be fine for us to stay with Clemmie. I don't care where it is as long as we can be together at last.

The weather here has been terrible. Ma and I have to hang laundry in the cellar and little at a time we bring pieces to hang around the warm kitchen to finish drying. The windows are so frosted over I can't even see my hill and snow too deep to walk there.

It will be so nice to see J.W., Mabel and Cookie again. But it will be a dream come true when I see you, sweetheart.

Lovingly, Jennie

*****

Dearest Jennie,   December 1, 1908

The time we have been waiting for has arrived. Here is a check for your train fare, money for food on the way, and to send me a telegram letting me know when you will arrive. Be careful and dress warm as the train will be drafty and I don't want you to get sick. See you soon, my little darling. Lovingly, John

John put the check and letter in an envelope addressed to Jennie Campbell, 401 Bay Street, Bay City, Michigan. He took pride even in licking the stamp and sticking it on the envelope. Just before dropping it in the mailbox, he held it once more close to his heart and sent it on its way.

*****

December 22, 1908

Jennie waited as patiently as she could. *He said he would send the money the first of the month. Maybe the bad weather has delayed the mail.*

*****

Hum-m, I should be hearing from Jennie by now.

*****

Why hasn't John sent me the money yet? He said he was going to mail it the first of the month. Oh, dear, I hope he hasn't had a relapse of the fever. What if he's been hurt? Or....she wouldn't think of anything worse! Maybe he's had second thoughts.

*****

December 22, 1908

"John, you got a letter in the mail," one of the men yelled out. " Looks like it's been run over by the train," as he handed it to John.

John couldn't believe it when he saw what it was. Between the wrinkles and smudges it had been stamped, UNDELIVERABLE. No such address. *What do they mean no such address? I've been there.* He read it carefully. He had addressed it correctly. Then he noticed, it was postmarked, Bay City, TEXAS. It had been sent to the wrong Bay City. *Can't those people at the post office read?*

*****

December 24, 1908

Here it is Christmas. Some Christmas this is. I haven't heard from John in over a month and he was going to send for me. What has happened now?

*****

John took off an hour special leave. He bought a big envelope, the biggest he could buy, and wrote a note to Jennie explaining what had happened. He put the crumpled letter and check in the big envelope with the new letter. She could see by the postmark he really had sent the money, when he said he would. He sealed it and addressed it.

Jennie Campbell, 401 Bay Street, Bay City and across the bottom of the envelope in large letters MICHIGAN.

*****

Jennie went to the general store to pick up the mail; one big envelope from John with the word Michigan in big letters. *That's strange, but at least I finally heard from him. But is it going to be the good news I'm hoping for?* Jennie opened it and found the note and smaller envelope with the check. She had to laugh when she read what had happened. *Oh, John, how many more setbacks and delays are we going to have to face?*

Jennie turned back to Mr. O'Hare who ran the general store. "Mr. O'Hare, Can you cash a check for me?"

"Long tis no too mush," he spoke with heavy Irish accent. "I no hav' mush munny ta'day. Aye an' do ya know if tha check signer tis good?"

"Yes, it's good. It's from my fiancé in Texas." Jenny happily announced. "He has sent for me. But don't tell anyone. I don't want Pa to know just yet."

"Aye, and tha luck o' the Irish ta ya, lovely Lassie. Ya're finally going, air ya?"

"Yes, just as soon as I can get to the depot." Jennie looked at the check again and handed it to Mr. O'Hare.

"Aye, Jenny, Love, tis sorry I am," Mr. O'Hare said as he shook his head no. "I naught hav at mush cash ta spare." He handed her the check back. "Ye hav ta 'wit a week when tha pay roll money come in from tha comp'ny office."

"Oh! No! Another week?" Jennie cried. "Please, Mr. O'Hare. I have already been waiting seven months. I've got to have the money to buy my train ticket."

"Tis sorry I am, Jennie. I hav' bus'ness an bills ta pay. I canna do it right now. I let ye know soon as I got tha money."

Jennie wanted to cry. Putting the check in her drawstring purse, she turned to leave. *How many more disappointments do I have to face? It feels like a lifetime, now.*

Mr. O'Hare felt bad. "I saved ye 'nother box, jest in case ye needed. Ye wanna I should git it fur ye?"

"Thanks, I do need one more. I have been packing my things, preparing to leave. Please don't tell anyone. I don't want Pa to find out. I guess I'll have to wait another week to leave." Jennie half heartedly replied.

*****

A week later, Jennie went to the store to get a bag of flour for Ma. She had the check in her purse, hoping to cash it, while at the same time trying to keep her expectations low, so she wouldn't be disappointed again.

As she walked in, Mr. O'Hare was waiting on two ladies, but he saw Jennie. "Please excoose me, lassies. While ye da'side whit purchose ta mak', I show Jennie sum new dress fabric jus' come in. I be righ' bac'." He motioned for Jennie to follow to the back of the store. Picking up a bolt of material, he turned his back to the ladies and whispered, "Ye look, til they leave, then I cash 'at check fur ye."

Jennie's heart skipped a beat and a smile replaced the sad look on her face. Speaking loud enough for the others to hear, she said, "Oh! How lovely. I must take my time and look at each piece before I decide. You finish waiting on the other ladies."

As soon as they left, Jenny dashed up to the front counter where Mr. O'Hare stood waiting. She took the check out of her purse and handed it to him.

Mr. O'Hare pointed to the back of the check. "Ye hav' ta sign yer name here."

Jenny was so excited her hand was shaking, but she managed to sign her name and watched with anticipation as Mr. O'Hare counted out the money and handed it to her.

"Thank you, Mr. O'Hare. It's been a pleasure to know you. I'll be leaving as soon as I can. Please don't tell anyone and act surprised when you hear I'm gone."

Jennie turned to leave, but stopped. "Oh, I almost forgot. I came to get some flour for Ma."

Getting the flour, she headed straight for the train station, hoping no one saw her. Elated, she could finally say, "I want a one-way ticket to Fort Worth, Texas, please."

Then she hurried home to finish packing, planning to leave the next day.

*****

John anxiously waited to hear from Jennie. *Did she finally get the check? Did she change her mind about coming?* He hadn't received a telegram yet, saying when she would arrive.

*****

By evening, it started snowing again. The next morning snow was up to the top step of the porch and still falling. They even closed the mine. Pa and the boys tried to shovel snow off the steps, but it became hopeless. There was no way they could get through the six to eight foot drifts. Everything was snowed in. All day long Jennie sat by the window, crying, listening for the train whistle, but there was none. The train could not get here. Not even a horse could get through. She couldn't get to the depot to send John a telegram. She was snow bound.

*****

John kept wondering why he hadn't heard from Jennie. He was as nervous as....., as a groom, he guessed. He hoped Jennie hadn't gotten sick or something. Then one day one of the firemen brought a newspaper with him when he came on duty. "John, look here at this article. It's supposed to have been telegraphed from a Chicago newspaper to our paper here. It says, *All over the mid United States has had six to eight feet of snow with drifts up to fourteen feet. All forms of transportation, including the railroad have been halted. Most telegraph lines are down, too.* Isn't your bride coming through all that on her way here?"

John grabbed the paper to read it for himself. *Oh, dear God. Did she make it out of Bay City? What if she is stranded on a train? What if she has to lay over a few days? Does she have enough money to eat? She hadn't sent a telegram yet, saying when she was arriving. What's going on now? Jennie my love, where are you?*

135

*****

There was nothing to do but wait out the storm. Jennie had lived through these storms before. She used to like it when they didn't have to go to school because the snow was too deep. But why did they have to have the worst storm in history just as she was about to leave?

*****

January 26, 1909

John woke early but lay in bed thinking. He was worried and feeling about half mad. He hadn't heard from Jennie in weeks. Had she decided to forget about coming and just keep the money? Yet, the check had not cleared the bank. Was she stranded somewhere in a snow storm? If he just knew she was all right.

The alarm went off. John and the others jumped out of bed and into clothes. By the time they slid down the pole, the horses had taken their places in front of the wagon and were ready to be hitched.

A gasoline stove had exploded at the Southern Hotel on Jones Street, across from the depot. As the firemen raced to the blaze, the crew of a street car stopped in the middle of the street and ran to the burning building to try to rescue occupants. However, this blocked the street. The firemen had to stop and move the street car out of the way, before proceeding to the fire. This delayed them getting there. The blaze was getting out of control and no one could enter the building. As a last resort the police began firing their revolvers, in an effort to waken the guests, many of whom jumped from the second and third floor windows. Three railroad men were later found dead. Many were injured from burns or from jumping out the windows. The explosion damaged six other surrounding buildings. It took a while to make sure there was no danger of another explosion or fire starting up again.

*****

Late January 1909, after one of the worst snow storms in history, the temperature rose and everything began to melt. The mine opened again and Pa and the boys went back to work. Jennie tried to shovel snow off the walkway, but it was no use. She had to wait another day before she could make it to the depot. The station master said her ticket was still good and the train would start running again tomorrow. The telegraph lines had been down, but should be working in the next couple of days.

Jennie sloshed through the snow and mud back home and started packing again. *Dear God, please don't let it snow for a couple more days.*

She woke the next morning and immediately jumped out of bed and ran to the window. No new snow. She dressed and ran to the kitchen to help Ma with breakfast. Ma was the only one who knew she planned to leave soon. Even though being of age now, she feared Pa would try to stop her again. She had packed her things in boxes and kept the boxes under her bed. After breakfast and everyone off to jobs and school, she told Ma the train would be running today and she would be leaving.

Ma had suspected it and made an extra loaf of bread the day before. She wrapped it up with some butter and a jar of last summers jelly, boiled eggs and a couple of pieces of ham and some cheese. Before noon, Jennie finished gathering the last of her belongings. She had bought twine and tied up each box. She carried two boxes to the depot. The train was still due to arrive and leave at four, but the telegraph lines were still down. About 3:20, Jennie and Ma carried her other box, her picnic lunch and her carpet bag to the depot. Jennie checked her other box and she gave the station master the message and money to send a telegram as soon as the lines were repaired. The train arrived, Jennie said goodbye to Ma and boarded, assuring Ma she could take care of herself. She had made this trip several times before.

From there on she delighted in seeing less and less snow in the scenery. Now, she just had to hope John got her telegram and is there to meet her. *If he's not,* she laughed at the thought; *I'll just call station six and yell fire.*

*****

January 29, 1909

The men were doing the usual maintenance at the fire hall, when the young boy from Western Union rode up on his bicycle. "I have a telegram for John Whittenburg."

"Here boy, that's me."

"Sign here, Sir."

John signed and tore open the envelope. *Snow over, Leaving Tuesday27, due Friday 30, arrive 9am. Jenny.*

"Whoopee!" John yelled. "Chief, Jenny finally made it. She comes in tomorrow. Can I call in a sub and take tomorrow off.?"

"Of course, John. You two have waited a long time for this day. Congratulations."

John went to the phone and called till he found a sub. Next he called Ida and Ma. "I'll pick her up at depot and go straight to the court house and get married."

"John, you will not," Ida disagreed. "Poor thing will be hungry and dirty from the trip. You pick her up and bring her here. Ma and I can fix her some breakfast and she can bathe and put on her wedding dress. You have waited this long and another hour or two is not going to hurt."

"Oh, I hadn't thought of that. I guess your right." John said. "I guess we'll see you then about 9:30, if the train is on time."

*****

January 30, 1909

John finished his chores and hitched both horses to his wagon. He went upstairs to shower and change clothes. He nervously waited on pins and needles till his sub arrived at eight-thirty. J.W. had called Mabel and they arranged to take off for an hour, so they could be at the court house when John and Jennie got married. When John went out to get in his wagon to leave, the other firemen had decorated it with paper streamers.

"Yea, Congratulations, John!" and they clapped their hands.

John felt a little embarrassed, but it was such a fun jester, he couldn't be mad. "Thanks, fellows. Jennie will get a real kick out of this." He felt a little foolish driving to the train station, but he thought it was funny too.

John paced the platform for twenty minutes before the train slowly pulled in. *She has to be on this train. She just has to,* he kept thinking. He kept looking in every window as the train slowly moved by. *THERE SHE IS!* He waved. Jennie had been watching out the window and began crying tears of joy and waving when she saw him. The train came to a stop and Jennie headed down the aisle toward the door. John followed on the platform till he reached the steps of the train. The conductor took her bags and she flew down the steps into John's arms. He lifted her off the ground and swung her around. Neither wanted to let go of the other and appeared speechless. The conductor put her basket and carpet bag down on the platform beside them, not wanting to interrupt the young lovers.

Finally, it was Jennie that faced reality. "John, you're going to have to let me go, I can't breathe."

"I'm sorry." They laughed as he set her down on her feet.

She took a deep breathe, "You always did take my breath away." She reached her arms around his waist and hugged him again."

"Am I dreaming?" John asked. "Are you really here?"

"I'm either here or we are enjoying the same dream."

"Well, let's get out of this dream and into real life. Where's your luggage?"

"Oh!" Looking around Jennie found her basket and carpet bag beside her. Reaching into her coat pocket, she retrieved 3 tickets. "Here's my claim tickets for my three boxes." Handing them to John, he took her hand to lead her to the baggage claim area. They retrieved her boxes and John carried them toward the wagon. "Wait till you see what the fellows did to our wagon this morning."

When the decorated wagon came into view, Jennie started laughing. Riding in it she said, "I feel like I'm leading a parade." She waved at passersby and they waved back. The sun felt so warm on her face, Jennie shed her heavy coat and just put her shawl around her shoulders. "I love the sun." After a while, she asked, "Where are we going?"

John told her of the plans to have breakfast and clean up at Ida's, then going to the court house and get married.

"Oh, John, that's perfect. You think of everything."

"Well, not really. It was Ida's idea."

"Ida and I are going to get along just fine together. I feel like I already know her from the letters she wrote me while you were ill." She squeezed his arm. "I was so worried when I didn't hear from you. I don't want us to ever be apart again."

"Well, you have to remember, you married a fireman. But, Chief Bideker is working with the city official to allow married men to have more time off and vacations."

"Oh, that will be wonderful. Oh, by the way, do we have time for you to show me the vacant lot you bought?"

"Not right now. We are to meet J.W. and Mabel at noon at the court house. He arranged special leave for an hour and they are going to be our witnesses. After we get married, I'll take you by and show you our lot on the way to Clemmie's house."

"That will be fine. I'm just so excited I'm getting in a hurry to see everything."

John guided the horses up in front of Ida's house and tied them to the hitching post. Then he went around and helped Jennie down out of the wagon. He handed Jennie her basket and carpet bag and retrieved her boxes for her. Ida and Ma had been watching for them and came running out onto the front porch.

"Oh, Jennie, dear, how nice to see you, again," Ma met her with open arms.

"Ma Whittenburg, it's good to see you again, too."

"Jennie, how are you? Did you have a nice trip?" Ida asked as she hugged Jennie.

"Ida, it is so good to see you. I feel like I already know you."

"I feel the same way about you. Well, come on in." Ida invited. "John, put Jennie's things in Ma's room for now. Let's get some breakfast so you two can be on your way."

As they sat down to eat, Ida asked Jennie, "Did you finish sewing on your dress? I'm so anxious to see it."

"You have to remember, I planned on getting married when the weather was still warm. So I added long sleeves and a little higher neckline. It's a light color but I think it will do for Texas, as warm as it is today. That's all I'm going to tell you for now since John is listening." Jennie chuckled as she looked at John with a big smile.

All the women laughed. Ma said, "I'll set up the iron and ironing board in my room and press your dress while you bathe. You don't mind us helping you, do you?"

"No, of course not! It would be an honor to have you both help, since my own Ma can't be here."

John teased, "I'll go outside with the horses, while you silly gals are giggling and carrying on."

John kept looking at his watch. Thirty minutes. Forty-five minutes. *How long does it take for a woman to bath and dress?* He found out, it was worth the wait, when Ida came to the door, "You can come in now, John."

"Gee, thanks, I was beginning to get cold out there."

Ida motioned toward the sitting room as he came in the door, so he turned and there was his bride, looking like a princess. John just stood there taking in her beauty. Her blush matched the pink color of her dress. She was wearing the cameo pendant, he had given her. With ribbons and bows and her hair up in curls, he couldn't believe it was the same girl he just picked up at the depot. "I am not believing my eyes. Gosh, I knew you were beautiful, but now you have just taken my breath away."

Jennie flashed a big smile.

"Now, you two run on, it's almost noon" Ida said. "Jennie, we'll gather your clothes and things and put back in your boxes. You can pick them up later on your way to Clemmie's."

"Thank you so much, Ma and Ida. I feel like part of the family already."

"You are, dear. You are." As each gave her and John a hug and sent them on their way.

J.W. and Mabel were at the Tarrant County Court House when John and Jennie arrived. It was just like old times with the four of them together. They found the office of Mr. T. J. Maben, Justice of the Peace, who performed the ceremony. John surprised Jenny with a plain, gold wedding band. At last, their dream had come true. They were married, January 30, 1909.

They said goodby to J.W. who had to go back to work. Jennie told Mabel she would come get her things that were stored at the Moore's in the next few days. They climbed aboard their decorated wagon and headed back to North Fort Worth.

As they neared Ida's house, John kept the horses going straight for another block. Turning right, they went just a little ways and John stopped the horses and pointed, "This is our land, Jenny."

"This is really ours? Oh, I can't believe all this is happening. My knight in shining armor has rescued his damsel in distress and is now going to build me a castle," she said, teasingly.

"Well, not exactly a castle." John admitted.

"It will be to me," Jennie said. "Oh, I meant to write and ask would you mind if we didn't have an upstairs and had everything on one floor."

"If that is what you want, Jennie, my love, it will be a lot easier for me to build. I thought you would want an upstairs."

"No, I am sick of running up and down stairs. I've done it all my life. I see it's getting harder and harder for my Ma, especially getting up to the third floor. I don't want to spend the rest of my life carrying laundry and babies up and down stairs."

"Then no two story house."

"I love it, John, simply love it. Have you started drawing any plans, yet?"

"Just in my head. I'm not good at drawing on paper."

"Well, I'm not either, but I bet between the two of us we can get our ideas on paper for the builder to read."

"I'm going to hire the foundation put in." John continued. "Then I'll hire a helper or two when I need help with things like putting up the roof trusses. We can save a lot of money by me doing most of the work. 'Coarse it will take a little longer to build, but worth it in the long run. Well, let's get back to Ida's and get our things, then we'll go on to Clemmie's and get settled into our room. Ugh! Did I forget to mention Clemmie's house is two story?"

Jennie laughed. "That's all right. We won't be there long."

John loaded all of Jennie's things and also had to get his own things that he kept at Ida' for when he spent the night there.

They arrived at Clemmie's and put their horses and wagon in the back corral. John made several trips between the wagon and their room upstairs to get everything moved in, while Jennie unpacked a couple of her boxes. Clemmie informed them dinner would be at 5:30 when her husband came home from work.

Jennie liked Clemmie all right, but she didn't feel as comfortable around her as she did Ida and Ma. She didn't know exactly why. Maybe once they got better acquainted things would feel different.

Jenny and John hung up some clothes. She would finish putting everything else up later. Right now she wanted to spend time with him. Jennie ran across her writing tablet. "No more writing letters. We can use this to start drawing the plans for our house."

"Why don't you do that this next week while I'm at work?" John suggested.

"I could put down some ideas, then your next day off, we can decide what we want to do."

"That will work. Meanwhile," John walked over and locked the door to their room. "It is only 4:30 and dinner isn't till 5:30. Let's consummate our marriage."

"Oh, John, I thought this day would never come."

10

Married Life and Promotion

January 31, 1909

The next morning, John woke early as usual. It felt so good to have his Jennie next to him. He knew she needed the rest after the train trip and full day of activities yesterday. So he quietly got up and dressed. He got her writing tablet and wrote her a note. "I didn't want to wake you. You needed the rest. I'll call you later. Your loving husband, John." He saddled old Clyde and rode him back to the fire hall that morning. The fellows did their share of teasing him about married life.

Jennie woke and realized John had already left for work. She lay there a few minutes feeling of the sheets where he had slept last night after they made love. It was wonderful to finally be married. She found John's note lying on his pillow.

Jennie dressed and made their bed. The last box she hadn't unpacked contained her summer clothes, so she would wait a while before unpacking it. Jennie gathered their dirty clothes and headed downstairs. Hearing Clemmie in the kitchen she went in "Good morning, Clemmie."

"Good morning." Clemmie answered without looking up from her task of kneading bread. "I guess you must be a late sleeper."

"Not really. I'm usually up by 5:30 or 6:00. Why? What time is it now?" Jennie asked.

"It's almost 9."

"Oh, my goodness, I had no idea I slept that late. I was so exhausted from the train trip and all the activities yesterday. I didn't even know when John got up and left this morning."

Clemmie didn't say anything and didn't even mention her getting a cup of coffee, let alone breakfast. After a few minutes of awkward silence, Jennie said, "Clemmie, if you don't mind telling me where the washing facilities are I'll do my and John's laundry."

"I normally don't wash but one day a week and that's on Monday." Clemmie said.

"Oh, I'm used to helping my ma and we wash every morning. It just takes a little while each morning and we're done, rather than take all day long to do it all."

"Well, suit yourself. The wash house is out back."

Jennie took their clothes and headed for the backyard. *Boy, she must have gotten up on the wrong side of the bed or something. I'll have to talk to John, but I thought we were paying her room and board. Maybe it's just for the room. Maybe that doesn't include being able to do my own laundry. Strange. I wish we were staying with Ida and Ma Whittenburg. It was so much fun having them help me get dressed yesterday. I'll ask Ida to take me over to see Mabel and pick up my things stored at the Moore's. I'll have to get John to teach me how to drive the wagon, so I don't have to ask people to take me. And while I'm at it, I'll buy a bar of laundry soap so I don't have to use Clemmie's. I wish I knew what was wrong. If she didn't want me around why did she offer to rent us a room?* Jennie thought the whole time she was taking out her frustration on the wash board and wringing out the clothes. She hung the clothes on the line, drained the water out the back door of the wash house and tried to leave everything as she had found it. Returning to the house, she asked, "Is there anything I can help you with Clemmie?"

"No, not a thing."

"Would you mind if I set up the iron and ironing board and press some wrinkles out of my packed clothes and then iron John's uniform in case he needs it?"

"No, go ahead. The iron and ironing board are in the pantry."

Jennie thought some more as she set the iron on the wood burning stove to heat and brought her clothes downstairs. *Clemmie's not exactly rude, but she's sure not being what I call friendly. John had said he would call and I hope it's soon. I hope Clemmie is planning on lunch, since I wasn't offered breakfast.*

The phone rang, Clemmie went to answer it. She came back in the kitchen, "It's for you. It's John."

Jennie placed the iron back on the stove and ran to the phone. "Hello, John."

"Hello, Mrs. Whittenburg. How are you this beautiful Texas morning?"

"Oh, sweet heart, I'm so sorry I was sound asleep this morning. I didn't hear you get up. You should have waked me before you left."

"You were sleeping so sound and I knew you needed the rest." John said.

"John, I.....," suddenly she heard Clemmie coming down the hall. "I just wanted to say I love you and to be careful." She had wanted to ask him about the room or the room and board agreement, but not where Clemmie could hear.

"I love you too. Is everything all right?"

"Yes, everything is fine. I'm pressing my clothes that were packed for so long and I'll iron your uniform so it will be ready if you need it. When did you say your regular day off was?"

"Wednesday, but if you need me, you call."

"I just miss you and look forward to seeing you. Oh, John,...." As if she just thought of something. She thought Clemmie had gone upstairs, but just as she started to ask him, Clemmie came walking by again.

"Yes, what is it?" John asked.

"Oh, I was just thinking. Do you think some time on your day off, you could teach me how to drive the horses and wagon?"

"Sure, it's easy."

"That would be wonderful and I wouldn't have to depend on other people if I need to go somewhere." Jennie declared.

"Well, if you do need to go somewhere and Clemmie can't take you, you call Ida." John advised.

"All right, I will."

"Well, I gotta' go. Can't tie up the line too long with personal calls."

"Be careful and call me whenever you can." Jennie hated to say goodbye but couldn't keep him on the line forever. She decided not mention her problem with Clemmie. If she could handle the wicked witch Florence, she could handle Clemmie.

Jennie finished her ironing and put the iron on the back of the stove to cool and the ironing board back in the pantry and took their clothes to their room. She was starving and not wanting to miss lunch, if offered, she hurried back downstairs.

Clemmie had put the bread in the oven to bake and it smelled so good.

Again Jennie offered, "If there's anything I can help you with Clemmie, please let me know."

"Well, the bread will be done in a few minutes. I made one small loaf we can have for our lunch. There was one potatoe left over last night if you want to cut it up and I'll chop a little onion and fry it for our lunch."

"Oh, that sounds good. I'll get out the jar of jelly my Ma gave me. Have you ever had any Huckleberry jelly?" Jennie asked.

"No, I never heard of it."

"I think you'll like it. Ma and I made it toward the end of summer. I'll have to admit I don't know much about cooking, but I'll be glad to help. And when you have time Clemmie, would you teach me? I'd really appreciate your help."

"That seemed to soften Clemmie's disposition. From then on they got along okay, but they weren't close like she, Ida and Ma.

Jennie called Ida a few days later and asked if she would take her over to the Moore's to get her things stored there. Ida said she would. Jennie asked if Ma would go too, but Ma declined saying her arthritis was bad that day. So, Ida came in her small one horse, one seated little buggy, so there wasn't room to ask Clemmie to go too. Jennie didn't want to be rude, but she was with Clemmie all the time. She wanted to be with Ida for a while. They went to the Moore's and Mabel fixed them a nice lunch. Then Jennie went to the sitting room to visit with Mr. Moore. He was glad to see her and to hear she and John were married. Jennie felt heart broken to see him wasting away to nothing by grieving himself to death over the loss of his wife. While Jennie visited with Mr. Moore, Mabel took Ida up the back stair case and showed her the mansion's beautiful bedrooms. They went on up to the third floor attic and got four boxes marked 'Jennie'. By then Jennie met them and helped carry everything down the stairs and out to the buggy. After saying their goodbyes, Ida trotted the horse and buggy back to Clemmie's house. One at a time Jenny carried the boxes upstairs to their room. She would gradually unpack them over the next few days.

*****

February 1909

The firemen ate their breakfast and did their chores. They were about ready to sit and have a midmorning cup of coffee when the alarm went off at 9:07am. Madden's Glass Factory. The fire started in the molding room and completely consumed the building before the firemen arrived. Nothing left to save, just extinguish as soon as possible. John and the men had just returned to the station when the alarm went off again at 11:29am, a house fire caused from knocking over an oil lamp. One bedroom was destroyed, but no one hurt. They returned to the station and had finished lunch when another alarm sounded at 2:34pm. This time, it was a grass fire on a vacant lot. By the time they returned to the station they were dirty from one end to the other. They all showered and put on clean uniforms. Just as they finished eating supper at 6:03 pm the alarm sounded again. Embers from a wood burning fireplace caught a rug on fire and damaged the floor. Minimal damage. No sooner had they returned to the station, when at 8:12 pm, another call came in. A man had fallen asleep in his chair, dropped his pipe and caught his clothes and chair on fire. Damage was minimal. Relatives took the man to the doctor's office. By the time the men got back to the fire hall, they went right to bed. At 11:22 p.m. they got another call, but it proved to be a false alarm.

The next morning most all of then slept till 8 or 9 o'clock. When John woke he called Jennie. "I need you to do me a favor. If Clemmie can't, call Ida but get one of them to bring you and bring me a clean uniform. We had a busy day yesterday and I need some clean clothes. Don't rush, just whenever you can make it will be fine."

Clemmie only had her big wagon, so Jennie called Ida first, to see if she could bring her little buggy and it would be faster. Ida said she would be right there as soon as she could get the horses hitched. Jennie was so excited she would get to see John earlier than his usual day off. She had time to freshen up and slip on a little nicer blouse before Ida got there.

*****

March 8, 1909

While answering a call at J. A. Capps barn at 120 East 12th Street, hose wagon hit Eagle Bakery wagon's tongue doing slight damage to hose wagon's fender. No damage to bakery wagon. G.W. Collop driver was not in wagon at time. Captain was off duty.

April 3, 1909

Two little boys decided to experiment with smoking tobacco. About noon, one barn, at Jennings and Tucker Street, began to burn. Aided by forty mile an hour winds, the fire began to spread from one wood shingled roof to another barn or house. By the time Central and station two could get there, the fire had spread too fast and too far. Chief Bideker attempted to set off a third alarm, but the fire alarm box wouldn't transmit. The intense heat had melted the copper wire. Bideker located a telephone and called out a general alarm to all stations.

Bideker had directed John on the phone, "Take your men and head south on Henderson. You'll know what to do when you get there." As John and his crew pulled out of their station they could see the heavy smoke blowing in from the south side of town.

"Looks like we got ourselves a big one," John said. Sure enough when they got to Henderson Street, John directed his driver to head east. When they were approaching the fire, they stopped at the nearest fire hydrant and connected. "The wind is blowing north. We can't stop it but we can keep it from spreading west." Just as they thought they were getting ahead of the blaze, the wind blew more embers to the next building and the next.

Engine 8 crashed into a telephone pole, killing their lead horse, in an attempt to avoid colliding with a push cart peddler. The men cut the dead horse loose. Using the one horse, all the men were able to pull the wagon out of the line of fire.

Number 5 station had a horse to slip on the pavement, breaking its leg. They cut it loose, knowing it would keep running on three legs away from the fire. They had to take care of the wagon and themselves.

Unit one got in place to attack a wall of flames. But the heat was so intense it began to melt their rubber hoses before they could get water pumped through the lines. The men pulled the wagon out of the path of the blaze.

The fire was spreading north toward downtown Ft. Worth and consuming everything in its path. The men were only able to keep the fire from spreading any farther east and west. As a last effort Bideker called Dallas for help. Dallas and a little town of Oak Cliff each sent a wagon.

The fire now approached the Texas Pacific Railroad round house and adjacent repair shops which formed a natural barrier between the south side and downtown Fort Worth. The fire slowed enough the firemen could begin to move in and gain some control. The round house and the shops were consumed by the fire, but it allowed fire fighters to gain control of the blaze and breathe a little easier.

Oak Cliff firefighters had barely arrived when they were called back for a big fire in their own area. It took all available firemen and equipment twelve hours of working desperately to gain control and get the fire completely out. When it was all over the damage covered an area of twenty-six square blocks and destroyed more than 290 homes, barns and businesses.

Chief Bideker called all his Captains together. "When you get back to your stations, check your equipment, and then call me with any repair or replace reports. Stations Five and Eight wait here and we'll get you another horse to get you back to your stations. Station one, come by Central and get some extra hose. Get everything taken care of as soon as you can and be ready for the next call, which hopefully won't be any time soon. You and your men did an excellent job today and most importantly no one injured. So far I have heard of only one fatality for the multitude of the devastation. Please convey this to your men. They deserve more than a pat on the back and believe me I am working with the city to get more and better benefits."

*****

Jennie could see the smoke blowing in from the south and knew there must be a big fire south of town. That wasn't John's district, but if it was really big, his station would get called out to help. John told her not to worry every time she saw smoke. If they had a big fire, he would call her as soon as he could to let her know he was alright. All day long she watched the smoky clouds blowing in the forty-mile-an-hour wind. All she could do was wait with mixed emotions. "Lord, take care of my John. Why isn't the smoke going away? What's taking so long to get the fire out? When is John going to call?"

Finally, near midnight that evening he called and told her what it was and they were back at the station and he was okay, but bone tired.

The next day, John called Central to give Bideker his report. "Chief, we did the usual clean up, inspection and maintenance and I'm glad to report we have no damage. Two wagon wheels needed to be greased and we fixed a buckle on one of the harnesses. The horses can wait a few more days and go in on their regular day to be shod."

Chief Bideker replied, "That's good to hear. By the way, John, I was going to call you in a day or so anyway. So when the horses need to come in, how about you bring them? While they are being shod walk on over to my office. There's something I need to talk over with you."

"Sure thing Chief. Will Friday morning be alright?"

"That will be fine. See you then."

*****

John called ahead of time and arranged for station five to cover for them while their horses were off duty. Friday morning, John dressed in a clean uniform and drove the horses in to the department's blacksmith's shop. He walked over to Bidekers office.

"Come in John. Want a cup of coffee?"

"No, thanks."

"Well, have a seat." Chief motioned toward a chair. "John, it's just been made official and you'll be hearing the news or reading it in the paper next week. North Ft. Worth is being annexed to the city of Ft. Worth."

"Oh, that is news. How's that going to affect the fire department?"

"The city is going to build three new fire stations. John, I want you to open #12 station, on the corner of Ellis Ave. and 24th St. Don't you have family that lives on the North Side?"

"Yes, I do."

"So are you fairly familiar with the area?" Chief asked.

"Yes, mainly between the viaduct, stockyards and Harrington Street and the cemetery, along in there."

"Good. You want the job?" Chief asked.

"I appreciate your offer and I'll do the best I can."

"I know you will, John. Now, another thing I wanted to ask you. Will you accept the promotion as Chief of #12 station?"

John was caught off guard and almost speechless for a few seconds. "I don't know what to say. You really surprised me there. I know I can do the work, but you know I didn't get much schooling."

"John, I have no doubt you can do the job, that's why I want you. You have the know-how. You can read and write and that's all you need to fill out the Chief's log book, keep a record of supplies and what and when you answer a call. I can give you twenty-four hours to think it over if you need to. But, I was hoping you'd say yes today, so we can get on with some other business."

John thought a minute. "I'll take that cup of coffee now, if you don't mind." John rose to go to the kitchen, "and I'll tell you my answer when I get back."

"Fair enough," Chief replied, "Bring me a cup, too."

"Sure." John went to the kitchen. A couple of the firemen were sitting there. "You fellows got any coffee left?"

"Yes, Sir and the cups are in the upper cabinet to the right of the stove."

As John got two cups and filled them with coffee he tried to sort out his thoughts. *It's a good promotion and probably be a raise in pay. I want the job, but can I do it?*

Returning to Bideker's office, John set the Chief's cup down and announced. "I'll take the job."

"Glad to hear that, John. You just took a load off my mind. Now, next thing, I want to ask you, who would you recommend for promotion to captain's for stations eleven and fifteen?"

"Whew, you're questions just keep getting harder and harder. I thought that was your responsibility to assign jobs?" John questioned.

"It is," Chief answered, "but I never make a big decision without first seeking advice from a trusted friend and co-worker."

"Well, let me ask you a question." John asked. "Who and how many men will be going with me to station 12?"

"That's another thing I was going to talk to you about?" Chief confessed.

"You got any more cards up your sleeve?" John grinned at his friend.

"I think that's all." Bideker replied with a slight smile.

"Well, let's see. If I picked the three good men to take with me to #12, it would be J.W. Kennedy, Floyd Harrison and Buck Buchanan. But, I think I'd recommend all three for Captains. I'd like to have Kennedy as my captain and second in command at #12. Are you hiring more men or moving men around?"

"We are trying to hire at least one new man for each station to work with other trained men to start."

"In that case, give me H.W. Russell; he's almost fully trained and a rookie and who ever else you want me to have."

"That sounds good to me. Now, keep this under your hat till it's officially announced May first. They are working on the station now and trying to get finished by then. But it may be another week or two before you fellows get to move in. You'll be getting a new wagon and new team of horses. Soon as the horses arrive, I want you and your driver to come over here every chance you get and get acquainted with the horses, so they know you. They will be used to you when you move them to the new station. Otherwise, they should be fully trained."

"I'll look forward to it. You got any more surprises for me?" John asked.

Chief smiled, "yeah, as a matter of fact I do. You didn't ask, but there's a $25. a month raise coming with your promotion."

"Oh, yeah, I did forget to ask. You were asking me too many other questions."

Chief stood up and stuck his hand out to shake John's, "Congratulations, John. I was hoping you would take the job. I know I can depend on you."

"Thanks, Chief. I'll do my best."

"By the way, how's that little wife of yours?"

"Just great. She'll be happy to hear the news. This will mean we can get a place of our own a little sooner."

John would be off Sunday and he told Jennie he would hitch up their wagon and take her for a ride and they would have lunch at Mrs. Simpson's Dining Room. He would then tell her the good news.

*****

Sunday as they left Clemmie's house, John showed Jennie how to guide the horses. They rode down Park Street to Ellis Avenue, where John told her to turn the horses left on Ellis. By then Jennie's curiosity was aroused. "Where are we going?"

"I heard they are remodeling a two story building down here close to the stockyards. I wanted to take a look at it." John said casually.

Soon the wood frame building came into sight. Jennie thought the design was odd, with one big door and one small door on the front. "That's strange. It looks a lot like....Ahh...Is that going to be a new fire station?"

"Yep, that's going to be the new number twelve fire station." John said as a matter of fact. "It's due to open in a few more weeks."

Jennie was thinking ahead, "Is there a chance you'll get assigned to this station?"

"Not a chance." He paused. "I already have."

"Oh, John, that's wonderful. We'll be closer together and when we get our house built you'll be closer to your work."

"Not only that, but you are looking at the newly appointed 'Chief' of number twelve station."

"Oh!" Jennie squealed. "John that's wonderful. I'm so proud of you." She leaned over and gave him a big kiss, not caring who saw them.

"Only thing is you can't tell anybody just yet, till its officially announced."

Jenny put her hand over her mouth, "Mum's the word." Removing her hand she said, "Oh, I'm so happy for you, John."

"Now, what you can be doing is looking for us an apartment or little house to rent. With this promotion came a raise. So we can afford to rent a place where we have more privacy and still be able to save some money to build our house."

"Yea!" Jennie yelled and laughed. "I'll start making a list of things we need, like a skillet and cooking utensils and …."

"Speaking of that, if you don't mind used stuff, I've got some stuff stored in James and Ida's barn. Go over there one day and go through it all. Throw out what you don't want to keep."

"Oh, another surprise; I feel like I'm hunting buried treasure, between my boxes over there and your boxes over there and our stuff over here." They laughed.

John said, "Let's head on downtown, I'm getting hungry."

"Oh, here you drive if we are going downtown. I'm liable to run over somebody." They arrived at Mrs. Simpson's Dining room. The last time they dined here John fell in love with Jennie. This time he fell in love with her even more.

*****

A week later, the new team of horses arrived and John and J.W. took turns going to Central and working out with the horses, Tom and Dan. They were big and muscular, but gentle as a lamb and better trained than any horses John worked with before. They were so friendly John stayed outside the fence till after he greeted them, for fear they would knock him down, not knowing their own strength.

He soon had them spoiled. The minute they saw John, they would run over to him and nuzzle at his shoulder. He would reach in his shirt pocket and pull out a carrot or sugar cube. Sometimes he had an apple in his hand and would get out his pocket knife and cut it in half for the horses to share. But when the alarm sounded, they were focused on what they were supposed to do.

Supplies arrived at Central in preparation for the move. The annexation of North Ft. Worth was announced in the newspaper with just a little sentence about the fire department expanding to cover the new area. But there was a whole paragraph about Fort Worth in 1873 was nicknamed Panther City. The fire department officials decided to add the impression of a panther head to their badges and other emblems.

The anticipated call came from Chief Bideker, "John, get ready to move next Monday. I'm sending a letter out to all the stations announcing the opening of the new station and who got promoted. You, Kennedy and Russell be at Central Monday morning to start loading up. I'll have your new man report that afternoon. You are all set to go."

John called Jennie, "its official now. You can tell anybody you want to. In fact, why don't you see if James will bring you, Ida and Ma down to the new station that morning and you can see our new horses and wagon?"

"Oh, I can hardly wait." Jennie was excited

11

Opening Number Twelve Fire Station

May 1, 1909

John received a call from Chief Bideker, "We got a wagon load of supplies for you for # 12. Also, the kitchen table and some other furniture are supposed to be delivered to today. Can you be there to sign for them?"

"Sure thing, Chief. I'll get there as soon as I can."

"And take a look around, make sure everything is in working order. They were varnishing the floor upstairs yesterday. I haven't had a chance to get out there to check it all out. If something is not done or not right let me know."

John told his men to take over while he went to the new station and caught the streetcar to the North Side. The plumber was there checking for any last minute leaks. John thought, *I'll get him to explain what all he did and how he did it, so when I build my house I might be able to do some of my own plumbing.* After going over everything, John signed the paper saying the work was completed.

By then the wagon of supplies arrived from Central. They unloaded boxes marked kitchen in that area. Everything else they unloaded in the sitting area, including 2 beds and 2 mattresses, till they could make sure the floor upstairs was ready for furniture.

A few minutes later, the Furniture Company delivered the kitchen table and chairs and the card table and chairs for the sitting area. Just as the wagon left, the builder showed up with two Negro women who came to clean cabinets and mop up the last of sawdust. While they cleaned, John walked around with the builder and inspected everything for flaws. It would be alright to move in upstairs tomorrow.

Everyone left, too late for him to get back to station six in time for supper. He had tomorrow off and he'd have to turn around and come back to the North Side again. The phone had been installed when they installed the electric alarm system, so John wanted to see if it worked. He called, Floyd answered, "Fire Station six."

John told Floyd what happened that day and added, "Since I'm already on the North Side, I'm just going to go on home. If you get a really big fire call me, otherwise ya'll handle it and I'll see you day after tomorrow." John walked a few blocks and caught the streetcar to Clemmie's. He could hear everyone in the kitchen when he arrived, so he walked on in, "Got any leftovers?"

Jennie jumped up and ran to hug him. "John, I didn't expect you till morning."

John explained what happened, as Jennie got him a plate, fork and glass of iced tea. They waited till he finished eating then Clemmie served the peach cobbler and they had dessert together.

May 2, 1909

When John woke, he called Central and told Bideker all the reports from the day before. He told Chief he had today off but would be back at #6 in the morning. Chief said, "While you are on the North Side, why don't you just stay there and go to work at getting #12 unpacked. The ice box is due to be delivered tomorrow anyway. When it gets there, call the ice company and start getting ice delivered regularly. Call in on the forth and everything should be ready to move officially on the fifth."

John thought, *Got that call off my mind, now I am going to get back in bed and enjoy my extra time with my wife.*

May 4, 1909

John and his friend and driver J.W., went to Central early that morning. Chief Bideker met them. "John, here is your log book. Start your entry. Then starting with the fire wagon, list everything as the boys are loading the supply wagon. It will be just the two of you today, then H.W. Russell will join you tomorrow and the new man Lee Roy Snow will report for duty day after. I will give you two or three days to get settled in before I tell the phone operator to put twelve on active duty for calls."

"Yes, Sir." John said. Since they were loading out the back door, John pulled out a chair and sat at the kitchen table.

No. 12 Station

Chief's Log
May 5, 1909

New station going into service as #12, at Ellis and 24th Street. Captain John Whittenburg promoted to Chief and transferred from #6 to #12 at 10:00 am.

One wagon Robinson Fire Apparatus Co.

Two extinguishers, 2 axes, one set double harnesses

2 horses Tom and Dan two ganters

1500 feet hose, 50ft garden hose, 2 bedsteads, 2 pair springs, 2 mattresses, 4 pillows, 4 quilts, 2 nozzles 3sp, 2 plug renches

J.L. Whittenburg, Chief; J.W. Kennedy, Capt.; H.W. Russell and Lee Roy Snow.

With the supplies loaded, John and J.W. put their own personal stuff on the wagon. John said, "J.W., I got to call Jennie and tell her we are on the way."

John guided Tom and Dan as they pulled the new fire wagon and J.W. followed with the supply wagon. Arriving near the new station, it looked like a parade. Word got out the new station was opening today. Neighborhood women and children lined the streets to see the new fire wagon and horses. The bells on the horses harness were ringing and everyone waving.

Jennie sat in the buggy beside Ma Whittenburg, James and Ida. Jennie hugged Ma who had tears of joy and pride in her eyes. Ma told Jennie, "The day he was born, I had a feeling someday he would make it on his own and be somebody."

"And you were right, Ma." Jennie assured her.

After everyone had seen the new wagon and children lifted up, so they could pet the horses, mothers began to take the little ones home for their lunch and naps. Jennie told John and J.W. "We brought you lunch, so you wouldn't have to fix a meal while you're moving in. John, you can bring the basket home later."

"Thanks, sweetheart," John said as he leaned down and kissed her cheek.

"Thanks, everybody," J.W. said.

After everyone left J.W. staked the horses in the vacant lot next door where there was plenty of grass. They ate their lunch of fried chicken, potato salad and pinto beans and corn bread. A lot better than the sandwiches they had planned. They began to unpack and by evening they at least had themselves and the horses settled. They found the coffee pot and coffee to get them going in the morning.

Chief's Log
May 6, 1909

Bucket polish, bucket axel grease, 4 sheets Emory Cloth, 5 bars laundry soap, 1 bar

Harness soap, 1 gal oil, 2 brooms and 1 hammer.

Russell reported for duty. They hung the horse's collars in front of the stalls, laid out harnesses and Russell made his bed and unpacked. John sent Russell to Central station for a few more supplies they missed yesterday. "Here's the list and on the way back stop by the grocery store on North Main and get us some groceries, staples and food for 3 or 4 days. And don't forget to ask for some carrots or apples for the horses. He saves back a few bruised ones for me to give the horses a treat.

Chief's Log
May 7, 1909

Greased wagon, out testing plugs, 1 hr. and 25 min., 24th and Refugio water main leaking, 24th and Prospect Ave. nipple broke off cap.

New man Lee Roy Snow reported for training. John decided to take the horses and the men out for a practice run. On 24th street there were several vacant lots and not many houses. John called into Central and asked for a false alarm, for the practice. In a few minutes, the alarm went off, the chain dropped, Tom and Dan put their heads in the horse collars and ran and backed up to the wagon. Russell and the new man fastened down their harnesses, while J.W. hooked them to the wagon. John took the drivers seat holding the horses back until they were ready to pull out of the station. They all worked together to explain every thing to Snow and take time to answer his questions. While they were out, John said they might as well tests some fire hydrants, since they had all ready found one was leaking. John made a note and when they returned to the station, he called the water department and reported it. J.W. and Snow greased the back wheels on the wagon. John called Bideker. "We are as ready as we will ever be. Put us into service."

"That's good to hear, 'cause Central is moving into our new building next door to city hall at 10th and Throckmorton. We have been in this old building at 8th and Throckmorton since 1899. We go off duty at 6 am in the morning. Station #2 and #4 will cover for us till we get moved and set up. You and your men will cover for them if they are both out on a call for us."

163

Chief's Log
May 10, 1909

Got 16 bushels oats from #5 Station.

They were running out of oats for Tom and Dan. John called some of the other stations and found too much had been delivered to station #5 and they could give him 16 bushels. He sent Snow to get them. He also had the men to decide what day of the week they wanted off and get a schedule set up.

Chief's Log
June 7, 1909

Tom and Dan shod at Eilenburger's Shop.

Tom and Dan were a good team. They were big and muscular but friendly and playful. They loved to be staked outside and run circles around their stakes. When approached, if you didn't pet them, they nudged you with their heads till you paid attention to them. The fire department contracted with Eilenburger's Livery Stable in the stockyards to shoe the horses. It was closer than taking them all the way to Central.

*****

June 1909

Jennie had been looking and asking people and recruited family to watch for a little house they could rent close to the fire hall. So far none were available. Meanwhile, Jennie kept adding to the list of things they would need to set up housekeeping. Little at a time she bought a few items, like cooking utensils, pot holders and dish pan. Their room at Clemmie's was beginning to look like a country store.

By mid-June she began to suspect a change about to happen in their lives. She wasn't sure so she didn't say any thing to anybody, not even John.

This morning, Jennie dressed and went downstairs. Clemmie had the coffee on and had just starting to fry bacon. Suddenly, Jennie felt a wave of sickness spread from her toes and coming up her body. She managed to say, "I'm going to be sick" and ran out the back door to lean over the porch railing to puke.

Clemmie came running out with a wet rag and glass of water. "The smell of bacon cooking got to me every time I got pregnant. Is that what's wrong, Jennie?"

"I think it might be, Clemmie. I've never felt this way before."

"Why don't you sit out here on the porch and get some fresh air. I'll finish cooking and bring you some coffee. I'll get everybody fed and off the work and then fix you a soft boiled egg and some toast. You'll feel better then."

Jennie did feel better later. The next morning, she didn't smell bacon but felt the same way. The next morning the same thing happened.

By the time John came home on his day off, he took one look at Jennie, "Sweetheart, what's wrong? You look a little pale."

"I've been sick every morning for the last 4 days. But, it will pass soon."

"No, I am taking you to see the doctor today."

"John, I don't need a doctor to tell me what's wrong. I'm pregnant."

"Are you sure? Are you sure you're all right? Oh, that's wonderful. I don't mean it's wonderful that your sick but it's wonderful we're going to have a baby and that's all that's wrong. Are you sure you don't need to see the doctor?" John rambled on.

"John, calm down, I will be all right in a few more days, once I get over this morning sickness."

"If your not, you be sure to call me and I'll take you to the doctor. You promise."

"I promise. I'll be fine. I just wish we could find a place of our own, before the baby comes. This room is going to be crowded,"

"We will sweetheart. I keep walking a different street every time I come home, looking for 'for rent' signs. We have everybody out looking for us. We'll find something. When's the baby due?"

"I think probably about the middle of January. What an anniversary present!"

"I think it's just great," and he gave her a hug and a kiss.

*****

Chief's Log
June 26, 1909

Snow on regular day off, while coming back from Lake Como, he was stabbed at 12:15 am., on right side, between 21st and 22nd St. at N. Main, by unknown Negro.

On Lee Roy Snow's regular day off, he went to Lake Como, southwest of Ft. Worth, to visit family. Coming back he rode the last trolley on North Main St. Near midnight he got off at 21st Street and walked toward 22nd Street to head up Ellis toward the fire station. All he saw from the faint glow of the street light was a Negro man jumping out in front of him. He felt a sudden pain on his right side and being knocked down, someone feeling in his pockets and footsteps of someone running away. Lee Roy tried to get up. His right side hurt and he grabbed it. Feeling his wet clothes, realized he had been stabbed. He pressed hard against his side to try to stop the bleeding and tried to walk on to the station. Luckily, a police officer, making his rounds came along and saw him. Seeing the fireman's uniform and blood he stopped. Lee Roy told him what had happened. The policeman took him to the nearest doctor. While the doctor tended to him, the officer called the fire station to report what had happened to one of their men. John immediately went to check on Snow. The doctor said the wound wasn't deep enough to hit any vital organs, but it still required stitches and he had too be off duty till 8 am July 4th.

Chief's log
July 1909

Chief Bideker got the first motorized vehicle, a chief's car, for the fire department at the cost of $2,140.00. It was a black, model A, Ford pickup with no top on the cab. It had a small tank in the bed with a hose just slightly bigger than a garden hose. This was mainly used for small fires or to put out embers left over from big fires.

Chief's log
August 2, 1909

Two children burned to death. Gracie Marie Reames age 8, and baby Arvol Reames. Fire at 2106 Ross Ave. Kerosene explosion. Captain Kennedy's day off.

There was nothing they could do. The explosion blew the mother out into the back yard. Seriously injured she didn't know what was going on. The firemen could only keep the fire from spreading to neighboring houses and get it out as quickly as possible. A neighbor said they would go get the father at work. John grieved as he and Russell carried the children's bodies out of the remains of the house. He always asked himself, "What more could we have done?"

Chief's Log
August 7, 1909

Broke butt off tongue of wagon. Taken wagon to Eilenberger shop 5x5 out one hour. At 2:30 pm gasoline explosion at 2525 Lake St. Mrs. Antone Coblake seriously burned, died at 8:45 pm.

Luckily the wagon was repaired that morning. Mid-afternoon the call came in for house fire. They arrived to find the back of the house in flames. Neighbor ladies were screaming, "There's an old lady inside."

John gave orders. "J.W., Lee Roy, go in with the big hose. Knock down the smoke and fire. Russell, we will follow. You look left, I'll look right. Stay low."

They opened the front door and started in with full force of water pointing to the ceiling. J.W. spraying back and forth and Lee Roy holding the hose, as steady as possible so the force of the water wouldn't get away from them. About seven feet into the living room, the water cleared the smoke and John saw the body. "Found her!" He yelled. John picked her up and Russell made sure John didn't trip over the fire hose and they found their way out. Both men were coughing from the smoke. John laid the lady on the grass in the front yard. Part of her clothes had burned and she was wet from the water. She coughed and John knew she was alive. "She's alive! Somebody go get a doctor." A neighbor lady came to help, "My boy went on horseback to fetch the doctor." Another lady brought a sheet. John told the ladies, Try to get her burned clothes off and cover her with the clean sheet while you wait for the doctor." John stood, turned and saw Russell had gone back in to relieve one of the other men. He grabbed another hose, connected it. J.W. and Lee Roy came out to breathe some fresh air. They had to concentrate on getting the fire out before it spread. J.W. caught a breath of fresh air and went back into the burning house to stay with Russell. John and Lee Roy pulled the other hose and started spraying water on the outside. The doctor arrived and they put the lady in his wagon to take her to his office. As soon as the fire was out, and before leaving the scene, John asked one of the neighbors to call the station and let them know what happened to the lady.

About 9:15 the call came in, she died at 8:45. John grieved that they had not been able to get there sooner and possibly save her life. What more could they have done or done better or done it faster?

Chief's Log
August 14, 1909

Received 10 blankets guaranteed pure wool from W.C. Stripling. (Apparently, Mr. Stripling who owned Striplings department store, donated blankets to each station or maybe just to each of the new stations.)

Chief's Log
August 21, 1909

Received 4 chairs from Ellison's Furniture Co.

These were good sitting chairs, not like the straight back wood chairs in the kitchen.

*****

Mid September, Ida called Jennie, "I just overheard two ladies talking in the grocery store. One said they had one side of a duplex for rent. I interrupted them and asked where. It's on Ellis and 23rd street. I told her your name and asked if she would hold it till you could get there. She said they would. Her husband is there now working on the house, doing some painting and wall papering to have it ready to rent by October first. Do you want me to come take you?"

"Oh, thank you, Ida. I'll just catch the streetcar and go see about it. Thank you."

Jennie grabbed her purse, told Clemmie where she was going and walked two blocks to catch the streetcar. She road down 21st. Street, getting off at Ellis and walked to 23rd. There was the duplex on the corner; a nice, white clapboard house. The door was open and she could hear someone in the back. "Hello, anyone here?"

"Yes, Ma'am," came a voice from the back and footsteps approaching. When he saw her, the man asked, "Can I help you?"

"I'm Jennie Whittenburg. I came to see about renting the duplex."

"Oh, yes, my wife came by on her way from the grocery store and said to hold it till you could get here. It's just these three rooms for $10.00 a month. I'll have the place ready by the first."

"I'll take it! It's perfect!" Jennie exclaimed. "Do you want the rent now in advance or first of the month when we move in.?"

"Not so fast. You haven't seen the kitchen yet and besides I need to ask you a few questions. How do I know you can afford more than just this months rent?"

"I'm sorry, I'm just so anxious to get a place of our own and not be renting a room from my sister-in-law. My husband is John Whittenburg, the chief at #12 fire station. This will be perfect since it's so close to the station. We own a lot up on Harrington Ave., but we need a place to live while we're building our house. It will be about a year before we get our house built. I'm going to walk on over to the station when I leave here. If John can take a few minutes, he may want to come look at the place."

"Well, little lady, you made yourself a deal."

"Do you want the money now or later?"

"I haven't got my receipt book with me."

"I'll go get my husband, he'll have some paper and we can write out a receipt and pay you today, if that's okay."

"Fair enough."

"I'll see you in a few minutes." Jennie said as she turned to leave, "Unless they get a fire call, then I'll wait till they get back."

Jennie walked the one block to the fire station. "John!" She called out as she reached the door.

John immediately recognized her voice and jumped up, "Back here in the kitchen." He yelled back as he started toward her. "What's wrong? Are you all right?"

"Nothing's wrong. I just wanted to tell you the good news. I just rented us a duplex on the corner of Ellis and 23rd street. The man is painting and papering it now and we can move in on the first. Can you take off a few minutes and come see it?"

"Sure. Hey, fellows, I'm just going down a block to 23rd. If we get a call, drive by and pick me up."

"Oh, have you got a piece of paper we can write out a receipt on? The man didn't have any with him." Jennie asked.

John wrote out a receipt on the tablet of paper on his desk and tore it off and stuck it and a pencil in his pocket. They started walking. "John, as anxious as I am to get there and seal this deal, you're going to have to slow down. I can't walk that fast. I'm carrying an extra load, remember." She happily reminded him of her condition.

"I'm sorry. I didn't realize I was walking fast. You set the pace. You all right? How did you get here?"

"I'm fine. I rode the streetcar after Ida called me when she heard about the house. It's just a few blocks here and there."

Arriving at the duplex, John and the owner exchanged introductions. John retrieved the paper and pencil from his pocket and a ten dollar bill and they sealed the deal. John walked with Jennie and saw that she got on the streetcar headed home. On his next day off, he promised to take Jennie to buy some furniture.

Chief's Log
October 1, 1909

Chief Whittenburg off duty today.

John hitched their horses to their wagon. As Jennie finished packing, John loaded their belongings onto their wagon. They arrived at their duplex before noon. Clemmie had packed them some sandwiches for their lunch. The furniture company wagon arrived shortly after to deliver their iron bed frame, springs and mattress, a three drawer dresser with mirror, a kitchen table and four chairs, an ice box, two big rocking chairs, a small table and an oil lamp. The house came with a wood burning cook stove. They had a few things that were Ma Whittenburg's, they had saved. Some things Jennie had been buying over the last few months. Ida and Ma had made them a quilt for a wedding present and Jennie had made one for her hope chest. Clemmie gave them a pair of sheets and embroidered pillow cases.

As soon as John and the delivery man put the furniture in place, Jennie began looking for the bed linens. Meanwhile, the ice man came and delivered a block of ice for the ice box and they signed up for regular delivery.

"Now all we need is food, so we can eat." Jennie surmised. "I can take my time unpacking and putting everything else in its place later."

John volunteered, "The horses are still hitched. I'll take you to the store so you can get what we need. Then when we get home, you are going to sit down and rest in those chairs we just bought and I'll fix supper. How does that sound?"

"That's so thoughtful of you, John. Have I told you lately, I love you?"

"Not since, um, let me see. Gee, I don't remember." John teased.

Jennie put her arms around his waist in a big hug as she looked up at him.

"Well, I'm telling you now and you better remember I love you."

"I love you too, sweetheart."

Returning from the store, Jennie lay down on their bed and took a nap, while John unloaded the groceries and unhitched the horses and staked them in the backyard. He found what he needed to put together a meal. After dinner John washed the dishes while Jennie put some food items up and laid out what they would need for breakfast in the morning and they called it a day.

*****

Chief's log
October 21,1909

Let Capt. O'Donnell have nozzle tips, Victor Maddox come after it.

November 11, 1909

Received one heating stove Nash Hardware, one taper joint of pipe. .

Chief's log
November 19, 1909

Changed Tom; Tom sick. Substitute horse taking Tom's place while he's off duty.

November 20, 1909

While riding horses at 4 pm. Saturday, Dan kicked baby Cunningham. Didn't hurt her. Driver Kennedy hollered at her to stop but she ran up behind Dan and he jumped and kicked her just touching her enough to knock her down, at alley between Main and Ellis Ave.

November 25, 1909

New locations for fire alarm boxes, 11th Ward school building and 12th Ward school building.

Chief's log
December 1, 1909

Put Tom back in service. He also got shod. Took Dan in to be shod. Received 2 bushels of hay. Gave station 5, half gallon wagon grease

*****

December 23, 1909

John kept telling Jennie they didn't need to buy a baby bed this soon. Unbeknown to her, he had picked up some wood apple crates from the grocery store. In his spare time at the fire hall, he made a baby bed. On his regular day off, 23rd, he and Jennie celebrated their first Christmas together. He surprised her when he came walking home with the baby bed. "This is why I didn't want to buy a bed."

Jennie was so surprised. "I wondered why you kept wanting to wait till last minute. Oh, John, it is beautiful. I didn't know you could make things like this."

"Well, to tell the truth, I didn't know either till I gave it a try."

*****

Chief's log
December 29, 1909

Received telephone call of fire, at Redwine house on Azle Ave. They stopped us out in the street. A woman and two young boys were out by the street waving when the fire wagon got there. The firemen were able to keep the fire contained in the kitchen. The husband arrived and family was safe. The firemen helped them clean up as best they could before leaving.

12

New Baby and New Home

Early January 1910

Chief Bideker called John to come meet with him at Central. He told John, "the city just approved a plan to replace all the old stations with new. They'll be built alike; all brick and as fire proof as possible. They're starting on the North Side with Station 12. Your new building will be on Prospect and 23rd Street."

"Well, I'll be." John was surprised. "We just got settled in where we are. When do we move?"

"You know how slow the wheels of politicians roll. Probably six to eight months." Bideker guessed.

"Good. I was afraid you were going to say in a couple of weeks. I got a baby coming in 2 to 4 weeks."

"Oh, yeah, how's the Mrs. doing?"

"She keeps saying she's feeling fine, just tired of carrying the extra weight and anxious for the baby to arrive."

"Well, take what time you need, when the time comes." Bideker advised.

"I've been saving my special leave time, so I got about six hours coming. On my next day off, I'm meeting a builder to level my lot and start the foundation for our house." John said with a little pride of accomplishment.

"Good to hear you're making progress. I'm proud for you. By the way, John, did you get a telephone at your house?"

"No, they only have four party lines available. I'm only a block away and the men know if we get a call, they are to come by and pick me up."

"Well, the fire and police departments have put in a request with the telephone company to give firemen and policemen and doctor's highest priority when it comes to installing private or one party lines for emergencies. As soon as that's approved, I'll let you know and you can apply again."

"That would be good, so if we are off duty, we can be called out sooner."

*****

January 29, 1910

Jennie woke about 3:45 am feeling full. She pulled the chamber pot out from under the bed and relieved herself and crawled back into bed. Just as she got warm again and about to go back to sleep, she felt a little pressure. Maybe it was just gas. She relaxed but it wasn't long till she felt it again. She began to wonder, *is this a sign the baby is coming?* She got up, stoked the coals and put more wood in the wood burning stove. She would need a warm house. *"What time is it? Hum, 4:30, what to do. I'll wait a while and see for sure if I am going into labor."*

Everything was ready for the baby's arrival. Mrs. Murphy next door had said when the time came to come get her. She would send her oldest boy to the fire station to get John. John would call Ida and Ma and then come home.

By 5:30, Jennie knew the baby was on the way. She saw the lamp light in Mrs. Murphy's kitchen window. Jennie put on shoes and wrapped a heavy shawl around her and hurried next door. While knocking, she called, "Mrs. Murphy, it's me, Jennie" and heard footsteps running toward the door.

Mrs. Murphy opened the door. "Saint preserve, Child, is it time?"

"Yes, get word to John please and remind him to call Ida?"

Mrs. Murphy, yelled, "Patrick! Patrick! Up lad and be quick 'bout it. 'Tis Mrs. Jennie." She grabbed her shawl and turned to Jennie, "Come now, let's get you home and to bed."

"I can make it," Jennie said, "Just get word to John."

"We will lassie, we will." Mrs. Murphy assured her as she yelled again, "Patrick, hurry Lad." She stepped out the door and took hold of Jennie's shoulder. Jennie felt a sudden gush of water run down her legs.

Patrick came running to the door still pulling up his suspenders with one hand and grabbing his coat with the other. "Yes, Mama, I'm going."

Jennie reminded, 'Tell chief to call Ida."

"Yes, Ma'am, I'm on my way." Patrick started running toward the fire station.

Mrs. Murphy helped Jennie into a clean gown and back in bed.

"Thanks you, Mrs. Murphy. I'll be alright now. You need to get breakfast for your family and get them off to work and school."

'They can wait another five minutes. I'll put the coffee pot on for your man."

Patrick came to the back door and opened it just enough to say, "Chief said he would make the call and be right here, Mrs. Jennie."

"Thank you, Patrick."

Mrs. Murphy had just started the coffee when John came in the door.

"Jennie, I'm here. Are you alright? Ida and Ma will be here soon. What do I need to do?"

"I'm alright. Mrs. Murphy has everything under control."

"Thanks, Mrs. Murphy."

"Glad I could help. Coffee will be ready shortly."

Jennie told her, "You tend to your family now and thank you, Mrs. Murphy."

"You come get me if you need me." She pulled her shawl over her shoulders and headed for the door.

'Thanks, Mrs. Murphy." John said, again.

John sat by the bed holding Jennie's hand.

Jennie said, "Go check the coffee and get you some breakfast. It will be a while."

"You sure you're all right? Can I get you something?"

Jennie cowered down with pain; then breathed easier. She had been sitting up in bed. "I think I better lay down now." And she slide down under the covers.

"You sure you don't need a doctor?"

"No, Ma knows what to do. They will be here, shortly. You go on and get you some coffee and fix you some breakfast." Jennie assured him, even though she was a little nervous and scared.

John got some coffee and came back to sit beside Jennie and hold her hand. The pains were coming closer now. *What's taking so long for Ida and Ma to get here? What if the baby starts arriving before they do? What do I do?* "Jennie, where's everything we need for the birth and after the baby gets here?"

"Everything is in that bottom drawer of the dresser," She grimaced with another pain, "rolled up in a cloth diaper, blankets in the baby bed."

John busied himself getting the things out of the drawer, stoking the fire in the stove to keep the room warm and running to hold Jennie's hand with each pain. He went into the living room. Looking out the window he wondered, *what's keeping Ma and Ida. They should be here by now?*" Looking at the clock it was 7:30. He went back to hold Jennie's hand. Her pains were almost constant now. A few minutes later, he heard the horse and buggy out front. "They're here, Jennie. Everything's going to be alright. I'll be back in a minute." He raced outside. Ida was in her little buggy, so neither really needed help getting down, but John wanted to make sure. "Am I glad to see you? What took so long? I was getting worried. It's getting close; she's almost in constant pain now."

"It's alright, John. There's plenty of time." Ma assured him. Ma went in the door followed by Ida and John. "Jennie, How you doing? What time did you start with pains?"

"Oh, Ma, I'm glad you're here. When I was sure the baby was coming, I went to get Mrs. Murphy at 5:30." Jennie managed to say between clinched teeth.

"Okay, let's get you ready to have that baby. Did you get everything together like I told you?"

"Yes, John just got it all out of the drawer and on top of the dresser."

John showed Ma as she began issuing orders. "Get me a chair

to sit in and another one for a pan of warm water beside me. Ida get a cold rag and sit on that side of the bed and keep bathing her face. John, I smell coffee, why don't you get us a cup? Ida and I just grabbed a bit of breakfast, but didn't take time for coffee. Did you get some breakfast?"

"I can't think of breakfast at a time like this."

"John, it may be another hour or more, so go get us some coffee and get you some breakfast now while there's time."

John reluctantly did as Ma said. After all she was the experienced one here. He got Ma and Ida a cup of coffee, then quickly fried him a couple of eggs and browned a piece of bread in the skillet. He ate quickly and put some water on to heat as Ma directed.

He went to sit by Jennie and let her squeeze his hand. Ma also directed, "Jennie girl, your doing fine. Now, when you feel a hard pain, take a deep breath and try to raise up. John get the pan of warm water ready and in the chair beside me."

Jennie did as Ma said, "Aagghh" she grimaced in pain and then relaxed. A few minutes later, Jennie declared, "I think its coming!"

Ma pulled back the covers, and the baby was indeed coming. "Come on, couple more tries , spread your legs, raise your legs up, feet flat on the bed and deep breath and raise up. Good, one more time." Jennie winced in an out cry of pain. Ma cried out, "It's a girl," as she began cutting and tying the cord. Ma checked the temperature of the water with her elbow and lifted the baby into the warm water bath. John and Ida watched in fascination, as Jennie lay back exhausted but breathing easier. Ma removed the baby from the warm water and the baby began to cry. "That's it little one, clear those little lungs and breath on your own." Ma dried the baby, wrapped a diaper around her little bottom and wrapped the blanket around the baby and handed her to John. "Here you go, hold her while I help Jennie get cleaned up."

John never felt as helpless in his entire life as he did holding that tiny little life in his hands. *Flesh of my flesh, he thought.* He was fascinated at the tiny dark eyes that blinked at him. *You are going to be as pretty as your Mama.*

Ma and Ida cleared away the dirty linens and covered a very tired new mother.

"Are you alright, Sweetheart? You want to see our baby girl? She's going to be as pretty as her Mama." John laid the baby beside her.

Jennie said, "Her mama isn't very pretty right now. But she is beautiful."

"Well, her mama is still beautiful, just a little haggard right now. You sure you're all right? Do you still want to name her, the name we picked?"

"Yes, I like Ella Louise, if that's all right with you. Can you take the baby and let me rest a while? I am so tired."

"Here, let me hold her," Ida spoke quickly, just dying to hold the baby.

Ma said, "I will stay with Jennie and the baby during the day. Ida will come spend the nights, until Jennie is able to be up and about."

"Thanks, Ma. I appreciate that. Wow! What an event!" John exclaimed.

"Let Jennie get some rest, then she is going to need something to eat." Ma said.

They went to the kitchen to have another cup of coffee and try to be quiet so Jennie could nap. John held little Louise as long as he could. When Jennie woke and asked for breakfast and he knew all was well, he went back to work.

Chief's log
January 29, 1910

Chief Whittenburg off duty four hours. Baby girl born.

John returned to the station in time to receive a call from the man putting in the foundation of their house. He finished the job and John told him to come by the fire station and he would pay him.

That evening John went home for supper and to check on Jennie and the baby. He told the men he would be gone about an hour, but if they got a call to drive by and pick him up. He arrived to find Ma had cooked a big pot of stew and cornbread baking in the oven. Jennie looked much better after resting all day. John picked up little

Louise, even though she was sleeping and held her as long as he could, then ate supper and returned to the station.

*****

February 2, 1910

John hired a carpenter to work every day but Sunday. On his days off, John worked with the carpenter to frame in the walls, get the trusses up for the roof and the roof on. He saved his special leave time to get an extra day off. With just the two of them working, it took longer, but it saved them some money. Shortly after they started their house, the doctor who bought the lot next door hired a builder to start his house.

*****

Chief's log
March 1, 1910

New Orders issued by Chief W. E. Bideker.

Order #1 Don't let men be wasteful.
Order #2 Be careful about special leave.
Order #3 Go to your meals and come back as quick as you can-conveniently.
Order #4 Don't go back and forth home between meal hour.
Order #5 Keep station and equipment as clean as possible and grounds also.

Chief's log
May 1, 1910

Fire at 211 W. 25th St. Owned by Ed Dillon and occupied by W.H. Atley and D.W. Brown, jumped from window on second floor on West side of house and broke both legs at ankle.

May 3, 1910

One Mane and Tail brush, 2 bolts for nozzle standards, 5 gal. oil from Central.

June, 1, 1910

Got 32 bushels oats from #4 station, 8 sacks bran and 25 bales hay from #11, Russell hauled them.

June 8, 1910

Tested plugs, out 1 hour 45 min. Corner 24th and Main cap is wore off, won't hold. Made inspection of gas cans.

June 13, 1910

Notified Padhorn and Al Gant to remove gas cans out of alley or complaint would be filed. Gant said they would remove them today or tomorrow.

June 24, 1910

Cans removed and approved.

June 28, 1910

New plugs in service at 20th and Main, 2013 Main, 2113 Main and 2223 Main, 3 way plugs.

Chief's log
July 11, 1910

New hydrants at McKinney and 24th, Bryan and 24th. Dr. Bittick left prescription for Tom. Tom must have eaten a weed from the vacant lot and his bowels were running off. They had to clean out his stall every few hours and wash the front of the wagon off after coming back from a call.

July 13, 1910

New Hydrant at 23rd and Loving.

Chief's log
August 1, 1910

Received 10 yds. Cheesecloth, one sponge, 3 sheets Emory cloth, ½ bar harness soap, 4 bars laundry soap, 2 buckets salt.

August 2, 1910

H.W. Russell off 8 am to 8 am on 4th, 48 hrs, getting married. Stanley sub.

August 9, 1910

Lee Roy Snow cut hole in chin with harness hanger, dressed by Dr. Covington while answering alarm at 200 E. 21st Street at 3:30 pm.

Snow accidently ran into the hanger that held the horse collars. He grabbed a towel holding it to his chin. As they headed to the fire, John told Kennedy to stop at Dr. Covington's office on the way and let Snow off. He could be treated and they would pick him up on the way back from the fire.

August 25, 1910

Took Tom in to shop, had horse shoe tightened.

September 1, 1910

New Orders, turn all sub money over to Captains, by order of Chief Bideker.

Chief's log
September 14, 1910

New Plugs in service Azle and Epheham, New plug at Azle and Franklin and Franklin and 27th and Franklin and 28th.

September 19, 1910

Occupied new fire hall 9 am, Prospect and 23rd St. Moved from 23rd and Ellis Ave.

They had been saving boxes to pack and looking forward to this day for several months. They were moving into a brand new brick building, with all the modern conveniences, indoor bath room, concrete floor.

September 20, 1910

Received supplies, 4 bedsteads, 4 pr. Springs, 4 mattresses, 1 pillow, 1 sponge, 1 chamoise, 4 bars laundry soap, 1 mop and harness soap, 2 brooms and 6 pkg. toilet paper. Made practice run. Put back into service.

September 31, 1910

Dr. Bittick come to give Tom a capsule at 10 pm.

October 1, 1910

Dr. Bittick come to give Tom a capsule at 4 pm.

October 13, 1910

Taken wagon to shop for single tree, made Gus Eilenburger shop.

October 14, 1910

Got #8 wagon and taken #12 to Bob Hoods shop for repair

October 27, 1910

Got wagon back from # 3 had new brake put on new tongue chains.

November 2, 1910

Report to Central 7 am. Special meeting for all Chiefs.

There was no special training, you just learned as you fought the fires. So Bideker occasionally called his chiefs together, asked what kind of fires they had had and did they learn anything new that could be passed on to the other firemen. They also reported any old equipment that needed to be replaced and discussed how they could shorten their response time.

November 23, 1910

Put in gas meter and tested pipes in new station #12.
Had a new gas burning cook stove installed and tested.

*****

December 1, 1910

John and Jennie moved into their new house. John had finished four rooms, more than they had at the duplex. They no longer would have to pay rent and that money could go to finishing the rest of the house, a little at a time. Firemen, policemen and doctors now had priority when it came to having a telephone. So the telephone company installed their phone right a way. Their bill would be one dollar a month. They also built a barn and bought a cow for milk and butter.

The day after they moved in, Doctor and Mrs. Hayes moved into their 2 story house next door. They were about the same age as John and Jennie and had a 2 yr. old daughter. They became instant friends.

*****

Chief's Log
December 6, 1910

Alarm from box 76 at 1:30 am, box 78 at 11:50 am. and box 68 at 6:20 pm. Reported to the police as possible arson, as each fire was small brush or trash pile.

December 25, 1910

Alarms at box 126 at 2:45 pm, box 189 at 7pm and box 32 at 2:05 am. All false alarms. Reported to police, possible pranksters.

Chief's log
January 2, 1911

Had 2 calls today. 8:10 am. and 10:50 am, box 136, both trash bins. Police called to investigate arsonist.

January 6, 1911

Got supplies: one broom 45 cents, 3 sheets Emory cloth 10 cents, ½ bar harness soap 35 cents, 10 yards cheesecloth 45 cents, 1 sponge 30 cents, 2 bricks salt 42 cents, polish 7 cents, one double hitch rein $1.80, 5 gal. oil 55 cents.

Mid January 1911 was a bitter cold month, with freezing temperatures. That meant checking the fire hydrants to make sure they weren't frozen, so they would have water in case of fires.

Chief's log
January 14, 1911

Water off on Ross Ave. from 24th St North. Water off on Clinton St. from Central to 20th.

Checked plugs. 26th & Lincoln Round valve stem. 22nd & Jones Valve stem leaking, same on 22nd & Ellis, 22nd & Clinton and 22nd & Ross. 24th & Market stuff in box loose. 24th & Lee Ave. leaking at bottom, same thing at 25th & Prospect and 24th and Houston. At

24th and Main need new cap on Nozzle, 25th and main leaking out of valve stem.

February 10, 1911

Received 5 new helmets from Central Station.

March 1, 1911

While at a fire at 16th and Lincoln, Russell got hit in ear with full stream of water. Rendered unconscience for few minutes. Had Dr. Barden treated him 1 visit and Dr. Haysett treated him 17 visits.

Chief's log
March 14, 1911

President Theodore Roosevelt was to speak at 9:00 a.m. at the Stock Yards coliseum. Meanwhile at 7 a. m. fire broke out in the feed barns at the stockyards. Firemen couldn't get control and called out three other stations. It spread too fast in the high March wind and consumed over six acres of stables. Prize winning horses, mules, sheep and hogs died before they could be rescued. It was a cloudy day, but only a few drops of rain fell. No help for the firemen, but they managed to finally bring it under control and extinguished.

March 18, 1911

Received new city phone directory.

April 1, 1911

Had 61 bales of hay delivered.

April 7, 1911

Supplies, one curry comb 20 cents, one broom 45 cents, 6 bars laundry soap 25 cents, one bar harness soap 15 cents, 6 light globes 55 cents each.

April 21, 1911

Got 5 gals oil 55cents. Took Tom and Dan in to be shod.

April 27, 1911

Got new pair bits for horses $100.

Chief's log
May 8, 1911

Received 33 ½ yards stockyards loam for park (vacant lot next door). J. M. Burkett hauled it 35 cents a yard.

May 11, 1911

Bought lawn mower for $9.60 and lawn hose $8.25 cents. The vacant lot next door was not only where the horses grazed but the firemen planted some trees, kept it clean for a park area. The neighborhood kids would play ball in the street. The firemen got them to play in the vacant lot and would sometimes play with the kids.

Chief's log
June 25, 1911

Went to stockyards fire. Carried 1600 ft. hose burned up.

After dragging hose the shortest distance to put out fire, the fire spread too fast from one dry shed roof to the other over the empty cattle pens. Before they realized what was happening, the roof collapsed on top of their hose. They had to pull another hose, connect to a different hydrant and get the fire out.

June 28, 1911

Dr. Bittick on call for Tom, sent powder for Tom's skin where harness rubbed.

Chief's log
July 4, 1911

When the firemen ate watermelon, they always tossed the rind over to the horses.

Tom and Dan loved watermelon rind. One typical Texas, hot, muggy day, one of the firemen came on duty and brought a big watermelon. The firemen all gathered around the table with forks and spoons in hand. Just as they sliced the melon in half, the alarm went off. The men scrambled to their places, the chain in front of the horses dropped. Dan went straight to his place in front of the wagon. Tom detoured through the kitchen, opened his big mouth and in one motion, scooped the heart out of one half of the watermelon, ran and took his place in front of the wagon. Without missing a step, he swallowed the last bite, just in time to get his harness in place. Lee Roy swore that horse grinned as he buckled Tom's harness.

July 5, 1911

While playing ball on the vacant lot next to the fire hall, one of the kids J.D. Franklin, Jr. broke a window pane over the horses stall. John told his Father not to punish him, it was an accident.

Later that afternoon a fire call came in on the phone.

Mrs. J.J. Lesley burnt up at 1602 Lincoln Ave. Coal oil or gasoline explosion. Died July 6 at 3 pm. It was suspected Mrs. Lesley, in filling her oil lamps, mistakenly picked up the gasoline container. When making sure the lamps worked, lit one and it exploded causing the others to explode and spread the fire.

July 20, 1911

The woman's aid society gave an ice cream social in the park.

Chief's log
July 31, 1911

J.M. Bennett killed while answering call box 148 at 3:20 am.

189

Thrown from wagon at Weatherby St. and 6th Ave. Wagon run over him.

The Woman's Aid Society took several baskets of food to his family.

August 8, 1911

Changed hose to reel, taken wagon to shop

Chief's log
September 1, 1911

Got wagon out of shop. New ladder on top.

September 2, 1911

Got two straps for ladder at Noby Harness.

October 7, 1911

Had prescription refilled by Dr. Bittick for Tom.

October 22, 1911

Had Tom, Dan and Dutch shod. Dutch taking Tom's place. Tom out of service.

December 2, 1911

Took Hays and Dan to be shod. Hays taking Tom's place. Sent wagon to #3, had new foot board put on.

Chief's log

From Jan. 1, 1911 to Jan.1,1912, 75 runs, 68 hrs. 40 min. 24556 ft. hose, 612 ft. ladders.

Chief's log
January 24, 1912

Let city street department have old Tom. Doc said Tom was developing arthritis and shouldn't run like he used to. John felt like he was loosing an old friend.

Chief's log
February 4, 1912

Mrs. Alonzso and Loncenia Pastor burnt face and hands, not serious. Antonio Alonzo 9 months old burnt up. 204 E. 22ⁿᵈ St. Two story grocery and rooming house.

Tears streamed down John's face as he carried the small burned body out of the remains.

March 1912

The call came in for stockyards, the horse and mule barns, at 25ᵗʰ and Main St. The fire spread so quickly very few horses or mules could be saved. When the firemen arrived, John found the train there getting ready to unload some animals. John told the engineer to move the train out before the wood box cars caught on fire too. John climbed on a near by shed roof over a pen to get a better perspective on where to direct his men. He didn't realize the roof was supported by rotting timber. Just as the train started moving, the roof started to collapse. John had no choice but to jump on top of the train. He made his way to the boxcar's ladder, climbed down and jumped off before the train picked up speed. The firemen worked all day putting the fire out, but still it destroyed a large part of the stock yards and dead animals covered over one-forth of a mile.

1912

Central fire station received the first fire truck. Rumors were the city would replace all horse draw wagons with motor vehicles over the next few years. One at a time men from each of the stations were invited to come to Central and see the new truck. Those that wanted to could apply and if chosen, start learning to drive the trucks. Mechanics being hired could also apply to be a driver.

Chief's log
April 16, 1912

Tom Shay burned about face and hands in gasoline explosion at 2469 N. Main St., Chili stand. John and Tom Shay, occupants.

April 22, 1912

Got one garden rake 75 cents. Got 17 loads loam from stockyards. With the help of the Ladies Aid Society set out 236 flower plants around fire hall and park.

Chief's log
June 10, 1912

Call came in for fire in stockyards, what hadn't burned before was now burning. Damage to pens was worse than before but very few animals lost this time.

July 9, 1912

J.C. Buchanan got foot blistered while at fire.

Oct. 1, 1912

Busted section of 1906 hose

December 1912

Had total of 59 calls, 49 hours 10 minutes in service.

Chief's log
January 23, 1913

Got new double tree and wagon tongue.

Chief's log
March 1, 1913

Wrote down locations of hydrants and main lines in stockyards and packing houses.

May 14, 1913

Checked hose invoice, one section 1903 bad, two sections 1906 one inch bad.

*****

After John finished their four room house and they moved in, he added a screened in back porch, a large front porch, a fenced in area for chickens and a garden. Being only 5 ft. 2in. tall, Jennie couldn't reach to hook up the two big horses to their large wagon. So John bought her a small, one seated buggy, like Ida's. Jennie could manage one horse and getting in and out with the baby was easier. She didn't have to depend on someone else or John on his one day a week off, to take her shopping.

*****

Chief's log
July 30, 1913

Chief off duty with sub C. Palen till Aug. 7th for vacation.

September 6, 1913

Hays fell and hurt hip. Dr. Bittick visited, gave him some linement. Got Bill from station #9 in place of Hays.

September 25, 1913

Moved alarm box 313 to Central and Boulevard

Chief's log
September 29, 1913

Put Hays back in service.

December 1, 1913

New man Louis Frowin off 24 hours special leave, his baby burned.
New subs, E.M. Pruitt and W.M. Bingham.

John & Jenny with baby Louise

Chief's log
February 22, 1914

Whittenburg off 13 hours, R. A. Killian sub.

*****

Jennie was expecting their second child. Ma and Ida were delighted to be on call as before. The morning of the 22nd, Jennie felt
fine. She did a little house cleaning and washed a few pieces. Little

Louise had just turned four years old the end of January. Jennie had prepared their lunch when she felt the first little pain. As soon as Louise finished eating, Jennie put her down for a nap. She called Ma and Ida and then called John. "John, I've started with the pains. I'm pretty sure the baby's coming. Ma and Ida are on the way. Louise is down for her nap, so why don't you wait an hour or so and then come home. You can take care of Louise while I'm having the baby."

"Call Doctor Hayes and just make sure he is available in case he's needed." John suggested.

"I'm okay, but, if it will make you feel better, I'll call." Jennie assured him.

Ida and Ma arrived shortly and began the waiting time. John arrived about an hour later. He took care of Louise when she woke from her nap, keeping her in the other room. Ida came every fifteen minutes to give him a report. When the baby came, Ida ran to tell John, "It's another girl." John went in to see Jennie and the baby and Ida took over caring for Louise.

"Are you disappointed this one isn't a boy?" Jennie asked.

"Not at all; boy or girl, doesn't matter as long as the baby is healthy and you are alright." John assured her. "And this one's got black hair and looks like her Mama, too." Teasing her he said, "But, you could have made one with blond hair that looks like me. Well, maybe next time. Did you decide on a name for sure?"

"Yes, I like Evelyn Rose, if that's okay with you."

"That's a pretty name, I like it."

*****

Chief's log
April 17, 1914

Took wagon to shop for repairs.

April 30, 1914

Got wagon back from shop and got 100 ft. hose on wagon.

July, 8, 1914

New Boxes 327 & 328 installed near Armour and Co. packing plant.

July 13, 1914

John hired an electrician to wire the house for electricity. The electric company connected them to service on July 13, 1914 for a $5.00 deposit.

Chief's log
October 10, 1914

Fort Worth Feather and Mattress Co. remodeled one mattress.

*****

December 1914

Money was a little tight, so John asked Mr. Lovelace at the grocery store to save some more wood apple crates for him. He took them apart and made doll furniture for his girls for Christmas. He used a draw knife, hand saw, hand plane, hammer and sandpaper. The furniture consisted of a four poster doll bed, a two drawer dresser with oval mirror and a little table. He also made a pie safe with two glass doors at the top, two drawers in the middle and two wood doors at the bottom.

*****

Chief's log
December 21, 1914

Put in underground gas tank and pump.

December 22, 1914

Received 60 gals gasoline from Magnolia Co.

December 29, 1914

Put new Chief's car into service. Taken place of Dan and Hays.

The fire department trained certain men that applied to drive the motorized chief's car, just as they had hired certain men to handle the horses. Most all stations received a chief's car first and each Chief had a driver. They kept a few horse drawn wagons for a while until they made the complete transition to all motor vehicles.

First truck at No. 12 Station

13

Family and Motor Vehicles

Chief's log
January 7, 1915

Let #3 have wagon and harness, Joe and Hayes shod

January 15, 1915

Received 50 gals of gasoline from Magnolia Oil Co.

February 12, 1915

Received new soft suction and mud chains for car.

February 20, 1915

Took car to shop 10 am out until 22nd at 4 pm. # 7 wagon in place.

April 10, 1915

Supplies received from Central, 6 bars laundry soap, 2 sponges, 2 bricks salt, and 1 blue print map of city.

April 30, 1915

Orders to give Subs 3 hrs. for each day he works for regular man.

May 10, 1915

Took car in for repair. Needed new radiator.

July 16, 1915

Chief Whittenburg off 8 am to 6 pm special leave, Markland sub.

*****

Louise, now age five and Evelyn, one and a half years old, were playing in the floor, while Jennie did some housework. She suspected she was pregnant again, but hadn't had any morning sickness yet. Suddenly she felt a wetness and pain. She was bleeding. She called Dr. Hayes next door and called Ma and Ida. Mrs. Hays came with the doctor to care for the girls. Ida called John who called in a sub and took the rest of the day off. Dr. Hayes took care of Jennie as best he could, but she had an infection and a miscarriage and spent the next couple of weeks in bed. John hired a lady to take care of Jennie and the girls during the day. Ma and Ida took turns spending the nights with Jennie when he had to work. When she recovered, the doctor said he didn't believe she could have any more children.

October 4, 1915

Car out of service 11 am to 5 pm. #2 in place.

Chief's log
January 18, 1916

Let #4 have riding saddle and double hitch reins.

February 26, 1916

One section 1908 Eureka hose busted.

March 25, 1916

Received nozzle pipe from Central and 2 small light globes for car.

April 27, 1916

Took car to shop, new gear. Get it back on 29th

June 19, 1916

Received 50 gals gas from Gulf Refinery.

June 30, 1916

Clyde May Scott burned to death at 2515 Clinton, age 3 yrs. Mother next door, child supposedly asleep. Unknown cause of fire. Arrived too late, fire out of control.

It always bothered John when anyone, especially children, were killed in a fire. Now that he had children of his own, it upset him even more. Many times he cried and agonized over what more could be done, to get there sooner or get the people out or put out the fire sooner. This was one of those times.

*****

1916

Sometimes people called the fire station on the phone instead of finding the nearest fire call box. So when the phone rang the men stopped what they were doing in anticipation of a possible call. Snow answered, " Number twelve fire station." Pause. "Yes, just a moment. Hey, Chief, you got a phone call."

John started walking up to the front to the desk. He wondered, *No one calls me at the station unless it's really important. Who could it be?* "Hello, this is John."

"John," Ida was crying. John's heart skipped a beat. "A horse stepped on James, we're at St. Joseph's hospital. I couldn't get here in time to see him before they started to operate. The men that brought him here told me the horse stepped on him several times before they could get the horse away. John, I'm scared. Can you come, please?"

"Hold the line Ida, don't hang up." John turned to Donahue who was just going off duty. "I've got a bad situation with my brother-in-law in the hospital having an operation because of an accident. Can you stay and sub for me, possibly the rest of the day?"

"Sure, Chief. You take what time you need."

"Thanks." John said as he turned back to the phone. "Ida, I'll be there as quick as I can."

John had been doing his chores, so he ran up stairs and cleaned up and put on fresh uniform. He slid down the pole and glanced at the clock. If he was lucky, he had just enough time to catch the streetcar that came by at 10 every morning on 21st Street. He walked as fast as he could and made it just in time. Time passed slowly as it seemed like the streetcar went slower than usual. He was anxious to get to the hospital and be with Ida in case of what might happen.

John got off at the hospital stop. He quickly walked in, told the lady at the desk, "I'm looking for James Ross. He had an accident earlier this morning and had emergency operation. My sister Ida Ross called me."

"Just a moment please." She looked at her charts. "Mr. Ross is still in the operating room. I believe his wife is in the waiting room down the hall. Look for the sign on the door to your left."

"Thank you, Ma'am." John said as he headed down the hall. He entered the door that said 'waiting room.'

Ida jumped up the minute she saw him, "John, I'm so glad you're here. The men that brought James to the hospital had to leave to go back to work. The nurse just came and said the doctor will talk to me in a few minutes. I'm so scared. They won't tell me how badly hurt he is but it must be bad for the doctor to operate immediately."

"We'll just have to wait and see, I guess." John hugged her to comfort her. "Is there a phone around here? I'll call Jennie."

"Ma was going to call Jennie as I left the house."

"Oh, good, just so she knows where I am."

They were about to sit down, when the door opened and the nurse said, "Mrs. Ross, come with me please, the doctor will see you now." She led them to the doctor's office. "The doctor will be here shortly," leaving them to wait again.

What seemed like an eternity, all of five minutes, the doctor came in, "Mrs. Ross, I'm Doctor Thomas" and he looked at John, "and you are?"

"I'm Ida's brother, John Whittenburg." The two men shook hands.

"Mrs. Ross, may I speak freely in front of your brother?"

"Yes, please do." Ida reached for John's hand. Expecting bad news, she needed his strong support.

The doctor sat down at his desk, "Mrs. Ross, your husband is stable for now. We had two doctor's operating and two observing because of the seriousness of his wounds." The doctor paused. "Mrs. Ross, he was torn up pretty bad. We were able to repair the rupture in his stomach. We removed the damaged gall bladder and repaired the tear in the bladder and intestines. He should be able to eliminate body fluids normally but," the doctor took a breath, "I'm sorry to say this, Mrs. Ross, but he will not be able to perform as a husband and not be able to father any children."

Ida and John both gasped. Ida started crying. The doctor continued, "I am so sorry. There was nothing more we could do." Dr. Thomas paused till Ida could absorb that much news then he continued. "Physically his chance of recovery is good. We don't know what effect this will have on him mentally or emotionally. We have to wait and see." He paused again. "Do you have any question?"

Ida spoke, "How long will he be in the hospital? Will he be able to go back to work and live a normal life?"

Dr. Thomas said, "I'm not sure at this point. Like I said, we four doctors had never seen anything like this before. We aren't sure how long the recovery period will be, but I feel like if he has a good mental and emotional attitude, he should be able to return to work. There again, mentally he may be afraid of horses from now on. I am sorry, but we just don't know what to tell you to expect. We will just have to take one day at a time and please call me any time you have any questions."

"Thank you, doctor." John spoke for Ida who was still crying. "When can we see him?"

"It may be another hour or so till he wakes up. If you will wait in the waiting room, I'll send for you as soon as we see he is awake and stable." The doctor said.

John helped Ida up and guided her back to the waiting room. Neither spoke for a while, not knowing what to say. The news was still soaking in.

"Oh, John, what am I going to do? We can't make love and now we will never have any children. How can I tell him its okay? That at least he is still alive and we have each other."

"I wish I knew what to tell you, Ida. But I just don't know the answer."

Two weeks later, Ida brought James home from the hospital. He didn't want to take hold of the horse's reins. Ida tried to show him she was glad he was alive and back home. He wouldn't accept her hugs and didn't want her near him. He moved away from her in bed and the next day told Ida to make up the bed on the screened in porch that John had used when he stayed with them. He would sleep out there. James withdrew like a turtle into its shell. When Ida tried to do something special for him he got angry. John was the only person James responded to that could handle him when his anger got out of control. After talking to the doctor Ida called John. The doctor recommended James be put in the insane asylum. John took one hour leave to take James to the institution.

It cost Ida $39 to $46 a month for his care. James had made good money and invested it in real estate. So Ida had money for her and ma to live on as well as take care of James's bills. She and Ma loved to sew and Ida spent many lonely hours making something to pass the time. She even began to take in sewing for other people.

One day, one of the other firemen mentioned he was selling his mother's estate since her passing. He asked if any of the other firemen would be interested in buying anything and named off several items, a treadle sewing machine being one of the items. John bought the sewing machine to make it easier and faster for Ida to sew and for her taking care of Ma.

By the end of August the doctor suggested James come home and see how he responds.

September 2, 1916, John took 1 ½ hours special leave to go with Ida to bring James home.

Ma Whittenburg did not like being around James in his mental condition. So when Ida wanted to bring James home, Ma asked to stay with John and Jennie.

October 3rd, John took 1 ½ hrs. special leave to take James back to the asylum. Ma went back to stay with Ida.

October 29th, on his regular day off, John brought James home again. Ma went back to John and Jennie's.

November 13th, John's day off, James begged John to take him back to the asylum and leave him there. He didn't want to come back home. He asked John to look after Ida.

January 15, 1917, the asylum called Ida early that morning. James had managed to hide a glass in his room. After bed check, he broke the glass and cut his wrist. He was dead when the nurses made the midnight bed check.

Ida paid all the expenses and bought the burial lot next to James for her self. John bought the lots next to hers for Ma, himself and Jennie, getting everything paid for in advance. They didn't expect to use them any time soon.

By late September, Ma's health began to fail. October 5th, Ma grew worse during the night. Ida called Dr. Hayes who told Ida it was just a matter of hours. Ida called John and Ma passed away at 4 am., October 6, 1917. John paid the remaining $30. for her casket. S.D. Shannon was the undertaker.

*****

Chief's log
January 30, 1918

Received one bath tub for # 12 fire station from Arens & Ott Manufacturing Co.

April 3, 1918

Hit Ford delivery grocery wagon, J.N. Ray owner. Tore off hub cap and skinned cason on fire truck.

June 1, 1918

J. C. Buckanan set up as captain #1 station. C.E. Whipple in place as lieutenant.

June 11, 1918

New man John Riley come to #12.

July 23, 1918

Richard Riley resigned, John Riley in place.

*****

September 18, 1918

Ida had grieved over the death of her husband James and again over the loss of her Ma. The doctor believed she grieved herself to death. James had made several real estates investments, leaving Ida provided for. Ida left a will leaving one house on North Fifteenth Street to John and making him the executor of her estate. She left the house on North Houston Street to their brother Charlie and her home place to her sister Clemmie. James had also invested in property in Sweetwater, Texas where he did some horse trading. Ida left that house and property to James's brother. Her other house was to be sold to pay for all debts, including her funeral. John paid her funeral expenses of $202.50, and other debts, but kept the house and inherited $929.69 from her estate. Jennie kept Ida's sewing machine. John took a weeks vacation on September 29th, to settle her estate and do some maintenance work around the two houses and rented them.

*****

Chief's log
October 8, 1918

Jim Riley resigned

December 1, 1918

Got bath tub installed at #12. They now had all indoor plumbing.

December 27, 1918

Received three new helmet's from Central.

1919

After Central getting the first motorized fire truck several years previously, by 1919 the fire department received ten more motor driven, LaFrance auto pump fire trucks, white with gold lettering and stripes. This completed the transformation of replacing all the horse drawn fire wagons.

John had mixed emotions about these machines taking the place of horses. The vehicles had no personality, roared down the street with flashing lights and screaming sirens. Horses had personality and performed with intelligence and skill, their muscles straining with strength and bells ringing with every move of the harness. But John accepted it as a new way of life. Being Chief he had his own driver and didn't have to drive the motor vehicle.

Chief's log
January 1, 1919

Got new battery for car. Mechanic brought the battery out from Central, put it in.

February 25, 1919

Received five gas masks. Whittenburg #90, Whipple #89, Pruitt #88, Matt Carroll #87 and Richard Riley #86

April 20, 1919

Let S.T. Bibb have 41 bales of left over hay, 3 were torn up.

June 5, 1919

Got two new tires on front wheels

June 23, 1919

Let North Texas Iron and Metal have iron material in horse stalls.

July 12, 1919

Exchanged old nozzle for new

July 17, 1919

Double Platoon went into service at #12 tire station. Thanks to Chief Bideker, more men were eligible and hired on the fire department, giving them 24 hrs on duty and 24 hrs off, with five men per shift: J. L. Whittenburg, C.E. Whipple, W. W. White, Dallas Bevil, Matt Carroll, E.F. Hines, E.M. Pruitt, Richard Riley, M.L. Honea, and Joe Fitzgerald.

September 10, 1919

Honea resigned O.C. Carter in place

September 22, 1919

O. C. Carter out sick. Put #12 car in shop for repairs, #5 car in place.

September 23, 1919

#12 car back in service at 9 pm, new gear.

When John went to pick up the car, Chief Bideker called him into his office and shut the door. Normally, Chief Bill left the door open, so John immediately knew it must be something serious he wanted to talk about.

"John, I want to retire in November. You are the first one I thought about to replace me. I would like to see you as our next City Fire Chief." Bideker announced.

"Oh, Wow, you really surprised me with that one." John stammered.

"John, you have the 'know how' and the integrity. I think you would make a fine City Chief. Every man on the department that knows you; respects you."

"That's nice of you to say that, but Bill, you and I have known each other for a long time. I consider you a good friend, not just my superior. I feel I could do the job as far as hiring and firing and transferring to the different stations and seeing the men got the proper training and equipment. But, Bill, to be honest, I don't feel comfortable taking the job. I don't have the formal education to do all the paper work. You have fought with the city politician to get us better benefits and done it in a dignified manor. I'm afraid, I would tell them politician I'd watch their house burn to the ground before I'd spit on it. No, Bill I know my limitations. I'm comfortable where I am. I thank you for the offer, but it's an honor that I have to refuse."

"Well," Bideker said, "I was afraid you would say that. I think you would make a fine City Chief, but I understand and I respect your decision. I also respect your judgment, so can I ask your opinion on who you think would be a good replacement for me."

"Hum," John paused, "Well, I guess the first one that comes to my mind would be Stan Ferguson. He's been on the department as long as you and I have. He's a good firefighter and the men like him. We got a lot of good men, so it's hard to say, except some haven't been on the department long enough and some just aren't leaders. So, I think I'd go with Ferguson."

"That's my thoughts, too." Bideker said. "He was my second choice."

Chief's log
September 26, 1919

O.C. Carter back on duty

September 29, 1919

O.C. Carter resigns

October 2, 1919

R.E. Daniels in place of Carter. W.W. White receives new pair of boots.

12:15 call to 2217 Commerce St., shed full of hay. 3:55 phone call 2213 Columbus Ave. weeds on vacant lot burning.

October 3, 1919

1:15 am. False alarm, out 10 min.

October 5, 1919

1:10 am. False alarm, out 10 min.

Chief's log
October 10, 1919

10:35 pm. False alarm out 10 min.

October 14, 1919

9:45 pm. False alarm out 10 min.

October 19, 1919

1:05 pm. False alarm, out 10 min.

After the third false alarm from the same alarm box, John reported it to the police. They must have caught the person by the fifth time, as no more alarms came in from that box.

October 20, 1919

Richard Riley resigned 8 am, J.H. Jay in place.

November 21, 1919

All firemen were issued pass books allowing firemen to ride the street car free.

Had 9 wool bed blankets laundered at Liberty Laundry for $2.70.

Phone call at 10 pm to Roanoke, Texas to get their assistance in gin boiler explosion, 3 men killed, 8 injured. 46 miles, 3 hrs. service.

November 25, 1919

City Fire Chief W.E. Bideker resigns.

Bideker was recorded to be one of the finest chief's ever known to Ft. Worth. He was known for his dry sense of humor and innovative leadership. When he assumed command, the department had 38 men, 7 stations and all fully horse drawn. Salaries ranged from $50 to $125 a month. The work schedule consisted of 147 hours per week with a full day off each month. Bideker's administration appointed the first Fire Marshall in addition to passing several fire prevention ordinances.

During the height of the horse drawn fire wagon era, thirty draft horses had filled the fire department stables. By 1919 the department's transformation from horse drawn steamers to motor driven pumpers was complete. Chief Bideker fought hard for labor reform, better salaries, training and better stations. During his fourteen years as city chief he transformed the Fort Worth Fire Department into a professional firefighting team. When he resigned he left behind a modern fire department of 13 stations and 100 firefighters, organized into an 84 hour work week with increased off duty time. The new schedule made it possible for men with families to pursue this noble occupation.

Chief's log
November 30, 1919

Phone call for fire at 2524 Azle Ave. Mrs. B.L. Hill, gas explosion. 20 min.

December 1, 1919

Standifer Ferguson became new City Fire Chief. He was one of the original 34 paid firemen in 1893 and boasted a service record of 46 years.

December 17, 1919

Joe Fitzgerald resigns, Z.M. Lee in place.

14

Realities of Life

Chief's log
January 19, 1920

Company #12
J.L. Whittenburg, Chief
E.M Pruitt, Lieutenant
C. Leaky, Driver
E.F. Hines, driver
Matt Carroll, lineman

W.W. White, lineman
Dallas Bevels, lineman
R.E. Daniels, lineman
J.H. Jay, lineman
Zaden Lee, lineman

Chief's log
January 22, 1920

Burnt indicator up, hot wire.
J.H. Jay resigned, Charley Potter in place.

February 28, 1920

Fixed indicator

March 28, 1920

Got new brakes on car.

June 12, 1920

A new man was hired and by the time his three months training was over all the firemen were tired of Harvey constantly pulling jokes on them. One day on his day off the men sat and talked about what they could do, to get back at Harvey. A plan soon took shape. They called Mathew who was coming on duty that evening and asked him to go by the store and bring three bottles of ketchup when he came to work. The next morning all the men put on their dirty uniforms from the day before. One of the men kept watch and when he saw Harvey get off the trolley, two blocks away, he ran back into the station and they all took their places.

When Harvey opened the door and entered the fire station, he saw one man laying on the floor, another in a chair laying face down on the card table, one at Chief's desk, slumped in the chair and one across the kitchen table with what appeared to be a knife sticking out of his back and all were splattered with 'blood.'

Harvey screamed, wet his pants and ran out the door. Just as they expected, he found a phone and called the police. The neighborhood patrol officer and friend had been told about the joke. He took his time before responding to the call. Playing along he told Harvey to calm down and tell his story, then they went to the station to investigate. The officer walked in first, "Well, howdy, fellows. Everything all right here?"

"Howdy, O'Donald, Yes, everything fine." "How are you?" "Got time for coffee?" The men all began to speak.

O'Donald said, "I think your man here must have got drunk last night and having nightmares."

Harvey heard them all talking and walked in to find all the men in clean uniforms, sitting at the table playing dominoes, with no sign of any 'blood' anywhere. The firemen never laughed or admitted what they had done, but seriously tried to convince Harvey he must have been dreaming. After they finished their chores, they had been sitting there having coffee and playing dominoes.

O'Donald said, "Under the circumstances I won't fill out a report this time. I wouldn't want to ruin a fireman's reputation." Harvey never pulled anymore jokes and soon turned in his resignation.

September 22, 1920

Z.M. Lee resigned, H.W. Franklin in place

November 27, 1920

Sent car to shop for overhauling. Back December 3rd, at 5 pm

Chief's log
March 1, 1921

Potter got leg broke. Lost balance on ladder, fell back, boot caught between rungs.

July 13, 1921

Got new siren for car

July 16, 1921

Went to Lake Worth with Chief's car, broke magnita. Went in shop until 19th.

August 18, 1921

Got new casing for car.

April 24, 1922

Sent car to shop, had radiator fixed, new front casing.

June 1922

Chief Stan Ferguson called #12 and asked John to come by his office. John had his driver take him to Central. He walked into Ferguson's office. "You wanted to see me, Chief?"

"Yes, John, come in. Shut the door behind you." Ferguson said. "John, I want you to be Battalion Chief and over see the four stations on the North Side; # 11, #12, #15 and later, a new station #22. This is just between you and me for now, it won't be in effect till August 1st."

"Gosh, Stan, I don't know what to say." John paused. "I guess I need to ask what responsibilities that includes?"

"Basically, just what you are doing now at your station. Only you will visit each of the other stations at least once a week. See what the men need. Make sure they are following the rules, keeping station and equipment clean and repaired. If one station has a really big fire and you are on duty, you might check it out and see if they need any more help, specially, if they are training a new man. You phone in supplies for #12 station now and you would be phoning in supplies for the other stations and making sure they get what they need. Assign days off, get replacements if one of the men get hurt or is off duty. Like I said basically just what you're doing now, but doing it for three more stations. I'm confident you can do the job or I wouldn't be asking you, John. It will take a load off my shoulders. I'm trying to get 3 more Battalion Chiefs, to over see the stations in each section of town, then you four can report to me, or I can issue orders to the four of you and you see that it gets to all four of your stations."

"Well, I think I can handle that. How soon do you need my answer?"

"As soon as possible." Ferguson answered. "But I can give you a couple of days, if you need it."

"I'd like to sleep on it. I'll let you know by tomorrow."

"If it will help with your decision, I'll tell you the job comes with a raise."

"I figured it would." John said with a smile.

The next day, John called Ferguson and told him he would take the job. Ferguson said he would be sending out official notices in July.

July 1, 1922

Notice from City Fire Chief Ferguson
To stations #11, #12, #15 and #22

Effective August 1, 1922, Chief J.L. Whittenburg is promoted to Battalion Chief for the North Side District. Any questions, problems, reports or supply needs will be directed to him as second in command to the City Chief.

Chief's log
August 1, 1922

H.O. (Dick) Osburn came to #12 as chief's driver. H.H. Kellough as backup driver.

September 12, 1922

While #12 pumper was returning from answering an alarm at 2015 N. Commerce, they collided with J.M. Clark in 2400 block of N. Main. No injuries or damage.

December 21, 1922

Received 2 new fire helmets and 100 feet of rope.

January 24, 1923

H. Franklin fell and hurt himself at fire at 112 East Exchange and taken to hospital 1:30 am, returned home 10 am, returned to work Jan 30th at 8 am. Off 6 days.

*****

May 1923

Jennie would take their cow out of the pen in the morning and stake it out in the vacant lot behind them, for the cow to graze during the day. Apparently someone threw an empty paint can into the vacant lot. The cow found it and licked the paint in the open can. The cow had green splatters on her face and legs when Jennie put her in the pen that evening, but didn't think much about it until she found the cow dead the next morning. She called John, crying she asked, "What will we do?"

"Well, I'll call the man that used to come clean out our manure bin here at the station. He sometimes picks up dead animals. I'll get him to pick up the cow, then day after tomorrow, I'll go down to the stockyards and buy us another one. Meanwhile, call Mrs. Hays and see if you can trade her some chickens or eggs for some milk for the girls." This was typical of the sharing between these friends and neighbors.

*****

Chief's log
December 24, 1923

H.W. Franklin sent to hospital for operation for appendix. Off 28 days.

April 30, 1924

Special adapter for line 2 ½ inch

October 12, 1924

One Dayton airless tire.

October 25, 1924

5 mattresses renovated and new ticking, Panther City Mattress Company

November 6, 1924

Call came in for 1006 N. Main, early Thursday morning. Ku Klux Klan hall.

Witnesses heard an explosion and saw fire rage out of control. Fire spread so rapidly, that a hamburger stand on south side of building also caught fire and burnt to the ground before firemen could gain control and get the fire out. It took two hours. Police suspected arson.

November 8, 1924

One section 1925 hose replacing one section 1918 from shop. Received four new tires.

November 11, 1924

New Dietz lantern on Chief's Ford in exchange for old one.

January 3, 1925

Supplies, 50 ft. chemical hose, 2 brooms, 1 chamois, 6 bars soap, 12 pkg. Toilet paper, 1 lantern globe, 2 electric globes, 6 acid bottles, 1 pkg. report blanks, 2 sponges.

Inventory as of March 21, 1925, station #12

Real estate and buildings, 1 motor com. Hose & pump, 1 motor com. Hose & chemicals, 1 Bat. Chief's car with 200 ft. 1923 fire hose, one 2000 ft. 2 ½ in. Eureka fire hose, one Mavel hot water heater, one heating stove, 1 writing desk, one 14 ft. ladder, one 45 ft. ladder extension, 100 ft. 1 in. rope, 6 iron beds, 6 bed springs, 6 mattresses, 2 pillows, 16 blankets, 4 window shades, 3 chairs, 34 cans oil and 1 funnel, 1 lawn mower, 1 wheel borough, 2 mops, 4 brooms, 3 sponges, 4 chamois, 7 fire helmets, 3 nozzels, 5 spanners, 3 hydrant wrenches, 1 fire record, 1 station journal, 1 steel sliding pole, 1 hose boot, 1 underground gas tank & pump, 60 gals gas, 50 ft. garden hose, one 2 ½ in. hard suction, one hydrant map, 2 tons coal, 6 acid bottles, 30 lbs. acid, 5 gal. lube oil, 70 lbs. soda, 9 pkg. paper, 5 gal. kerosene, 1 old hot water heater, 1 feed box, 1 siren, 1 hose strap, 10 joints stove pipe, fore 3 gal. chemical tanks, 3 axes, 6 lanterns, 50 ft. 1 ½ in. rope, 2 sinks, 1 bathtub, 2 commodes, 50 ft. 1927 hose, 1200 ft. 1918 hose.

May 19, 1925

Received one Stillson wrench

June 14, 1925

Bob Head Six sections 1924 Eureka Fire Hose to shop, Old hose back from shop same day.

July 22, 1925

Two Lee Cord Standard Casons 34X41/2 for #12

Chief's log
September 7, 1925

#12 truck in shop. Returned Sept. 10th

November 22, 1925

Monday 2:45 pm. Riverside fire mistake on box 612. One story frame residence. Chief did not respond by order of R.M. Ferguson.

June 10, 1926

Chief Whittenburg off 10th to 17th

John was on one side of a roof, opposite the side that was burning, when the roof suddenly caved in. He fell through the roof and through the ceiling, feet first. He hit his ear and nose and skinned up the side of his face pretty good. Doc said the cartilage in the top of his ear was broken and his nose, also.

Chief's log
July 8, 1926

Got 100 ft. rope

Men at No. 12 Station - 1930

Front row (left to right)	*Back row (left to right)*
Chief John L. Whittenburg	*B.F. Sullavan*
Dick Osburn	*W.W. White*
Thurman 'Pat' Patton	*Elmer Hines*
Dallas Bevil	*Walter Markland*
(name was either Franklin, Johnson or Southerland)	*H.H. 'Hob' Killough*
Henry Layton	
Chief John O'Donnel	

As Of August 1, 1926, the men of number 12 station consisted of:

J.L.Whittenburg, Chief	John O'Donnell, Chief	W.E. Markland, Captain
E.M. Pruitt, Liet.	H.O. Osborn, Chief Driver	H.H.Kellough, Driver

| T.W. Patton, hose man | E.F. Hines, hose man | J.A. Johnson, hose man |
| W.W. White, plug man | H.W. Franklin, engine driver | Dallas Bevil, plug man |

August 5, 1926

Captain Buchanan left the fire department and Lieutenant Markland was appointed Captain in his place.

September 5, 1926

H. Kellough hurt left knee at fire on 2305 Lee St. He took sick with flu on Friday 10th, back to work on 14th.

December 14, 1926

Chief Whittenburg off sick with flu, Sharp sub. Chief back Dec 21st.

Once a month they had 50 gals gasoline delivered from Magnolia Oil Co. and some times Cities Service Oil Co.

Model A Chief's Car

January 1927

Dick Osburn drove John in the chief's car; a black, Model A, Ford pickup with no top on the cab. It had a small tank in the bed with a hose slightly bigger than a garden hose, mainly used for small fires, if they didn't need to hook up the big pumper truck. On the way to a fire, a guy pulled out in front of them at 21st & Clinton Streets. Dick swerved to miss him and the car slid head on into a telephone pole. The pole broke and fell right between Dick and John. Neither one hurt. Station 12 received a new chief's car.

February 1, 1927

T.W. Patton and G.W. Coonrood were Rookie's and considered extra's. They went from station to station filling in for those out sick or on vacation, until permanently assigned to a station. Patton became almost a full time substitute at #12.

March 1927

Kellough hurt left shoulder, Osburn hurt stomach, Markland hurt right shoulder and Bevil hurt left side of back, all of them on the new training tower. With more multi-storied buildings being built, the firemen had to learn how to fight fires in a different and sometimes difficult situation.

June 5, 1927

D.W. Bevil quit.

Chief's log
August 11, 1927

W.W. White hurt testicles and C.O.Wilkins hurt leg when # 15 fire truck ran over their hose and knocked them both down.

Chief's log
January 22, 1928

C.O. Wilkins hurt eye sliding down pole. He hit it on ceiling.

January 24, 1928

Bevil went home to check on his sick family. Doctor was there and quarantined him with his family for 7 days.

February 7, 1928

W.E. Markland hurt back at tower pulling hose over hose roller, right side.

February 18, 1928

Pruitt was off 12 hours with sickness in family.

March 25, 1928

Johnson quarantined with sickness in his family. Big flu epidemic all over town, many people dying from it.

April 30, 1928

Took pumper to shop for new tires. Met new mechanic L. B. Bounds

July 28, 1928

Chief's car hit coming back from Riverside at Clinton hit by Negro in Buick, R.C. Woods driver. Chief Sharp driver of Chief's car. Witness L.B. Howard of Stripling Dairy, and S.M. Allen 306 W. 25th about 3 pm.

City Chief Ferguson called a meeting of all his Battalion Chiefs. Chief Sharp of the Riverside area drove over to pick up John. Their drivers could stay on duty while they were gone to the meeting.

September 3, 1929

W.W. White run bailing wire in finger on right hand second finger at Swifts hay fire.

November 30, 1929

Chief O'Donnell sore eye off 3 days. Hurt at fire.

1930

The roster of men at #12 fire station, their wives names and there addresses were:

John Whittenburg, Jennie, 1605 Harrington,

Walter Markland, Willie, 1512 Harrington,

Willie White, Mattie, 2107 Roosevelt,

Homer Franklin, Aline, 2413 Prospect,

Harvey Kellough, Fay, 2317 Roosevelt,

J.R. Johnson, Leslie, 2205 Prairie,

Burnard Sutherland, Eva, 2721 Prairie

John O'Donnell, Burch, 3030 Jennings,

Henry Layton, Norma, 2215 Columbus,

Dallas Bevil, Laura, 2121 Gould,

Elmer Hines, Alta, 2208 Gould,

Henry Osburn, Elsie, 1403 Lagonda,

Thurman Patton, Alma, 1815 Harrington,

Chief's log
April 5, 1930

Pump went to shop and had a new rotary pump installed.

April 8, 1930

Inspection of tank at 3205 N. Main, not passed on by Chief O'Donnell, owner C.T. Mayo, No. 75037 Pump.

Extra Work, #12, from Oct. 1, 1930 to Oct. 1, 1931

10 hours inspection of buildings in our district

2 hours cutting weeds away from hydrants.

2 days distributing circulars (on fire prevention supposedly, since a Bureau of Fire Prevention had been set up Oct. 1, 1925)

1 hour burning grass off vacant lot.

First Aid work, E.F. Hines called by neighbor to stop a nose bleed on child, Succeeded.

January 15, 1931

Chief's car in shop for two new Goodyear tires on front wheels.

July 6th received new oil in pump, but pump was not drained. Dodge was drained. On 15th pump went back to shop and had new cylinder gasket put on and developed knock in motor, nothing done about it at time. On July 23 took pump back to shop at 10:30 am, Mechanic Bounds this time. Four new cylinders in place and back in service 12:30 pm.

August 16, 1931

H.E. Layton burned his hand at fire at Boso Brothers hay fire, not off duty.

*****

Sometime in the early 1930's, John's sister, Francis Keith, called Fanny, died out in West Texas. John got a call from one of her daughters. "Uncle John, she has named you to be the executor of her will. The farm is all she had. The house isn't worth much but she has quite a few acres of land. All four of us girls want to sell our share, but our brother Claude wants to hold out for more money. Money is tight and buyers are scarce here is West Texas."

"Well, tell you what you do." John advised. "First hire a surveyor to see how much land you got and how best to divide it five ways. Send me a copy of the will, the report from the surveyor and send me the telephone numbers of each of you girls and Claude. Then I will get back with each one of you, later."

John received the copy of the will and the report from the surveyor showing the land, divided equally. They designated Claude's share to include the house. John called and talked to each one. Claude did not want to sell, but said it was okay if the girls sold their share. So when a buyer came along, John sold all the land and paid each of the girls their share. That left Claude with his land and the house right in the middle, with no access to his property, just like his sisters wanted.

*****

Chief's log
November 14, 1931

Answering alarm at 1401 Gould on a wet street, No. 12 pump slid into curb and broke right rear well in service with 4C pump at 5:25.

Summary of service in 1931

October, Drill tower 20 hours, 960 blocks

November, Drill tower 3 times 1st half, 480 blocks939 hours

December, J.A. Johnson rendered first aid to lady that fell down steps at Leonard Bros.

January, at 2:20 pm., 25 minutes service at 24th and Pearl St. Pumping out a man hole.

June 17, 1933

Alarm came in for 24th St. and Rosen St. The Hackberry Grove

Dance Hall burned to the ground. Probably caused by a cigarette left burning.

The great depression hit in 1929. By 1935, the fire department received its union charter and appointed Lieutenant C.C. Killian as temporary president. The union pushed for a minimum wage law and the bill passed in 1937, resulting in a division between management and labor. Meanwhile, the city went bankrupt and salaries were reduced to $114. 85 per month for a first private. Paychecks had to be discounted 3 percent in order to be cashed. The city, unable to pay the minimum wage of $150.00 per month, appealed the bill to the Texas Supreme Court. The Fire dept. had to cut back on the number of firemen on the payroll. Chief Ferguson called John into his office.

"John, I hate to do this but, we have to lay off a bunch of men. The only reasonable thing to do, I guess, is to go by seniority. Here's the list of men with the least amount of seniority," he said as he handed John the list. "You and I have been through a lot together and seen a lot of changes. I value your opinion and if you have a better idea, let me know. I hate like the devil to have to do this."

John looked over the list and thought a minute. "As for my stations, Pruitt and Wilkins are single men and don't have a family to support. I'll let them go. But men like L.B. Bounds have a family to feed and besides he is the best mechanic you have, right now. I would rather see a single man go than know I caused a man's family to go hungry. Now, I know you can fire me for disobeying an order, but I won't let any of my family men go."

"I hadn't thought of that. That's why I wanted to talk to you John. You have integrity. All right let's go over the main list and fill our quota with all the single men first."

Word leaked out of the office and the men with families heard, 'Chief John had saved their jobs.' They had an even greater respect for him after that.

Chief's log

In 1935, the Isis Theatre at 2300 North Main, burned. Damage bad inside but repairable.

Chief's log
November 1935

Gas stove explodes in apartment house. Six burned to death, 11 injured. Only 5 bodies recovered by firemen, a week old baby missing.

John had all the men to go through the remains of the house again after they brought out the five bodies. They found nothing in the ashes resembling a baby's body or the other victim. John went back to the station, downhearted and grieved.

March 21, 1936

Alarm came in for Liquor warehouse on 15th Street. Local newspaper reported: "Bystanders risked lives and singed eyebrows to try to rescue liquor as a matter of principal, before firemen arrived. Only two pints were saved as thirsty flames drank 57,000 pints of whiskey. A violent fire, it took 11 fire companies to finally put it out."

*****

As of July 19, 1939, City Fire Chief Stan Ferguson retired and July 20th Captain Coy. C. Killian was appointed the new City Chief. The economics of the '30's prevented the fire department from replacing outdated and worn equipment. Fortunately, prior to World War II, the fire department was able to acquired six new 750 G.P.M. "Mack" pumpers. Master mechanic John Oliver, conceived the idea of installing a forty-gallon booster tank, with power take off, driven off the transmissions of the new 1938 Buick Century coupes. This immediately enhanced the flexibility of the Battalion Chiefs and was a first for Ft. Worth. Chief Killian's conflicts between management and the Firefighters Union caused tension within the department. The City manager demoted Killian back to Captain and he was reassigned to station #19. Killian later became Fire Marshall. Chief Whittenburg was content to stay where he was, out of the political arena.

*****

To help supplement his income during the depression years, John started sharpening hoes, knives, scissors, anything with a blade that someone needed sharpened. He had a grinding stone set on a frame much like a spinning wheel. He sat at one end with his foot peddling to make the grinding stone turn. He would make ten to twenty cents for each piece he sharpened.

Newer truck at No. 12 Station

15

Working toward Retirement

1936-1947

T.E. 'Pat' Patton became John's driver for his chief's car, after Dick Osburn retired. John became used to the motor vehicles and finally decided to learn to drive. Pat taught him and soon John had his driver's license. Horses and wagons were becoming obsolete and almost dangerous to have on the streets with all the motor cars.

Chief Whittenburg & driver Dick Osburn

*****

John and Jennie's old horse was ready to retire, so John sold the horse and wagon and bought a car. Jennie flat refused to learn to drive 'one of those machines.' However, Louise and Evelyn were old enough and John taught them. Between the three of them they took Jennie where ever she wanted to go.

Jennie's Aunt Bell lived in Frontenac, Kansas. Aunt Bell was 5 ft. tall, like Jennie and her mother, only a little round in the middle and always wore her long, gray hair pulled back into a tightly braided bun. Her small eyes almost shut when she smiled and she smiled a lot. She wore plain, house dresses and a full length apron. She married a Mr. Burns and they had two sons John and Bob. She was widowed when her husband died in a mine cave in. Bell later married Mr. Hay. They adopted a little girl, Ester. Mr. Hay bought Bell a big diamond ring. He was later killed while bootlegging during prohibition era.

In 1936, on John's vacation, he took Jennie to visit Aunt Bell. John decided, while Bell and Jennie visited, he would walk up the street to see the strip mining operation and take a look at the new, big shovel the miners used in digging for coal. Aunt Bell's son, Bob told him about it before he left for work that morning. John was 6 ft. 2 in. tall and about 220 lbs. and wore a white, straw, cowboy hat, tan khaki pants and khaki shirt. He walked around looking at the mining area and decided to walk a different route back. He followed the rail road tracks a ways, cut through town, past the general store on the corner and crossed the street and back to Aunt Bell's. He had enjoyed the walk and the nice weather.

Later that evening, Aunt Bell's son Bob went over to the general store to buy some cigarettes and came back roaring with laughter. The store owner asked him, "Who is that big man in the white hat at your house and why is he here?"

Bob said, "That's my uncle from Texas and he's a fireman. Why?"

Well, it seemed most drinking men, in those days and in that little town, made their own home brew; beer or bathtub gin they called it. The store clerk told Bob, "When every body saw that big stranger in the white hat, walking around town, they all went home and poured out their brew, thinking he was a lawman."

A few years later, John and Jennie went back for another visit. Aunt Bell needed some money and asked John to buy her big diamond ring. At that time it was worth about $500 dollars. The pawn shop offered her $200 and she offered to sell it to John for $300. He gave her $400 for it. Jennie wore it for special occasions for many years.

*****

About the time World War II started, mid 1940's, radios were installed in the fire trucks and chief's car. This required a birth certificate to get a license to operate the radios. When John was born, no birth records were issued. Like many other people, he applied for a delayed birth certificate. This required 'proof' he was born when and where he said. Luckily, John had an aunt that could swear "his mother was pregnant when they left for Dublin and she had the baby while gone and in her arms when they returned to Stephenville." He received a birth certificate on August 5, 1941 and his radio license.

*****

The fire trucks and Chief's cars could talk to each other or to Central Fire Station's operator on the radios. But if they needed to call in extra men that were off duty, they had to use the telephone.

One evening, on John's day off, he was sitting at home with Jennie and their daughter Evelyn. The phone rang. Central Fire Station's operator said, "Chief, we got a big one. The railroad bridge over the Trinity River by Riverside Drive. We called #12; they got there and requested #11 to come help. You might want to go. You want me to send the Chief's car for you?"

"No, I'll have to go by the station and get my gear. I'll get there soon as I can." John hung up the phone. "Daughter," he called to Evelyn, "I need you to drive for me, so I can be putting on my boots and gear while on the way."

Evelyn jumped up and John pulled the keys out of his pocket and handed them to her as he said to Jennie, "Now don't worry Mama. We'll be all right and be back as soon as we can."

Jennie anxiously replied, "Ya'll be careful."

Evelyn went around to the driver's seat while John opened the garage door. They drove to the station and he ran in to get his gear. He started putting on his boots and telling her which way to go. It was getting dark, so she turned on the car headlights. They were coming to a red light up ahead and John told her to flash the lights back and forth from dim to bright and honk the horn and make sure every body stops then keep going. Meanwhile he waved his fireman's helmet out the window. As they got closer he told her the next turn to make. They could see the flames now. He told her to watch for a dirt road to the left. As they headed down the dirt road leading right to the fire, a policeman stood there blocking the road. Evelyn flashed the lights and honked the horn and John waved his helmet out the window. The policeman wouldn't move and Evelyn finally slammed on the brakes to keep from running over the man. John yelled, "Move, Dam it! Can't you see me waving my helmet? I've got a fire to get to."

The policeman came to the side of the car, put his foot on the running board of the car and said with all authority, "I can't let any-body past here."

John looked at his badge on the front of his shirt, "Well, Mr. Badge fourteen, I'm sure that's going to look good on your record in the morning when Chief Maddox hear's you wouldn't let the Bat-talion Fire Chief go to the fire. Now get your dam foot off the car before I knock it off." With that, he motioned to Evelyn to "drive on." A little further he said, "Pull over here, stay in the car and lock the doors. You stay here till I get back."

The fire trucks were there, #12 on one side of the river and #11 on the other side, hitting it at both ends with water full force and working toward the middle. John found his 'on duty' captain. "Looks like you've got your hands full. Did anyone inform the railroad com-pany?"

"Oh, hadn't thought of that, yet."

John waved acknowledging he would take care of it and walked over to the Chief's car to get on the radio. "Central, this is Whit-tenburg. Do you hear me?"

"This is Central. What you need, Chief?"

"That railroad bridge over the Trinity River off Riverside Drive,

I need you to call the railroad dispatcher to reroute any trains. They will probably want to send out their inspector, but this bridge is going to be too weak to hold up a train."

"Will do immediately and get back to you."

John waited a few minutes. "This is Central calling Chief Whittenburg."

"Whittenburg here."

"T and P said thanks for the warning. They will reroute trains and send inspector immediately. Anything else you need?"

"That's all, Thanks."

John went back to #12 truck. The nearest fire hydrant was far enough away that it cut down on their water pressure. The tanks were running low too. John told the man working the pumps, "I'm going to pull the siphoning hose down to the river. When you see the other end, connect it to the tank and start using river water." John came back to the Chief's car and got on the radio again. "This is Whittenburg, calling #11. Can you hear me?" He waited a half minute. He could see the man checking the gauges on the truck on the other side of the river. When he saw him walk back toward the cab of the truck he called again on the radio, "This is Whittenburg, calling #11 pumper" he yelled.

He saw the man jump into the cab and answer, "Yes, Chief."

John asked him, "Is your water pressure dropping?"

"Yes, Sir, it's dropped a little."

"Connect your filtering hose and start pumping water out of the river."

"Will do!"

John walked over to his captain and told him what he had done. "You should be getting more pressure in that line soon."

"Thanks, Chief."

John waited and watched till the fire was out. He was proud of every one of his men, at both stations. They were good men as well as good firemen and he never missed an opportunity to tell them so. When they started to pick up hose, John called his men to gather round. "You fellows did a good job. I'm proud of the way ya'll work together. Hope you get a good nights rest tonight and I'll see you in the morning."

"Thanks, Chief. See you later."

John got on the radio, "Whittenburg calling number eleven."

"Yes Chief."

"Gather your men around the radio."

"Just a minute." There was a pause as he watched from across the river at the men gathering round the truck "We're here Chief."

John spoke loud so maybe all could hear him over the radio, "You boys did a good job and I want you to know, I'm proud of you. Hope ya'll get a good night's sleep and I'll check with you tomorrow."

All the men across the river turned and waved and John waved back. John walked back to his car, where Evelyn waited. As they drove out toward the main street, the police man had someone stopped. John told Evelyn to pull over. He went to inquire and sure enough the policeman had stopped the railroad inspector. John told him, "The fire is out now, and all the trucks are packing up getting ready to leave. You won't have any lights and this is a bad neighborhood to be out alone. It would be better if you came back in the morning to make your inspection and you won't have a rookie cop delaying you. If you need me, I'm Chief Whittenburg at #12 station."

"Thank you, Chief, appreciate that."

The next day, as soon as John reported to work, he called the police chief. "Maddox, I'm not going to point a finger at any particular one of your Rookies, but you need to make sure they understand, when told to keep people away from an emergency situation, that does not include fire chiefs or inspectors."

*****

During the time of World War II many items were rationed, like car tires, shoes, sugar and beef. Everyone was issued coupon books and you were allowed to buy these items but only in certain amounts. Many families would trade coupons. A couple with no car might trade their tire coupon for shoes or sugar.

Sometime in the early 1940's, Jennie developed diabetes. Because she needed to eat more protein she was allowed extra meat coupons. For years, she gave herself insulin shots every day and she continued to live a full life for several more years.

In the hot summer time, with no air conditioning in the house,

John and Jennie would get the old iron beds out of the barn, wash them off and set them up in the backyard. John would tie a canvas tarp over the top to catch any dew that might fall and they would sleep outside until cool weather returned or it rained. With a white picket fence around the yard, they didn't worry about prowlers bothering them.

John always had a garden, nearly year round. He enjoyed it and it helped supplement their income. John tended the garden and what they didn't eat, Jennie would can or they gave to Louise and Evelyn (who were now grown and married) or the neighbors next door. They also raised chickens to eat and for the eggs. Again, if they got too many eggs, the next door neighbor would buy or trade for the extras.

They had one neighbor named Kate who took in every stray cat that came along. Not only did John have chickens, but the neighbor on the other side of Kate raised Bantam Prized Show Chickens. On a regular basis the cats would pick the middle of the night to get into their yards and kill a chicken or two. After talking to Kate a number of times with no results, John came up with a secret weapon. He made a wire cage trap. When he caught a cat the first time, he put the tea kettle on to heat. When the water was hot but not scalding, he poured it over the cat then let it go with a warning not to return. If the same cat was caught the second time, it somehow 'disappeared.' Kate never suspected a thing. One day the other neighbor remarked to John, "My chickens haven't been bothered by cats in a long time." John said, "Mine neither, but every time I stick a pitchfork in my garden, it meows."

The Chicken feed came in cotton cloth sacks, each about one yard square. Many times flour and sugar also came in cloth sacks, only smaller. These were often an off white color and Jennie would bleach them white and make underpants for herself and the girls. Later, the Chicken feed came in colored print cloth. Jennie would always go with John to buy feed so she could pick out the prettiest color or print sacks. These were used for kitchen or bath curtains, cup towels, aprons, pot holders or blouses and the scraps saved for quilt making. Later, she made dresses or summer play clothes for her granddaughter.

In winter time John and Jennie sat in their big rocking chairs in their big back bedroom next to the kitchen. They had a small gas stove for heat and would close the doors to the other part of the house, living mainly in the kitchen, bedroom and hall to the bath. They would listen to the radio while Jennie cut out scrap material into different shapes and layed them out on the bed to match shapes or colors. Then she would sew the pieces together. After John finished reading the newspaper, he would sometimes cut out some pieces for her.

John made Jennie a quilting frame and a stand. After she had sewed all the pieces together, he would set up her quilting frame in the living room. John connected some small pulleys and narrow rope in each corner of the high ceiling of the room. If company was coming, he could pull each corner and lift the quilt in the frame up to the ceiling out of the way.

*****

In 1943, after 38 years of service, at age 62, John received his certificate that he was eligible for retirement. Most young and able bodied men had been drafted into the military for World War II. John's peers convinced him he was needed and talked him into staying another year or two. Still in good health and the pay good, he decided to stay on the fire department a while longer.

In 1945 Chief Claude Ligon was appointed City Fire Chief. He came to work on the fire department the same year as John.

Chief's log
June 1946

Call came in for house on fire at 2217 Prospect. A neighbor saw flames and reported it. Owners not home. Fire contained to kitchen in back of house.

*****

By early 1947, the war was over and a flood of young men were coming home from overseas and looking for jobs. John decided it was time for him to retire. He turned in his request and set the day July 1, 1947 as his last day at work.

June 4, 1947

Thursday morning, after breakfast and all their chores done, John was sitting and talking with his men at #12 Station. The sound of a big truck in front of the station caught his attention. The sound seemed familiar. He got up to investigate when the sound grew louder. The big truck from Station #11 pulled up, followed by station #15, both loaded with men. Behind the trucks came a Chief's car with City Fire Chief Ligon and another car with Amon G. Carter, owner of the Star-Telegram newspaper and prominent philanthropist in Fort Worth. Following them, in his own car, was Jennie and Evelyn. As the firemen began getting off the trucks, John asked, "What's going on here? Where's the fire?"

About 25 of his fellow firemen gathered around to shake John's hand. Chief Ligon said, "John, your men came and asked me, if the other stations could cover for them for a couple of hours. They wanted to give you this little surprise party for your retirement." Ligon turned and extended his hand to Amon Carter, "Mr. Carter, we would like for you to be first on our program."

Mr. Carter stepped forward carrying a large hat box, opened it and took out a Shady Oaks Stetson hat. "Chief Whittenburg, it is an honor to meet you, Sir, and it is my privilege to present you with this hat for your 43 years of service and dedication to the Fort Worth Fire Department. On behalf of the citizens of Fort Worth, I thank you for serving your community."

"Thank you, Sir." John managed to say, "I was just doing my job."

"Well, you did a mighty fine job according to what your men tell me."

John put his hat on. Mr. Carter remarked, "Now, you look like a cowboy with out a cow." They laughed and Mr. Carter continued. "Now, let my reporter get a picture of us for the newspaper. We will be doing an article on you and it will be in the paper in a few days. We understand tomorrow is your day off and you like to work in your garden and sit on your front porch. I'd like for my reporter to get some pictures of you in your garden. Is it all right if he comes by your house tomorrow morning?"

"Yes, Sir, that would be fine." John replied with a smile. "Thank you, Sir."

"Thank you, Chief and Congratulation." Carter said as he shook hands with John. "Now, I believe your men have some more surprises for you."

"Oh, my!" was all John could say. "They surprised me, all right."

Chief Ligon reached as one of the firemen handed him a wrapped gift and he stepped forward. "The men asked me to do the honors, but they all had a hand in this."

He handed the present to John.

John began unwrapping the package and looking for a place to put the paper.

Chief Ligon turned to Jennie, "Mrs. Whittenburg, can you come help John? He seems to be all thumbs."

Jennie had been standing to one side, but walked over and stood beside John and took the paper wrappings. John looked at the framed scroll. It had a picture of him standing beside his Chief's car with these words:

> *Some men come into this world, occupy their small niche and leave small regret behind them when they pass on to other endeavors. Then there are those men...men who stand out above the crowd like pillars of strength...men who are in the front line when danger threatens. Such a man is our friend and comrade, Chief John L. Whittenburg.*
>
> *Those who have known him through the long years of service, as well as the man who met him yesterday, cherish his warm handshake, his friendly smile and wise counsel. Chief Whittenburg is retiring to the easier life he has so richly earned...and with him goes all our regard and affection...his memory will always be fresh in our hearts.*
>
> *From your Friends and Comrades*

Station No. 11	Station No. 12	Station No. 15	Station No. 22
Capt. J.W. Buckland	Chief J.C. Allison	Capt. M.G. Hess	Capt. E.E. Redford
Lieut. J.W. Fuller	Capt. C.A. Senior	Lieut. G.M. Greenwood	Lieut. G.G. White
H.H. Trowell	Lieut. H.M. Huddle	W.E. Bellamy	H.V. Stockton
H.L. McDaniel	T.W. Patton	G. Wallis	R.E. Kennard
H.E. Barham	R.H. Rogers	J.R. Jameson	P.V. Bankston
J.B. Kimberly	R.E. Fickle	C.I. Crick	C.L. Fromm
H.B. Heath	E. C. Burns	W.L. Clark	C.E. Luttrell
J.V. Smith	Vlody Novak	W.R. Allen	W.C. Webb
L.R. Hale	J.W. Harper	O.D. Rogers	E.F. Johnson
E.W. Scott	B.F. Sutherland	J. Solomon	H.R. Golden
E.L. Webb	R.B. Jameson		W.B. Long
T.S. Williams	Joe Meadows		J. J. Ellis
H. M. Anderson	H.H. Killogh		
E.F. Hines			
G.H. Brown			
E.W. Kelley			
A. (Fat) Munskey			

John finished reading and glanced over the names and handed it to Jennie, not knowing what to say and afraid if he would cry if he did.

Chief Ligon handed John another gift. He opened it, handing Jennie the paper and ribbon. It was a hand-tooled leather belt. Opening the other, he found a hand-tooled leather billfold. The men had paid Terry Williams, a 20 yr fireman at No. 11 station, to make the belt and billfold. John, surprised and humbled by all the attention, was at a loss for words. All he could say was, "Oh, my.....Oh, my."

Jennie whispered to him, "John, say thank you and tell them how much you appreciate all this."

John cleared his throat, wiped his eyes with his shirt sleeve and finally found his voice. "Boy's, I just can't say enough. I thank you all and I really appreciate this party and the nice gifts. You really surprised me. And thank you, Mr. Carter. I ....I don't know what else to say."

Mr. Carter asked, "Will you be coming back to visit and play dominoes with the boys?"

"Yes, but I don't think they will let me win now." John replied.

Someone else asked, "Are you going to buy a farm?"

"No. If I wanted to keep working, I'd stay on the fire department." When the laughter died down, he added, "My garden is all the farming I'm going to do."

Another asked, "Any idea how many fires you fought?"

"Well, the first 38 years it was about 19 thousand. I lost count after that."

The reporter asked, "Did you rescue many people?"

"I had my share."

The reporter asked, "Do you still slide down the pole?"

"Oh, yes. At my age, I can slide faster than I can walk."

16

Retirement Years

1947-1973

After John's retirement party and his last day at work, he and Jennie prepared to make the trip to Seattle, Washington to visit their oldest daughter, Louise.

They talked to some neighbors who had driven over the mountains in Colorado. Taking their advice, John mapped out a route. Driving the speed limit and averaging 55 mph, John figured it would take five days. John took his 1941 Ford to the repair shop and had it checked over, including lube and oil change. Jennie packed their clothes and prepared their 'grub box.' They planned a picnic lunch at roadside stops or city parks. Most motels had kitchenettes, so she packed the skillet, coffee pot and one saucepan. Along with a small container of flour, sugar, Crisco, mayonnaise, butter, salt, pepper, cooking and eating utensils and tablecloth.

Their ice chest was a box lined with an oil cloth (like plastic or vinyl), holding about a 10 lb. block of ice. John would chip off some for their iced tea at lunch and dinner. The rest was just enough to keep a few items, like lunchmeat, bacon or eggs from spoiling. (A year or two later, they bought a new Coleman, insulated, metal ice chest.)

After all the planning and packing, John and Jennie left mid July. John wanted to leave early in the morning, like about 4 o'clock, and drive while it was cooler as the car didn't have air conditioning. John did all the driving, stopping for gasoline and 'potty breaks' and for their picnic lunch. By two or three o'clock in the afternoon, the hottest part of the day, they looked for a motel with a kitchenette. After checking in and asking where to find the nearest grocery store, Jennie bought what groceries they needed for that night, breakfast and lunch the next day, while John went to a service station to fill the car with gasoline. They returned to the motel to rest a while. After supper and cleaning up the dishes, it was early to bed, so they could get up early the next day.

Jennie enjoyed the trip except for the day they crossed the Rocky Mountains. The roads were narrow, winding and sometimes S curves. And either high up on the edge of a mountain or down in a deep canyon with signs, "watch for falling rocks." They couldn't drive as fast and didn't drive as far on that day. On the fifth day, John and Jennie arrived at Louise's house about three or four o'clock in the afternoon. They called her at work that Friday afternoon and she finished cleaning off her desk and left early.

Louise and her husband Carl, took a weeks vacation that following week, to take them sightseeing. This was the first chance John and Jennie had to get to know Carl and see the little house they built next door to Carl's sister and brother in law, Millie and Kenny Gillman.

Saturday was scheduled for rest after their long trip. John and Jennie were introduced to all the neighbors and to Millie and Kenny and their three children. The kids were rather disappointed when John wasn't wearing boots and guns. He explained that not everyone in Texas wore guns and besides he had been a fireman, not a cowboy.

Louise and Carl took them down to the Pike Street fish and produce market by the docks. Their shopping bags were soon full with Salmon, Halibut and fresh vegetables.

During the week they took side trips each day driving to Mount Rainier, Whidbey Island and Vancouver, Canada. One day trip they went by boat to Victoria, Canada.

Carl's brother-in-law Kenny was a commercial fisherman. The boats would make two or three trips a year to Alaska. In between, the men fished the outer coast of Seattle. Kenny's boat docked in the inland bay, so each time the boats went out or came in, they went through the locks. One afternoon, Kenny's boat was due to come in about four o'clock. Louise and Carl took John and Jennie down to the locks to watch the boats coming in. Having never seen anything like it before, they were fascinated watching the boats come in between the thick concrete walls and the big steel doors close behind them. The water would rise, then the steel doors in front of the boats would open and the boats would go into the inland bay. When they returned home that evening, Kenny came over to Louise's house.

"John, I cleared it with the others on the boat. How would you like to go deep sea fishing with us tomorrow?"

John was a little hesitant, "I don't know, Kenny. The last time I went fishing it was with a cane pole at the river bank, sixty years ago."

"That don't matter. We got all the equipment and I'll show you how."

"I didn't bring any heavy clothes, just this sweater."

Kenny said, "I have a heavy jacket and toboggan you can wear."

Carl spoke up, "I got some long underwear and rubber boots that will fit you."

"Well, it seems like ya'll got me fixed up. I'd love to. What else do I need; a sack lunch?"

"Nothing." Kenny said. "Got it all taken care of. One of the guys will be by to pick us up at four in the morning. We'll be coming back through the locks about four in the afternoon. By the time we dock and unload the fish, it'll be about five-thirty when we get home. And what ever you catch you can keep if you want."

John was excited now. "Sounds good. I haven't had good fresh fish in long time till we got here the other day and Louise fixed that Halibut."

The next morning everyone was up and getting John a big breakfast and seeing him off on his new adventure. That afternoon, Louise and Carl took Jennie to the locks and watched for the boat to come through. John waved when he saw them. When the water raised the boat up where they could see each other better, John walked back to the ice bin. He raised the lid and lifted out the big fifteen pound Salmon he had caught and held it up for them to see. John grinned from ear to ear.

Back home, John showed them the other fish he caught that was a little bit smaller. Louise got her camera and took his picture. He wanted to take the picture back home and show his fellow firemen, next time he visited with them.

Jennie asked, "What in the world are we going to do with all that fish?"

Kenny's wife spoke up, "Why don't you can it and take it back to Texas with you, to eat this winter?"

"I have no idea how to can fish." Jennie admitted.

"I'll show you." Millie offered. "First thing in the morning, you go to the store and buy some jars. We'll have it all canned before dinner time."

The next morning, Louise and Carl left to go back to work. Jennie cleaned up the kitchen and John went to the store and bought two dozen, pint size, canning jars. Arriving back home, Millie came over and the three of them started preparing and canning. They filled the two dozen jars and still had half of one Salmon left. Millie suggested, "Why don't you bake the rest for your dinner tonight?"

Jennie said, "I have no idea how to bake fish."

"Here, I'll show you," Millie said, as she went to the refrigerator and took out the jar of mayonnaise and a package of pecans. Laying the piece of Salmon in a baking dish, she spread mayonnaise all over the top and sprinkled it with chopped pecans. "Now, put this in the 'frige till Louise gets home. Then put it in 350 degree oven and bake about 30 minutes."

Jennie was surprised. "I had no idea, cooking fish was that simple."

Carl never learned to drive a car. Louise worked downtown, so it was easier for them to take the bus back and forth to work. Between their house and the bus stop was a huge area about the size of six vacant lots. People going and coming to work, bus stop or the neighborhood grocery store, had worn a path through the middle for a short cut.

One day Jennie said, "We are going to need bread and butter from the store."

"I'll just walk to the store if that's all we need." John volunteered.

He came home saying, "Jennie, that vacant lot is covered with blackberries. If I go pick some will you make us a berry cobbler?"

"Oh, yes, that sounds good. We haven't had a fresh berry cobbler in long time."

While John went to pick the berries, Jennie started making the dough. That evening everyone rushed through their supper, so they could dig into the cobbler.

Carl said, "Jennie, I have never had cobbler that tasted that good. But there is just one thing wrong with it." He paused and added, "There's just not enough of it."

They laughed and she promised to make a bigger one next time.

John asked, "Is it okay, if we pick the berries? I haven't seen anyone else picking them and it's a shame to let them go to waste?"

Louise said, "Once in a while I see someone picking a few, mainly kids eating them. Go on and pick as many as you want. Nobody ever sees the land owner."

John went back the next day and picked more berries and Jennie started making another cobbler. John came into the kitchen. "You known, Carl likes to come in from work and have a cup of coffee and wait awhile before supper. How about making a little pie, just for him and me to have with our coffee and have the cobbler for after supper?"

"I can do that. No trouble at all." Jennie replied. "You know I was just thinking, it sure would be nice to make some jelly with those berries. We could leave a few jars for Carl and Louise and take a few jars home for ourselves and to give to Evelyn and Erie. But have we got room in the car for jelly and fish?"

"I don't see why not. We got the whole back seat we can load up."

"We'd have to buy some more jars and sugar."

"Yeah, but just think about enjoying that good jelly all winter. When you get through baking, get cleaned up and we'll go to store and get what you need. First thing in the morning I'll go pick some more berries and we can get started."

That afternoon Carl came in from work and was surprised and

delighted to sit down with John over coffee and share the little pie. He ate another big helping of cobbler after dinner too.

Jennie began to tell Louise about making jelly the next day. Louise was glad they were finding something to do and not bored sitting at home with her and Carl off to work. "Daddy, after we do the dishes, I'll take you down toward the beach and all along the railroad tracks there is wild Raspberries, if you want some of them and not all Blackberries."

"I don't know that I've ever had any Raspberries before." He turned to Jennie, "What do you think, mama?"

"Let's go see and taste them." Jennie said. "We might just make some jelly out of both kinds of berries."

One taste and they were hooked. All of them began picking raspberries and came home with two buckets full. The next morning, John picked buckets full of blackberries, while Jennie started on the raspberry jelly.

They loved the weather in Washington. It might get up in the 80's during the middle of the day for a few hours, but the mornings and evenings were cool enough for a sweater. Even when it warmed during the middle of the day, there was a cool breeze blowing in off Puget Sound. They were enjoying getting away from the Texas heat. They planned to stay two weeks and head back home. But come closer to time to leave, they were enjoying themselves so much, Louise talked them into staying another eight weeks. She assured them they could still get back across the mountains before it snowed. For the next nine years John and Jennie went to Seattle in late May and stayed till early September to get out of the Texas heat. Every year, they loaded boxes of empty jars into the car and came home loaded down with jars of jelly.

After the depression and World War II, people began to be more prosperous. Some time around 1948-1949, John and his aunt Molly Whittenburg Neal received a letter from what looked like a lawyer in Germany. They were being informed; they were the only heirs that could be found to the Whittenburg Castle in Whittenburg, Germany. Aunt Molly called John who said he would do some investigating. John first called a lawyer friend of his, who said it could be true, but he recommended checking into it further before sending the lawyer's fee. John talked to the local butcher, Joseph Groshup, who was born in Germany. He said he had seen the Whittenburg Castle and knew it existed. But Mr. Groshup warned, "Since the war, there is a lot of fraud and you are 'rich' Americans to anyone overseas, no matter how poor you might be over here."

The letter stated they were to send $500 for the paper work to be processed. John and Aunt Molly thought it not worth the money, when it didn't cost that much in Texas to transfer a deed. They neither one had any use for a castle, especially that far away. And they had no desire to go there. They also thought it strange for the letter to say, 'they were the only heirs that could be found.' Many other Whittenburg relatives were listed in the Ft. Worth phone book, census records and other simple methods. They didn't follow up on it and the German lawyer was never heard from again.

In October 1956, Jennie fell, twisting her ankle, breaking her arm and fracturing her collar bone. John took care of her, along with the help of Evelyn. Because of the diabetes, complications set in. Jennie passed away March 10, 1957. Jennie and John had been married for 48 years.

John went to the bank to draw money out of savings to pay for Jennie's funeral. The clerk said, "I'm sorry, Sir, I can't let you have that much money at one time. There is no blue card signed authorizing more than five hundred dollars to be drawn out at one transaction."

John, surprised, not to mention a little upset said, "Lady, I have had this account since 1904. Nobody has ever told me I had to have a blue or any other color of card."

"I'm sorry, Sir. That's the bank policy."

"Well, as a long time customer, it looks like I would have been notified of any changes in my bank's policy."

"I am sorry, Sir."

"Lady, I need the money to pay for my wife's funeral. So, I guess, if you won't give me but five hundred dollars at a time, I have to walk out and back in the revolving door and come back two more times and fill our two more withdrawal slips. Now, looks to me like that is going to take a lot of your and my time and a lot of paper work for you."

Just then the Vice-President of the bank walked by and saw John and heard part of what he was saying. The VP walked up behind the clerk, "What's the problem here?"

The clerk told him her side of the story and John told his side of the story. The VP told the clerk, "Give this man a blue card and post date it a week ago. Give him whatever amount of money he wants to draw out of his account and put on there, I authorized the transaction. You won't find a more honest man than Chief Whittenburg."

John was surprised the Vice-President knew who he was.

The VP turned to John, "You don't recognized me, do you Chief?"

"No, I'm sorry, I don't."

"I'm J. D. Franklin. I used to play ball with you on the lot next to the fire hall. I broke a window and you told my father not to punish me, it was an accident."

"Well, my goodness. It sure is good to see you. And you're the Vice-President of my bank now. I am real proud of you, son."

John grieved over the loss of his Jennie. He lived alone in the home place for another two years, working in his garden, tending to his chickens and weather permitting, sitting on his front porch, waving at friends or neighbors driving by. To any one who would listen, he would tell stories of his youth or his adventures on the fire department. He could still tell you how to repair most anything. He was still active; putting a new roof on one of his rent houses. He still did his own yard work. It just took him longer.

In 1970, Erie and Evelyn remodeled the kitchen and bath at the home place and moved in to look after John.

September 25, 1972

The sound of applause rose and John forced his mind back from the past, to face the reality of the present. All these people, men he had trained and worked with, here to honor him. At ninety-two years old, he was the oldest living fireman in 1972. The speaker asked John to stand. John slowly rose up out of his chair and the applause rose with him. A waitress came over and set a cake in front of him. It was decorated with a fire chief's cap and the words, "Happy Birthday,

Chief Whittenburg." John smiled, nodded and waved his "Thank You." The events of the evening were more than he expected.

Slowly, over the last three years, his body became weaker, even though his mind was still sharp. Then little blood vessels in his head began to rupture, causing him to have a lot of dizziness, sometimes pain and sometimes passing out. He passed away of a massive hemorrhage on July 12, 1973, at the age of 93. He was buried next to his beloved Jennie.

Sources of Information and Acknowledgements

I had always thought my grandfather led an adventuresome life. After John passed away, my aunt and my mother were clearing out his possessions. They found his original Chief's log book, when he first opened #12 fire station in North Fort Worth. When I decided to write his story, in February 2009 and began gathering information, I started with the family genealogy. When going through his log, I realized that book was 100 yrs old in May of 2009. I have included many of the entries from that log book. The family remembered him talking about the Southside fire, the T & P depot and the stockyards fire as the three biggest fires he fought, but we didn't remember the details. Thanks to researching on the internet, I found some details.

I found one web site about the fire department and it had a picture of my grandfather and his men in front of their horse drawn fire wagon. On another web site I found a picture of him and his men in front of their 'modern, motorized' truck. I have those original pictures and included some in this book. It seemed information was being handed to me on a silver platter and I was meant to write his story.

I have my grandfather's dress uniform and badge and wondered why the fire department used the picture of a panther in their logo and could I use the logo in my book without infringing on their copyright. This is the story behind the panther logo.

The economic disaster and hard winter of 1873 dealt a hard blow to the cattle and railroad industry of Fort Worth. Many people left town in search of a better opportunity. Robert E. Cowart, a lawyer, moved to Dallas and wrote a letter to the *Dallas Herald* newspaper in

1875. He commented, "Fort Worth had become such a drowsy place that he saw a panther asleep in the street by the courthouse."

Rather than be offended by his comment, the nickname Panther City was enthusiastically embraced. Panther names began to appear on businesses; Panther Meat Market, Panther City Saloon and Panther Oil and Grease.

A fire company organized about that time, naming their steam engine *The Panther*. Two Panther Cubs were secured by the local newspaper and housed in a handsome cage at the fire station. The fire department adopted a picture of a Panther head as part of their logo on their badges. That logo was never copywrited. My grandfather served under that badge.

Thanks to the fireman I talked to at the Fort Worth, Texas Firefighter's Association and the Fort Worth City Fire Chief. Thanks to my husband, retired Lieutenant of Indian Harbor Volunteer Firefighters in Granbury, Texas, for technical advice. My thanks to Randy Schmeltz, Battalion Chief, Arlington, Texas Fire Department and Chief of the Indian Harbor Volunteer Fire Department for his advice.

I apologize to anyone who may be offended by my use of the words Negro or nigger. That is history, those words were used in those days and I used them, but with no intention of being derogatory.

Some of the names I used are fictitious. Either I didn't know their real names or wanted to protect the innocent, or guilty, as the case may be. This book is based on true events. Although, in most cases, the dialogue is fictitious, it is based on what the family remembers being told.

January 29, 1954, the day before John and Jennie's forty-fifth wedding anniversary, their granddaughter (me) married Douglas Hall. Doug was the grandson of L.B. Bounds, the mechanic who worked on John's chief's car and fire truck. "Pappy" Bounds told me and Doug, "If it wasn't for John Whittenburg, I would have been out of a job during the depression."

When I was doing research for the family history book, I located a man by the name of Jim Noah. Mr. Noah was gathering information and writing the history of the Fort Worth Fire Department. He answered my query with a copy of my grandfather's service record and included the following note:

> *"When John retired in 1947, his men gave him a retirement party that few if any of his peers ever received. If I am correct, many top civic leaders of the time attended the extravagant farewell party, including Amon G. Carter, Sr. From what I heard throughout the years was that he had the respect and admiration of his men more so than any other Battalion Chief I have heard of."*

No man could ask for a better eulogy. This man did not ask, but he received.

Whittenburg's Corn Doggers

To one cup of corn meal, add about one teaspoon baking powder, a half a teaspoon salt and 1 big heaping tablespoon of flour. Mix together. Now pour in some hot, boiling water, about two tablespoons at a time, till a stiff dough forms. Wet hands in cold water and dip a big tablespoon at a time into palm of hand and flatten slightly to about half inch thick. Keep hands wet for each patty. Lay patties in hot grease, as you make them. Enough grease (vegetable oil) to cover bottom of skillet. Fry till browned and turn over and fry till browned. Drain on brown paper sack. (or paper towel) Serve hot with butter. Good with stew, soup or ham hock and beans or salt port and Collared Greens.

Feed the Crew Stew

Cut up about one pound beef in one inch cubes. Salt and flour meat. Pour enough cooking oil into a Dutch oven or stew pan to cover the bottom of pan. Heat oil and add meat and one large chopped onion and brown lightly, stirring to brown on all sides. Add one can, undrained, cut up tomatoes and enough water to cover meat. Simmer till meat starts getting tender. Add 6 to 8 sliced carrots. Cook about 10-15 minutes, making sure water level still covers ingredients; stirring occasionally. Add 3 or 4 cubed potatoes. Season with salt and pepper to taste. When potatoes and carrots are done, stew can be served as is. Or you can add a can of whole kernel corn, and a can of peas. Depending on how many you want to feed, you can add a can of green beans or handful of macaroni. Make sure macaroni is done and serve hot with corn doggers. Oven baked corn bread is okay, too.

About the Author

 Janie Hall grew up in Fort Worth, Texas. Through the years she has written talks, devotions and newsletters for Baptist Marriage Encounter. An interest in genealogy prompted stories about her family's ancestors. She has been published in Texas Outdoor Sports News, Senior Circle, Western Woman and Granbury Showcase magazines. Her first book published was a children's chapter book, "Scooter's Adventures." She is a member of the Fellowship of Christian Writer's of Oklahoma and Writers Bloc of Granbury, Texas where she lives with husband.

LaVergne, TN USA
22 April 2010
180145LV00002B/5/P